OATH

BLOOD BROTHERS
BOOK FOUR

HEATHER LONG

*This book is for the promise-keepers—the rare beasts who say
they'll do the thing...
and actually do the thing.
For the follow-throughers, the finish-liners, the mythical
creatures who make plans and show up. You glorious anomalies
in a world built on "sorry, I totally forgot."
Keep being unsettlingly reliable. It's weirdly powerful.*

SERIES SO FAR

Burn
Lure
Own
Oath

FOREWORD

Dear Reader,

Welcome to the fourth of five books in the Blood Brothers series. This is a series that should be read in order so if you have not read the first three, please pause and begin there. If you are curious about where the Blood Brothers story came from, I shared some background on that in the foreword of *Burn*.

Previously in Blood Brothers: Rescued from human traffickers, stunning model Grace expects freedom and wants desperately to find her twin sister—but what she gets is a team of dangerously skilled men who saved her... and don't plan to let her go.

Own opened with Grace and Bones on the run along with Goblin as Lunchbox, Alphabet, and Voodoo dealt with an invasion at their safe house in France. From there, the two groups remained separate for a few chapters as Bones and Grace managed to bridge the distance between them and the others worked on tearing apart the trafficking operation in the region.

Even as Bones and Grace grew closer, he still didn't let

her touch him though he took care of her. The two protected each other, when they finally reunited with the team, they continued their investigation into the wealthy participants like Maurizio Gallo.

They also come face to face with enemies of the team from the past, one who betrayed them and another who might have. They also rescue another group who were being held for sale. Eventually, after a break in Paris at a friend's place, they close the books on several of these enemies.

Lunchbox and Grace take their relationship to the next level, and he tells her his real name: Legend. She also confesses that she's fallen in love with all of them, while they don't say the words back, it's clear they are very invested in her. A message that is driven home at the end when she and Alphabet are on the way back to Montana while the team takes care of other potential dangers. They receive a call from Doc who needs their help, and while she has no compunction about helping to protect their family as they have helped her with hers, Alphabet reminds her that she is theirs too.

That brings us to Oath... and the journey gets bumpier from here.

Please be aware this book contains content with dark themes and intense situations intended for mature audiences only, including but not limited to: sexual assault, dubious consent, physical violence, emotional and mental abuse, as well as kidnapping, stalking, manipulation, and other potentially triggering topics.

And now, as always, the housekeeping notes:

For those of you who have never read a why choose, or reverse harem before, first let me thank you for picking this up and giving it a shot. Second, the heroine will not make a choice in this book or any other between the guys in her life. It may take her a while to reach that conclusion, but it's the journey that drives it. There are many ways to frame this kind of relationship, currently why choose fits it very well.

I'll see you on the flip side.

xoxo

Heather

P.S. The dog doesn't die.

PROLOGUE
BONES

There are some calls a man never wants to get. And some calls—well, you know they're coming. Whether you're the guy who enlisted or the one left behind, fate doesn't skip your number forever.

Me? I didn't have anyone waiting for me. Not for a long time. No one to devastate. No one to disappoint. I liked it that way. Cleaner. Safer. For them, and for me.

Over the years, I'd made a lot of those calls. Delivered bad news. Knocked on too many doors. The Army always sent someone, but if I could, I followed up. Reached out. Spoke to the families, the wives, the kids—the survivors.

My words couldn't bring anyone back. But sometimes, they could serve as a shield. Let grief punch something. Let guilt land somewhere. When I could, I told stories. Gave them a piece of who that soldier was—who they were to us. It wasn't much, but it mattered.

Stephanie James and I had spoken four times.

The first time was fifteen hours after the ambush that took the lower half of Alphabet's right leg and burned forty percent of Doc's body. Both men had been medevaced out. We followed.

The second call came after the doctors confirmed Doc would live, though his road ahead would be long and brutal. He'd be heading back Stateside. The third call wasn't mine—it was her returning *my* message after he arrived.

The fourth came when he started school. He was out of the hospital, trying to build something new. We kept tabs on him. I'd never leave one of mine behind. His sister was all he had, so I made sure she knew how to reach us—any time, any reason.

Doc called a few times over the years. Nothing big—intel, help with something small. We handled it, no questions asked. He'd done the same for us, more than once. When he asked for help with those prisoners they freed, we showed up.

And that's when Grace entered our lives. Doc gave her to us, and for that, we probably owed him more than I can ever repay.

So when he called again, needing help, there was never a question.

"Doc?" Lunchbox said when the line went quiet.

"I'm here," Doc answered, voice low.

Lunchbox asked, "How bad is it?"

A breath. Then—

"They killed my sister."

The words hit like a gut-shot. Four syllables—just four —but they carried a weight that bent the air. Grief. Rage. The kind of pain that leaves you hollow and burning at the same time.

"We'll be there in twelve hours," I said. "Don't move without us."

CHAPTER
ONE
BONES

The weather had turned cold, damp, and miserable. Fitting for a funeral. Grief clung to everything, soaking into skin and bone.

Doc's "gang" had been kids when he enlisted. Now they were older, harder—but still a mess. His girl was nearly half his age, and the fact that the rest of them were also involved with her made our job... complicated.

"Sorry," Doc said as he stepped out into the warehouse. The others were still inside. Voodoo, Lunchbox, and I were already suited up. Funeral black. Anonymous. We'd blend in, stay watchful.

This time, we weren't there to fight.

We were there to protect.

"You don't have to apologize," I told him. Didn't matter what he thought he was apologizing for. "You need us. We came."

End of story.

He ran a hand through his hair and gave me a tired smile. Doc had always been steady under pressure—the kind of medic who fought like hell for every life. Even under fire, he never flinched.

"You're not happy to be here," he said. Not a judgment. Just a fact.

"No," I admitted. No point pretending. "But we're here. Until it's done. You focus on you and your girl. We've got your back."

"Your girl?" It was the first time he said it out loud. Maybe he hadn't fully processed it before. But I'd seen it— the flicker of understanding in his eyes every time he looked at Grace.

"She's fine." That was as much as I was going to give him. "She and Alphabet will stay behind while we're at the service. They'll pull out before we return."

I'd been reviewing the security here, and I didn't like what I saw. Doc's people were loyal, sure—but they were also tangled up in criminal shit. Not my place to judge.

But Grace was ours.

Mine.

"Bones—" He exhaled sharply. Our eyes met, and beneath the exhaustion was a storm of grief, fury, and fear. "I should be more worried about this. And I will be. Later."

"Noted."

"For now... thanks for being here."

I gave a nod. "Let us worry. You take care of your girl."

Fifteen minutes later, we were on our way to the chapel. Alphabet had installed cameras the day before. We'd been watching the feed all night and again that morning.

No ambushes. So far.

Inside, we fanned out. One of us stayed within reach of Doc and his girl at all times. If they split, we adjusted. Doc's crew added a buffer, but grief made poor sentries. They were coated in it—thick and oily.

I wouldn't count on them to see danger coming.

The room was nearly full. We wouldn't sit. Voodoo moved to the doors. Lunchbox posted up front for a wide view. Once the service began, I'd rotate Voodoo out for an exterior sweep.

"Minister says we're starting soon," Lunchbox said over comms. "Thinks everyone's here. Want to confirm with Doc?"

I moved toward him, where he stood with his girl. "Doc..."

"Yeah, Bones. Thanks. Stick close to Little Bit if I get pulled away?"

I glanced at her. Pale, drawn, eyes wide. She looked like someone who'd barely survived a war.

"We've got her," I said. "And you. The minister says we're at capacity. He's ready to start—unless you need more time."

Delaying wouldn't change anything, but I understood the instinct. Every second stretched out the goodbye.

"We're good," he said finally, reaching for her hand.

They moved to their seats. The rest followed, one by one.

I gave the room one more sweep, nodded to Lunchbox, then stepped in to relieve Voodoo.

"I've got all angles," Alphabet said in our ears. "We're covered."

Yeah. We were.

No one was going to interrupt their mourning.

DAY one after the funeral went smoothly enough. Doc and his people were locked down, and we rotated security at the warehouse where they lived. The existing setup—both perimeter and internal—was decent.

We made it better.

Alphabet combed through the surveillance feeds, flagged weak spots, and we got the upgrades in. Cameras now covered the front, back, and interior. Inside their living quarters, the system remained separate—for privacy. Alphabet left that setup alone, working within its limits.

Trip alarms were in place. If someone failed the code twice trying to access the clubhouse, we'd get pinged. That also gave them a way to signal us under duress—fail on purpose, cameras kick in, the alert goes out.

It was solid. Temporary. Once we dealt with the bigger problems, we could remove ourselves as the first failsafe.

My phone buzzed as I reached the apartment we'd taken—three blocks out, top floor of a cleared building.

Voodoo: *Doc wants to take his girl to his place tomorrow. He needs a break.*

Me: *Understood. Just give me a time.*

Voodoo: *Done.*

I was at the door when the next message came through.

Voodoo: *You talk to Grace yet?*

Me: *There now.*

Voodoo: *Good luck.*

I snorted. It wasn't luck I needed.

The door swung open and a book came flying at my head. I barely caught it and eyed the chaos gremlin on the other end of the room. Wild blue eyes glared at me, her hair pulled up in a high ponytail, sunlight catching the dark strands like a warning flare.

"Good morning to you too, Dollface," I said, keeping my voice even.

The color on her cheeks deepened—fury now, but it looked a hell of a lot like the flush she got when she came.

"There's nothing good about it, Boney Boy."

Well. That answered that. I glanced at the book. Sick Boys. Heavy. "Bad book?"

She grabbed a marble frog and hurled it at me. I caught that too. The edges bit into my palm. Good arm on her.

Setting it down, I crossed the room.

No, I didn't need luck.

I needed body armor.

"Don't you dare," she growled, pressing a hand to my chest.

"Dare what?" I raised an eyebrow, then lifted her by the hips so I could sit and settle her in my lap.

She twisted, straddling me. That worked.

"This." She waved her hands in agitation. "Sticking me here like I'm in time-out."

"You don't like the place?" I glanced around. It was clean, quiet, and decent. Voodoo had stocked it well—a coffee machine, her favorite beans, all the bells and whistles.

She let out a long sigh, tipping her head back. Her neck arched, breasts pressing against her cotton top. I kept my gaze on her jaw.

"It's not about liking it," she muttered. "It's about being sidelined while you guys are out there."

"We're running security, not chasing targets," I said. "If anything, we're bait."

She smacked my chest again—no heat behind it, just frustration. "Exactly. You're out there taking hits while I'm stuck in here twiddling my thumbs."

"Then maybe don't throw your book," I said. "You'll have something to do."

The glare she gave me sent a wave of heat through my blood.

"Are you *trying* to piss me off?"

I tightened my grip on her hips, ignoring the itch to tear those little shorts off and *change the subject entirely.*

"Dollface," I said. "I don't have to try. You've got a temper—and you like losing it."

Her mouth formed a perfect little O, and I almost laughed. She growled, tried to push off of me. I pulled her back. A short tug-of-war ended with her throwing a punch.

I caught her fist, then the second. Hands pinned behind her back, I wrapped one arm around her. I was careful, the last thing I wanted to do was break any of those gorgeous nails she'd just gotten manicured along with the pedicure that Voodoo took her to get. That bit of pampering had put her in a better mood.

If only it had lasted.

"Right," I said, voice low. "You're in a mood. Let's fix it —*then* we'll talk."

"Excuse me?" Warning echoed in those syllables and I just slid my free hand down into her shorts and found her soaking cunt. Her pupils dilated and her nostrils flared. "This does not mean we're done fighting."

"I know, Dollface," I promised as I began to massage that swollen clit of hers. I guided the movements to the responsiveness of her reactions. The first orgasm had her crying out and riding my hand. By the time the second one hit her, I felt safe in releasing her wrists.

The third left her hanging onto me and shuddering. My cock was in hell, but I left it there. I needed to keep my head and getting her off was also the best way to curb that temper of hers, every bit as much as it helped chase away her fears.

With her breath hot against my throat, I licked my fingers clean and savored the sweetness of her. "Feel better?"

"I hate you," she muttered.

"No, you don't."

"Yes, I do."

"No," I murmured and stroked her back. "You don't."

At her silence, I smiled.

"Want another orgasm?"

"I might die."

"Well," I said and lifted her over onto the sofa and onto her back, I peeled the shorts right off and stared down at that pink pussy of hers. "Let's find out."

I kept it only to my fingers, but I used both hands this time and when she surged her hips up as she cried out, some of my control frayed.

We needed to get her home and somewhere secure.

Then I could take the time to explore her the way I'd discovered I really wanted.

THAT NIGHT, after she'd gone to sleep—sated, warm, finally relaxed—I sat by the window, one foot braced on the ledge and my hand curled around a cooling cup of coffee. City lights blinked out across the blocks like a bad heartbeat.

Alphabet had come back with Goblin late that afternoon, but he'd left us alone until after the quiet settled over the apartment like dust.

"She's not happy," he reminded me as he stepped into the room, scratching behind Goblin's ears. The mutt gave a grunt and flopped down with a groan.

"I'm aware. Her happiness is not my primary concern at the moment."

"Bones..." Alphabet sighed and grimaced, rubbing his thigh. Goblin had dragged him for a full mile at least—he needed the break. Voodoo and Lunchbox were on perimeter. I'd relieve them in an hour. I preferred the overnights. They let me think, or at least pretend thinking did any good.

"I'm listening," I said, not looking at him.

"You know this isn't all on you, right?"

I didn't answer immediately. That was the kind of thing people said when they meant well, but didn't understand. Or did—and didn't want to deal with what came next.

"I put Doc on that job," I said quietly. "I put all of you out there. Told you we had your backs."

Alphabet exhaled, slow and tired, like he'd been holding that breath too.

"You did have our backs," he said. "We're both alive because you had our backs."

"He went home. Rebuilt a life and now someone took his sister. He wants us here to protect his girl, his kids, him—he's the walking wounded in that warehouse and under guard like a civilian. That's not who he is or was."

"People get hit in this world. He's alive, Bones. He's not blaming you." Alphabet stared at me and waited until my gaze drifted back to him. "I don't blame you either."

"I don't care if either of you do," I said, and I meant it. "I blame me."

Alphabet rose, grimacing again as he stretched. "You're carrying all of it. That's not tactical. That's emotional."

"Everything about this is emotional," I snapped, then lowered my voice as I glanced toward the bedroom door. No sound. No movement. Grace was still asleep. "You think I'm splitting hairs because I want to? This is personal. But Grace..."

My throat locked up for a second. I pushed on.

"She's different. I can't risk her being part of this, Alphabet. None of us can. It's one thing when we're working her job, but this one is about standing in front of the bullets. She's not built for that." Even if she was, I wasn't.

"You sure about that?" he asked. Not antagonistic—just curious.

"She's survived a lot. Doesn't mean I want to add more to her list." I tapped my fingers against the ceramic mug, tension ticking in time. "Every time I see her upset, every time she glares or throws something or tries to argue her way in, I see it—she thinks I'm locking her out. I'm not. I'm keeping her alive."

Alphabet was quiet for a long beat. Then, "You love her."

I gave him a look.

"Yeah, yeah, I know. Don't say it. Doesn't mean it's not obvious."

"It's not about love," I muttered. "It's about obligation."

He snorted. "That's a lie you tell yourself so you don't have to admit how much this is fucking with you."

I didn't argue. Couldn't.

"I need the lines clear," I said instead. "She doesn't belong in the same world as the Vandals. They're Doc's kids and they might not be the worst people but they're criminals."

They came with their own enemies. Grace had enough problems, she did not need these.

"No one's about to let that happen to her." Alphabet glanced down at Goblin who'd come to lean against his leg. "She matters to us too, you know."

"I'm not blind." It came out clipped. "This fight isn't hers."

His expression tightened. "I get it. You're on edge. But if you shut everyone out trying to control the chaos, you'll miss something. You can't see every angle."

"I have to."

"You *want* to. But that's different." He leaned forward, elbows on knees. "Let us carry some of it. That's why we're here. And Grace? She's smart. She's fierce as hell. You give her a little more clarity, she might stop throwing frogs at your head."

That drew a half-huff of a laugh out of me. "That thing hurt."

"She's got good aim."

I ran a hand down my face, exhausted but still very much wired beneath the skin.

"She asked me today why I stuck her in the apartment like it was a cage," I said. "I didn't tell her it's the only place I can breathe when she's not in the room."

Alphabet gave me a long look, then stood, joints popping.

"You going to tell her that?"

"No."

"Maybe try it. You don't need to give her the whole op. Just the truth."

I didn't answer. He didn't wait.

"Wake me before your shift's up," he said, and whistled for Goblin. "And Bones?"

I raised an eyebrow.

"We've got your back. Always have. Don't forget it."

The door clicked shut behind him. I sat there, watching the lights blink and blur until my reflection stared back in the darkened glass, all sharp lines and heavier eyes.

I didn't forget.

That was the problem.

CHAPTER

TWO

VOODOO

Braxton Harbor smelled like rust, salt, and old lies. Felt like home, in the worst ways. The kind of place that didn't ask questions, just kept swallowing what people dumped in it—bodies, deals, regrets. Each day spent here pulled memories I'd buried deep, ones I'd stopped trying to scrub out. Not nostalgia. Just familiarity. Like the ache of a healed break when the weather shifts.

The warehouse was quiet—too quiet, if you asked me. Grief hung like low lying fog over everything. Doc, his girl, and his people—kind of funny that one of the most standup guys I knew not only hung out with an actual gang, but seemed very much at home with them.

I trusted Doc. For the most part, I trusted Doc's judgment. If it came down to trusting him with my life? I would. But I didn't—and wouldn't—extend that trust to everyone else around him. I wasn't alone in that decision. When Bones made the call to distance Grace from the Vandals and their trouble? None of us argued.

With that in mind, I took care of setting up an apartment where she could be comfortable. Neutral ground, no links to the people here, good sight lines, and private enough to keep her shielded from anyone looking for her too. We were taking turns watching over her, playing musical chairs with paranoia. She didn't like it. Not even a bit, but so far, she focused her irritation on Bones.

Probably because he'd been the one to drop the bomb on her about sitting out the next week or two. Hopefully, the job here wouldn't go longer. If it did, it did, but I suspected Grace's cooperation would be stretching it to go even one week without a solid reason beyond—we would prefer she kept her distance.

Funny thing was, most people probably assumed she'd be high-maintenance, fragile. A model wrapped in designer threads and glass expectations. But she'd adapted. Fast. Slotted in like she'd been around this world longer than I had. Joked with us. Looked after us when we needed it. Knew when to keep quiet. Knew when not to.

Firecracker was fierce, and more, she was tough as hell. Still, none of that meant I wanted her near the Vandals. They weren't just criminals—they were chaos barely held together by blood and code. They had a long and bloodied history, and, based on recent patterns, dangerous enemies. You didn't throw someone like Grace into that fire, no matter how well she walked through smoke, without a damn good reason.

It was nearing midnight when my phone buzzed. Unknown number. I sent it to voicemail. Three more calls. Three more declines. After the fourth call, the unknown number sent a text message.

Answer the phone, Asshole.

I almost smirked, but no, I didn't answer it. I didn't know the number and I really didn't give a fuck if they wanted to call me an asshole. Definitely didn't encourage me to answer the call sooner.

Five minutes elapsed before another text came through. *We need to talk. One more call, then I don't bother. DOR*

DOR.

I knew why *he* was reaching out to me and no one else. I was the one person who *might* answer the call. Then again, I wouldn't have a problem slitting his throat after what happened in France, either. So maybe not the win he was going for.

This time when the phone rang, I answered it. "Yeah?"

"I want to talk," Declan O'Rourke said. No hello, no buildup. Just that voice, like concrete grinding under a boot.

"Course you do," I muttered, stepping away from the warehouse gate.

"Just you and me."

I paused. Looked out over the water. Tankers floated out there like sleeping giants, waiting for orders. Just like the men in this business. Just like me.

"Not real fond of private meetings with people who leave bodies behind."

"You think I'd waste a bullet on you?"

"No," I said. "But I think you'd let me bleed if it made your point."

He didn't argue.

I exhaled through my nose, rolled my shoulders. "Fine. We'll discuss a spot. Somewhere I can see every damn exit and don't have to check my six."

"You don't trust me."

"Like you're surprised."

He chuckled, low and humorless. "You always this charming?"

"Only on special occasions."

Call ended.

I stared at the phone for a second too long before sliding it back into my pocket. Thought about Grace—how she'd asked earlier if she could come with me next time. Said it like it was nothing. Said it like she didn't see the weight in the spaces between the words we didn't say.

Not this time. Not with O'Rourke circling like a shark who smelled something familiar in the water. Not when the danger stalking the Vandals promised bloody retribution. Not when we still had to find her sister and deal with the rest of the sick system trafficking in people.

Bones arrived after midnight with coffee and a grim expression. At my raised eyebrows, he just shook his head. "SITREP?"

I sipped the black coffee without complaint. It was fresh and he'd brought it from our apartment so at least it was good quality. "No external movement. If anyone is watching them, they are doing it from a distance. Did two internal sweeps. No activity and no bugs. The cars are clean. We did have a couple parked a little close out here, had them moved after I swept them for explosives."

Overkill? Maybe. But our job was to anticipate what could go wrong in order to make sure it didn't.

"O'Rourke called."

Bones frowned. "What does he want?"

"To talk." I downed more of the coffee. I could go back to the apartment with the boys and Grace or I could crash here as backup for Bones. Part of me just wanted to see Grace, but O'Rourke's call made me leery.

Was he watching us? Not out of the realm of possibility. If anything, it was likely. O'Rourke dealt in intelligence. A lot like we did. Making a move with too many unknowns on the board was just not good for business. Either he knew exactly where I was or the location didn't matter.

Both made me antsy.

"I don't want to lead him back to Grace." It should go without saying, but she'd already been in close proximity to the son of a bitch. I'd prefer to keep her out of his crosshairs.

Bones' grim expression tightened further. "Agreed. We may need to reorganize her security."

No may about it. "We should. Take her off the board entirely, send her back to base with one of us." Alphabet would be our best choice. Most of what he did he could do remotely and we had the setup for it at base.

"We might need him on site and base is too far in an emergency." Bones grimaced, likely tracking possible outcomes from multiple scenarios. None of them were the best. How could they be? Of course, this was why he made captain first, not that I cared. If they promoted me, I'd have been off the team to lead my own.

I liked where I was.

"Can't be me or you," I reminded him. Bones would no sooner walk away from Doc than I would, but we needed Bones' tactical prowess and they needed me for sourcing supplies and more.

"He'll never go," Bones said in direct response to the remaining one of us that could take her. "I won't ask him."

I sighed. No, Lunchbox wouldn't go and asking him, especially using Grace as a lever, would be a shitty thing to do. "Then we need some fail-safes for her. The longer we're in place, the more risks this job takes, the greater the likelihood we pull her into the line of fire."

That was not a spot any of us were willing to put her in. Bones stared into the darkness and when he started to walk, I fell into step with him easily. The sweep took us from one end of the block that was home to the warehouse to the other.

"We need to do a full threat assessment." That didn't take long. "We also need to offer them options."

Not a bad plan. If they could just eliminate the source of the problem, that would ratchet down the threat. I finished the coffee. "I'll talk to Alphabet and to Doc. Get a list behind the who and the what. Maybe we take his girl out of this equation too. That would free them up to deal with the problem."

"Maybe." Oddly, Bones didn't disguise his distaste for the idea. "She should have a say in whether we take her into protective custody. We also need a new safe house for that and it could split our focus."

Could? No, it would. But I got it. "Then we talk to Doc, go over the potential outcomes and what they need to have happen to take the target off their backs." I wouldn't mind a few minutes with the assholes who killed Doc's sister. Yes, one man had ordered it.

We had that information.

I wanted the ones who carried out the orders. The ones who actually, physically killed her. People died in wars. Casualties happened. Civilian casualties, however, should be avoided at all costs. Everything I knew about his sister said she was definitely a civilian. Taking out the trash would be satisfying.

"Whatever you're considering over there, make sure you brief me before you do it." Bones' cool tone amused me.

"Where's the fun in that?" I didn't wait for an answer

and jerked my head toward the warehouse. "I'm going to crash here. Do a four-hour rotation, then wake me up. That will keep us both fresher for tomorrow."

He shot me a look that had me raising my eyebrows. "We need to get Grace into training."

"For?" I had an idea, but it was always better to check.

"Self-defense. Basic combat. Handling a gun." He scratched at his jaw. "The taser is good, but she needs more options if she's going to stay."

If.

"You still trying to drive her away?" Despite the dour look he gave me, I didn't retreat from the question. Instead, I met him stare for stare, and waited.

"No."

Good enough. "Do you want me to talk to her about it?" She might take it better from me. But the crackle of conflict that had electrified the air between her and Bones seemed to have abated.

"No."

"Well, don't spit it out all at once. You get chatty like this and I don't know what to do with it."

"Get some sleep, Voodoo. We'll work out a plan tomorrow."

I gave it a beat. "It's my turn to ask—you good?"

While he hadn't asked me about my mental state specifically, SITREP did cover it.

"Yes." As succinct and terse as his earlier "nos" had been.

"Why don't I believe you?"

"Because you're a pain in the ass." The deadpan, dry delivery made me grin.

"Sometimes. Particularly when you need me to be one."

It came from years of working together. We all had our own rhythms. We could adjust and adapt for each other. And had. Grace's arrival had shifted the balance entirely, something we all needed to remember and make room for, particularly if we planned to keep her.

"She may not want to stay once it's all resolved." The simple sentence was utterly devoid of all emotion. "She has a life. Had one. If she goes back to it…"

It would require that we shift what we did if we kept her. "I'm aware. Not a contingency we can begin to plan without talking to her. Something you've carefully avoided."

"Have you three made long-term plans that I'm unaware of?" The steely focus in his eyes put me on the spot. When I didn't answer, he nodded. "I didn't think you had. Planning ahead is necessary, but her future is not where her focus is."

No. It was on her sister. Or had been before this came up with Doc. "One good way to make sure we keep ourselves in the loop is to bring her in on part of this."

"You don't want her here anymore than I do."

"Then we talk to her about the whys. Instead of just making the arbitrary decision." Otherwise known as orders. We were used to it, she was still on the fence. Who the fuck was I kidding? She didn't like orders at all.

"She hasn't thrown anything today." The hint of humor in the faint curve to his mouth made me grin.

"Don't take this the wrong way, Cap," I said before bumping him on the shoulder. "But you just might need a better love language."

I headed for the doors, almost certain he wouldn't respond. He didn't until I was at them.

"She doesn't seem to mind it." The quiet words held an

odd kind of *hope* to them that made me bite back my immediate response of *yet*.

We could blast that bridge when we got to it. With my
firecracker? I was pretty damn sure that would be sooner
rather than later.

THREE

ALPHABET

Leaning back in the seat with my head resting against my interlocked fingers as I stared at the data scrolling over the screen. I'd released a few different search bots to collect data on Mark Sinclair, the head of Amorette Black's law firm along with, Bradley Sharpe, the sleazy uncle of Doc's girl, as well as her adoptive father—I'd already located the last.

Hunting this way was absolutely tedious, but ultimately satisfying. Once lined up, we could knock them all down. In addition to Sinclair, I'd gone ahead and added every other lawyer at the firm from the partners to the associates to the legal assistants. Couldn't hurt to turn over every single rock to see what slithered out.

The roll of the information was almost hypnotic. A soft snore from Goblin burst the meditative silence just in time for the front door to open and let Bones and Voodoo in. After cutting a glance at my watch, I scrubbed a hand over my face. The night had flown by. Fuck.

Pushing back from the desk, I unfolded myself and stretched. I could practically hear the creak in my joints like they'd gotten stiff from how long I'd been in the same position. Rolling my head from side to side, I appreciated the crack and the release.

Goblin sat up, one ear up and the other down. It was like having doggy bedhead. He blinked at me, then at the other two then yawned before he turned in a circle and collapsed back to sleep.

God, I felt that.

"You guys are back early," I said, barely suppressing my own half-yawn—thank you Goblin—as I picked up my coffee mug. One swallow and I grimaced, it was cold.

"Any updates?" Bones asked as he diverted into the kitchen with Voodoo and I followed them.

"Some," I admitted, smothering another yawn as Voodoo eyed the prepared breakfast plates that Lunchbox had made before he left to relieve them. "I have a lot of data coming in. Still sorting it. I've tracked Reginald Sharpe down to Vegas. He's rotating between three different casinos, playing his role as a whale and dropping a small fucking fortune."

"Losing more than he's winning?" Voodoo popped one of the thermal lids off and grunted at the waffles and bacon that were waiting. They were still hot. Lunchbox had left less than an hour ago.

"Pretty much. He's got steady funding paying off his debts. Doesn't seem to have noticed anything about his daughter or his wife from what I can see." I waited for Bones to get his own plate before I headed to the coffeemaker. "Frankly, he's a piece of shit. Drinking and gambling his way into oblivion."

"Not the first guy to bury his trauma in vice." Nothing in Bones' tone conveyed sympathy. The apartment wasn't huge, so both men stayed in the kitchen to eat while I made coffee.

"Not the first to piss away the lives of the people around him in pursuit of his addictions either." Voodoo's candor held a hell of a lot more anger. "How long has he been there?"

"Three days," I said, waiting a beat while I ground coffee to fill the portafilter. My blood would probably register more coffee beans than white blood cells at this point. "From researching previous binges. He's going to be there a while unless his brother cuts him off."

Which didn't seem likely. Bradley Sharpe might hold control of all the finances, but he paid a hefty sum to keep his brother out of the way. The pathetic coward let his piece of shit sibling pay him off, selling out his wife and child.

Disgust was far too mild a word for what I felt. There were assholes in every walk of life. But this guy was a special kind of shithead.

"Tag him and keep him under surveillance. I'll update Doc." Bones dug into his food, eating through it steadily like a man on a mission. Probably a good thing that Lunchbox *wasn't* here for that, though to be fair, he was never that fussy about whether we paid culinary homage to him.

A faint snort escaped me as I got the milk steaming. "What's the plan for today?"

"Sleep," Bones said, checking his watch. "We'll spell Lunchbox out later. I want you to stay on the searches."

"Limiting to just three of us is going to cut into your rack time," I reminded him. Normally, I wouldn't argue, but we'd been burning the candle at both ends since arriving. They hadn't even had time to do more than a casual debrief about the target elimination they'd been on before we got Doc's call.

"A few nights won't kill us. We might need some down days before we return to the mission at hand." A shrug. "We'll make it work."

Voodoo had finished his plate, rinsed it off, then grabbed a glass of water to down before he leaned back against the counter. "You have anything new on Sinclair?"

"I've begun a comprehensive dossier. I'll know what kind of porn he downloads at home and when he's away by the time I'm done. I'm also pulling everything on everyone else in the firm. Where there's one dirty bird, there's probably more." I wanted to know everything before Grace went in. If we could find out what we needed to know without ever exposing her, I'd take it.

"One more thing—" Voodoo cut himself off as a door opened deeper in the apartment. It had the faintest of squeaks. We'd made sure the hinge did squeak whenever she opened it so we'd know she was on the move.

"Good morning, sweet boy." Grace's sleep-husky tones drifted toward us as I poured the steamed milk into the cup. I'd just made a flat white. When she appeared in the doorway, the imprint of her pillow against her cheek declared she'd just gotten up. The disheveled tumble of her dark hair combined with the t-shirt hanging off one of her shoulders and those too sexy for their own good legs softened every sour note the night of research had left behind.

"Coffee?" I held out the flat white and her drowsy expression brightened.

"Oh, thank you." She reached for it, but I pulled it back to me and tapped my lips once.

"After you pay the toll."

Laughter dispelled her scowl, and probably saved my

life, but she slid between Bones and Voodoo to rise up on her tiptoes and pressed a kiss to my mouth. It was more of a sweet buss than something open, tongue swapping, and hot.

"I haven't brushed my teeth," she warned as she dropped back down. "Raincheck if you need more than a deposit?"

Yeah, Gracie made the whole goddamn day better. "I'll save it to collect later," I promised and handed her the cup.

A real smile curved her lips as she wrapped her palms around the mug. She gave me a blissful look as she took her first swallow. I swore, the warmth in her eyes was a stroke right along my cock.

"Do we get a good morning kiss?" Voodoo asked in a droll tone.

Bones watched her with this cool, almost predatory stillness to him. Cap really didn't know what to do with Grace. She threw him off his game so damn hard and it was entertaining to watch.

Most of the time.

Pivoting while she took another sip, Grace faced Voodoo and Bones. "Maybe. Have you done something to merit a kiss?"

With a snort, Bones flicked his gaze up to me. "I'm going to log some rack time. Wake me if anything breaks. I'll be up in five hours."

On that, he pivoted on his heel and left the kitchen.

"Ahh," Grace said with a long sigh. "Someone sat on that stick we keep taking out of his ass, I see."

A snort of laughter almost escaped me.

"I can still hear you, Dollface," Bones said from the other room.

Voodoo didn't seem to be fairing much better. If

anything, his compressed lips suggested he was barely containing his own amusement.

"Good, then maybe you can dislodge it before you have to ask Doc for medical assistance."

That did it, I laughed and Voodoo grinned. When Bones' only response was the closing of a door—the one that squeaked so he definitely took the bedroom we slotted for Grace. Lucky bastard. I could have been cuddled up with Grace last night, but no, I'd had to work.

"Point to me," Grace said, almost smugly as she took another sip of coffee.

"I don't have a stick up my ass," Voodoo said as he grinned at her. "Does that count as worthy of earning a kiss?"

"It'll do," she murmured, then put a hand to his chest as he dipped his head and she pushed up on her tiptoes again. Fuck, she was so damn tiny. I kept forgetting how small she was, cause her personality was just so much more.

Like me, Voodoo only got a quick kiss.

"You should get some sleep too," she was saying as I got the coffee going to make myself another cup.

"Yeah," Voodoo said with a sigh. "Be good today, Firecracker?"

"I'll think about it."

His light groan only made me smile. Grace had been enormously patient with all of us. It wasn't like we were here to vacation and she seemed to know that.

"Wait..." At the sudden sharpening of her voice, I glanced over at her and found Voodoo in the doorway to the kitchen. "Where's Legend?"

I did *not* roll my eyes. Ever since he told her his name, that was what she used. Just reinforced my determination to *never* admit mine. I did *not* need her using it. Though she didn't call Voodoo Bryant, so maybe there was something there.

"He took over at the warehouse," Voodoo said easily. "He'll be back later, when we spell him."

Her shoulders went so rigid, I had to swallow a sigh. Well, Voodoo just drove that bus right over Lunchbox. I told him cutting out before she woke up was a bad idea.

"Almost wish you were still asleep so I could go in and wake you up," Voodoo continued, then he blew her a kiss before he strolled out.

She didn't say anything, just stood there staring after where they went. Once I'd finished steaming more milk, I stopped avoiding the topic. "He has a job to do, Gracie."

"He also said I could go with him today."

"Point of order," I said with a wince. "He said if you were up for it when he left, we could work it out for you to go for an hour or two."

The icy blast in her eyes threatened to give me blue balls. "So, he just left extra early so I would still be asleep?"

When my second cup of coffee was ready, I faced her. "Yes." No point in sugar coating it. I could be diplomatic. "We're tired of telling you no, Gracie. Right now, none of us want you in the middle of this. We've explained why. You're not stupid and you're not this much of a diva, so what's up?"

Okay, so I could be mostly diplomatic. "I feel useless here." The confession didn't surprise me, not once she said it. Maybe I should have gotten that sooner, but the frustration edging each word dragged at my nerves. "All I'm doing is sitting around, watching movies, or reading, or staring out the window while you guys do the hard stuff."

"Sweetheart, I promise you, guard duty is boring as

fuck. You're usually alone, you have to stay awake, you can't relax, and then you get to do it all over again."

The mutiny in her fierce expression masked something more. Hurt.

"Gracie... If you go, you're a distraction. It also could end up with you in the line of fire."

"You just said it was tedious and boring as fuck."

"It is, until the moment it isn't."

Head tilted, she glared upward for a long moment. "Accepted." It took her a minute, but she got there. "However, I would like you take me there today, not right away, but when you have a minute."

Oh, there was a warning sign if I'd ever seen one. "For?"

"To see Legend," she told me. "Also, I want to check on that girl. She looked like hell the last time I saw her. Maybe I can't do anything else, but making her feel better is a way of helping."

She wasn't wrong. "I'll think about it. Now, are you done with your coffee?"

It was her turn to grow suspicious. "Why?"

"Because," I said after downing half of mine. "I want to take Goblin for a walk and I think you could use one too. There's probably somewhere we can grab something to eat —outside of the apartment. That will help with some of the restlessness."

The guys wouldn't like it, but I could hardly blame Grace for being on edge. I had my phone and she had hers. They could track us if they needed us.

"Really?" She brightened up and I knew I'd made the right call. Yes, she was pushing to get out of here, and to help, but it was also because she had literally nothing to do. We needed to fix that.

"Yep, and you can fill me in on how you'd like to

approach your sister's boss. I want to work out all the kinks before we do it. We have time now."

She drained the last of her coffee, then hurried over to brush another kiss to my jaw. "I know I'm a pain in the ass, but thank you for putting up with me."

I patted her ass before I wrapped an arm around her to pull her back against me. "I like your ass, whether you're being a pain or not. I never want to hurt you, Gracie. None of us do, not even Captain Stick in his Ass."

Her giggle was music to my ears.

"I'll work on listening better, you work on telling us what you need better. Deal?" I pressed another kiss behind her ear.

"Deal," she said on an exhale, then leaned her head back to look up at me. "I still want to see Legend sooner rather than later."

Yeah, well... "Like I said, I'll see what I can do. No promises." Though, a drive by wouldn't take long and later in the morning would be better than in the dark. We could make it work.

"Thank you."

I dropped a kiss on her nose. "Go put some clothes on, and then we'll go."

She scooted out almost lightning fast and I shook my head. My phone pinged as I made my way back to the computer. I was already dressed, just needed to get Goblin's harness and leash. The message was from Voodoo.

I frowned.

Voodoo: *O'Rourke called when I was on watch. He wants a meet with me. I put it off, but we need to talk it out. No, not lying to Firecracker, we'll involve her in the discussion. Make sure you're armed, since you're taking her on a walk and I put transmitters in the soles of her shoes. See you in five.*

Well, fuck.

Also, in her shoes?

I was still mulling that over when she returned in a pair of running shoes, sweatpants, and an oversized hoodie that managed to both dwarf her and look chic. Well, on her everything was "chic."

"Everything okay?" She paused, then held up a hand. "Rephrase, are we still good to go?"

I grinned. I knew what she'd meant, but clarifying was a solid first step. "Yes, we are. I need to get away from the computer anyway. I'm starting to see data in my sleep."

"Okay, I have my taser," she said, patting her hoodie on the right side. "And my phone." She patted the left side.

My smile just grew. "Getting my gun. Get Goblin's harness?"

"On it." Just like that, the tension melted away and we were out the door in under five minutes. It was dawn, gray light not quite having given away to the sunrise, but the city was already waking up. We'd gone a block when she said, "As for her boss, I want to rattle him. If she 'really' quit, then he'll be annoyed but not freaked out."

None of us believed the bullshit story. "But if he was behind her abduction?"

"Yes, that will freak him right the hell out. Or so you'd think, either way, I want to do it in broad daylight, maybe right there in his office with a lot of witnesses. Just totally screw over his whole day..."

Gracie had a vicious side to her.

I kind of liked it.

Eh, who was I kidding? I loved it.

CHAPTER

FOUR

LUNCHBOX

"**G**racie," Alphabet called, his aggrieved voice my first warning that she was even at the warehouse. Pivoting, I wanted to swear. It was bad enough that Doc's lady was just out here *wandering* around to get some air. Now Grace was *here*?

"Grace," I said as she charged right toward me. The air around her seemed to practically crackle with energy. Her brilliant blue eyes were narrowed as she closed the distance. Then before I could say anything else, she cracked her right palm against the left side of my face so hard, my eye watered.

The blow stunned me more than it hurt. With a wrathful glare, she darted around me and didn't let me reel her back in and made a beeline for Doc's dancer.

"Son of a bitch," I muttered, then cut a look at Alphabet. "Thanks for the warning."

His bland expression was less than helpful. "Told you not to ditch out on her this morning."

Really? An *I told you so?*

35

"Grace Black," she said as she introduced herself to the dancer and I didn't groan, I really didn't. "I know you," she continued. "You're Emersyn Sharpe."

"Goddammit, Gracie," Alphabet said, though his crooked grin held a lot more amusement than irritation.

"You're a dick," I informed him under my breath.

"A dick she isn't pissed at." Alphabet clapped me on the shoulder. "How sad for you."

"Ignore them," Gracie said with determination. "I intend to."

To her credit, Doc's dancer seemed to study her for a moment before she shook her hand. They weren't even five full feet away so it was hard to miss any nuance.

"Nice to meet you." Emersyn shot me a wary look before she released Grace's hand and resumed the "walk" she'd come out here to have.

Grace fell right into step with her, because of course she did. "Sorry to stage a raid on your—what exactly are we doing?" The openness in her question, and the genuine warmth was like an itch on the inside of my brain. The shift in positions also gave me a fantastic view of her ass which was beautifully shaped by the jeans she was wearing.

Jeans and—why was she in *heels*? They weren't particularly tall heels, but still.

"Walking," Emersyn told her. "And I don't mind. I already had company." Well, company was better than labeling me the watchdog that I was. "I'm sorry if we met before or if I should know you. You look familiar, but..."

"Why did you bring her?" I shot Alphabet a look, every single nerve on alert now that she was *also* present. Because it meant if a threat showed up, we had to protect both of them. If it came down to Doc's lady or ours—no, we didn't let it come down to that. It was the *other* reason we kept her from being here. "We discussed this." No way Bones signed off on this little jaunt.

"We haven't really met," Grace answer, her voice drifting back to tease me. The long braid she'd pulled her hair into highlighted her delicate cheekbones and just made her look even more fragile if that was possible. "Well, we met briefly when we got here, but that was before the funeral, and it's been a little busy."

A very brief meeting while we made a united front for Doc and kept his—and by extension the Vandals and his girl—covered.

"I recognized you because I've been to one of your shows." The wistful note in Gracie's voice intensified the itch in my brain. "And I probably look familiar because I did the campaign for Enchanté last year."

"You're a model," Emersyn said unhurriedly. "I never knew your name—sorry."

Rubbing a hand over my face, I dug my phone out of my pocket, but caught Alphabet typing on his. When I raised my brows in silent inquiry, was he pinging Doc? Alphabet nodded. If Doc could secure his girl, we could take care of ours.

"It's fine. It's the face that sold." Gracie just shrugged. I never forgot her face, but I had learned her name. "I guess you're not performing anymore?"

"Taking a break." The girls weren't really sharing much and that still seemed like too much for either of them at the moment. "I'm guessing you're not modeling?"

"No, at least not right now. I might go home— eventually."

Might go home? I didn't miss the frown on Alphabet's face. That was news to him.

"Nonetheless, I want to find my sister, and these brutes

are certain someone is looking for me." Despite her use of "brutes," there was still affection in her voice that made me sigh. She wasn't pushing us to wrap this up.

There was also no denying that she was in a holding pattern.

"I'm sorry," Doc's dancer said. "Where is your sister?"

"I think she was taken by the same type of people who took—"

"Little Bit," Doc said, the interruption stopping both women. The dancer spun and she locked her stare on Alphabet briefly before looking to where Doc approached. "Can we talk?"

"You okay if I step away?" Emersyn asked. It really wasn't an unfair question considering the icy lasers Grace fired our way.

"I'll be fine," she said. "It was nice to meet you again. Maybe *next* time, some people can mind their own business and let us walk."

"You are our business, sweet cheeks," I told her, a little over the attitude. I got it. She was pissed. I could take the lumps, *after* we made sure it was safe. "And so is the little dancer. Now stop proving how difficult you can be, and let these two go talk."

Far from chastised, Grace rolled her eyes but it was hard for her to hide the hint of a smile on her lips. She might be pissed at us, but it was more about the moment.

I could work with that.

As for Doc's girl, she just snorted. "I'd like that—being a little dancer and all—I need my little walks."

Alphabet huffed a laugh even as Gracie grinned. Right. Those two didn't need to become friends. We had enough trouble keeping Gracie's sassy mouth out of trouble. Doc lifted his chin as he guided the dancer back inside the security of their residence and Grace folded her arms as she faced us.

"I'm not apologizing," she informed me after Doc and Emersyn were secure and I could focus on her.

"Fine." I shrugged. I'd taken worse hits. "You being here is bad for me."

She frowned. "AB mostly explained that." It wasn't an apology so much as an acknowledgment. "But you should have still *told* me rather than sneak out."

"Accepted." I nodded once. "Tactical error. Won't make the same one again. Doesn't mean I'll ever apologize for wanting you to be safe."

"Fine," she said, the soft bow of her mouth pursing into the hint of a smile as she mimicked my earlier tone.

"Excellent," Alphabet said as he slung an arm around Grace's shoulders. "You've seen him and lodged your complaint. Time to go, Gracie."

She tilted her head back to look up at him, but he wasn't playing. In fact, he was deadly serious. As much as I wished he *hadn't* dragged her right into the middle of this, I got it.

"Okay," she answered in a low tone before she glanced at me. "Do you need anything? Before we go? Food? Drinks?"

"Back massage?" It was a tease and I had to remind myself to keep my head on a swivel rather than just stare at her like I wanted.

"Hmm, you'll have to earn that reward." The invitation to play was right there in her voice.

"Yeah, I made her coffee and got a kiss." Alphabet grinned. "You're lagging behind."

I just flashed him a middle finger without taking my gaze off Grace. "I just need you to be safe and secure so I can keep my mind on this job. I'll talk to you when I'm back and I promise, if you're asleep when I plan to leave again, I'll wake you up."

It was a concession and based on the very real relief sliding through her eyes, I wanted to kick myself.

"Alphabet?" I asked in quiet undertone.

"I got it. Take five," he gave Grace a squeeze then pressed a kiss to the side of her head. "You be nice. He's taken his punishment like a good boy."

Her snort in no way detracted from her smile. Even as Alphabet took the perimeter, I narrowed the distance to Grace further and cupped her face in my hands.

"I'm sorry if I worried you," I said. "While I'll never apologize for putting your safety first, I shouldn't have hurt you to do that."

She covered my hands on her face and let out a shaky breath. "I know I'm not easy."

"Don't see any of us asking for easy, do you?"

"No." Her tremulous smile wavered. "I just need to do something and to feel useful."

The itch in my brain started up again. "Or you feel guilty because you're basically sitting still."

"And Amorette seems to get farther and farther away." She licked her lips. "I'm not saying we need to drop helping Doc or these people and leave. You have been helping me look for and protect my family. I meant what I told AB, I want to help you with yours."

"But you're not doing anything." Yeah, fuck, I could see that. Looping an arm around her waist, I picked her up so we could be face to face. That and I loved the feel of her pressed right up against me. "I get it, Gracie. Waiting is the hardest damn thing any of us does. You may think you're doing nothing, but you're not. You're staying secure so we can focus on protecting them and digging up the assholes who killed his sister and are threatening his girl."

"And you guys don't want me around…" She waved at the warehouse.

"Yes, but none of us want to have to choose who we protect, you or them." Because I loved Doc like a brother and I would do anything, but I wasn't losing Grace to do it.

"Don't come at me with your passion-fueled logic." She wrapped her arms around my neck and hugged me. "I am sorry I slapped you so hard."

"No, you're not." I teased her and her soft laugh told me I was right. Then I nuzzled a kiss to her jaw. "Now, do me a favor and get the hell out of here. Go work on research with Alphabet or we'll find another task for you. As hard as staying still and doing nothing is, Gracie, you are helping us. I promise."

She stroked her fingers over my scalp, the caress light but it still sent electricity through my my system. "I do want to help—I want this to work. Whatever this is."

Yeah, so did I. "You know we want you."

"AB said I was one of yours too." A small smile. "Still not one hundred percent sure how it will all work out. There are four of you and then there is me and—"

"We'll make it work," I promised her. Another kiss and then I made myself put her down. "Be good for Alphabet, okay?"

"No promises." She wrinkled that adorable nose of hers. "Sweet Cheeks?" At the doubtful tone, I laughed for real.

"You were trying to get under my skin."

"And it worked." She practically dared me to deny it.

"Hence the sweet cheeks." When I raised my eyebrows, her grin just grew almost impossibly wider.

"I know, I'll go and be good."

She took three steps and I caught her arm to tug her back to me. "Grace…" Wrapping an arm around her shoulders to pin her back to my chest, I dipped my head to murmur. "Do you still love me?"

"Yes." No hesitation. Not even an element of teasing to make me work for it. "Yes, I love you, Legend. I love all of you."

Honestly, every fucking time she said it, it took me out at the knees. The ease, the way the words flowed off her tongue, but more the depth and the meaning.

"That's how we make this work," I said more determined than ever. "Trust me?"

"You drive a hard bargain." But she rubbed her sexy little bottom right against my crotch as if to emphasize the words.

"You really are asking for it," I growled and she laughed.

"Time for me to go now." She pressed a kiss to my jaw before she pulled away. "Off to be a good girl with AB." The jaunty little salute just made me shake my head.

Brat.

She was a brat and I didn't want her any other way. She was also—happier. Color flushed her cheeks, and I made a mental promise to *not* ditch the conversations next time. Grace had all the words for us. She was putting herself out there and I needed to do the same thing.

Alphabet lifted his chin as Grace reached him and I nodded. "Look after her," I mouthed the words and he nodded. No arguments there.

I made my way across the warehouse as they left via the side door. I needed to return to my circuit, but I also wanted to make sure they got off safely. Once they had, I returned to the quiet of the warehouse and resumed my vigilance.

Grace deserved a hell of a lot more than we were doing right now. Once we got all this done, once we wrapped this for Doc, found her sister, and dealt with the traffickers. I would prove to her how we could make this work.

FIVE

GRACE

It seemed to take months, though it had really only been a matter of weeks for the guys to wrap up their mission for Doc. Even when I wanted to pace the walls, I fought against my own restlessness and impatience. They were doing exactly what they needed to do.

And me? I was keeping my promise… I stayed put when they needed me to stay put. I worked with Alphabet when he needed it, locked down when he had to go with the guys. I was never *far* from them, but I wasn't on the front lines. I wasn't a distraction.

Every single day I kept that promise felt like a betrayal to Amorette. One thing to come out of all that time, I found out how to haunt Reddit, Substacks, and more. I found all these nooks and crannies that dug into attorneys, their work, and their ethics. I learned things about the firm Amorette worked for that puzzled me.

They weren't *bad* exactly, but their reputation in the area of law she focused on wasn't the best. If anything, they were more known as high-powered criminal and corporate attorneys. The kind of work Amorette did for women in bad situations—almost all of it pro bono—was just public relations for the firm. Something they could use to scrub up their image.

Former associates who worked for them shared deep cuts on buried subreddits that AB found for me with his bots. The more I read, the more it *pissed* me off. Most of them were socially conscious, morally upright people—at least based on their posts. They'd gone into law looking to *help* others.

They were the Amorettes of their time.

Most associates were expected to put in eighty hours a week, they had to also deliver on minimum billable hours and most of that was doing grunt work for the other senior attorneys in the firm. The pro bono was a carrot to keep them sweating up the hill and so the firm could bank their sweat equity in both directions.

But when it came time for promotion? They weren't the ones invited to buy in and eventually, they figured it out. They were phased out or driven out so the next crop of idealists could be put through the grindstone.

A knock on the desk next to me jerked me out of my reverie where I was doom scrolling through the subreddit. My heart hammered against my ribs, the shock more than a little jarring. Bones stared down at me, his expression unreadable and his eyes almost glacial.

Nobody deserved to be that damn good looking. None of them. But Bones? He needed to get laid but since the only time he touched me was to get me off—and who thought I'd *ever* think that was a bad thing—but he *never* let me touch him. At this point, I'd stopped offering.

You could love someone and not like them. Most of the time, we got along. But lately? I swore, being around him was like wearing the itchiest, cheapest polyester. "Yes?"

"We've got a date. Let's go."

I blinked slowly and then leaned back in the chair. I scrolled through my mental calendar, it being so full and all that, but I didn't recall even the suggestion of a date. After leaving Braxton Harbor, we'd ended up at some *new* safe house, this one in New Mexico not far from the Colorado border. I almost asked them if there was a bingo card for their various domiciles. Almost.

Ultimately, I'd decided against it. They were all tired, bruised, and more than a little battered. They'd been running on vapors, and I wanted them to *rest* even more than I wanted back on my own search.

"I'm going to go with my first thought," I said after a beat. "What date?"

Instead of answering, he nudged the rolling chair back and closed the laptop that Voodoo had sourced for me and AB set up.

"Let's go, Dollface."

"Go where?"

Rather than answering me, he just held out a hand. The silent demand of *let's go* just rolled off of him.

Blowing out a breath, I clasped his hand and let him pull me out of the chair. I was in a pair of marble colored yoga capris and a black Y-back sports bra. "I'm not dressed to go anywhere."

He swept a cool look over me. "What you're wearing is fine." A beat. "You need shoes though. Put them on."

Just... shoes.

Helpful.

"Okay, gimme a minute." I sent him a bright smile. It was one I'd worked on for the camera. The one that would light up my eyes whether I was feeling it or not. When his eyes narrowed in suspicion, a little burst of joy filled me but

I made a beeline for the bedroom they'd given me in our new place.

The square—well rectangle really—sprawl of the adobe structure surrounded a center lap pool, that in itself, surrounded a meditation garden with a koi pond. It was kind of tranquil. The spill of the water into the lap pool circulated it and added a soothing rhythm. The koi were lovely and I could tan if I wanted to, but I made sure to use plenty of sunscreen the two times I'd been out there.

It was better at night. The house was far enough out that we had a decent night sky, but nothing like the view from "Base." A wistful sigh escaped me as I found the shoes I wanted in the closet. I slid into the four-inch heels. We hadn't actually made it back to their Montana after returning to the States.

More and more it looked like we wouldn't and—I was in this odd place of wanting to both go there and find Amorette simultaneously. Shaking off those competing sensations, I headed back out to where Bones waited for me at the end of the hall.

He dragged his gaze over me as I sauntered toward him. Despite his earlier wariness, his expression barely shifted. Oh well, I still had fun wearing the shoes. "Ready to go."

"Follow me." He was already striding away. Though for a split second, I thought I caught a hint of his lips curving. Probably just the light. Instead of the front door or even the garage, he headed toward the opposite wing where another structure jutted off from the main house.

I hadn't been out there, no reason to and as far as I knew, they weren't using it. When he opened the door to a full-on gym right down the free weights, weight machines, and mats, I raised my brows.

Lips pursed, I shook my head. "Well played, Boney Boy. Well played."

With a light snort, he curled his fingers in a beckoning gesture. "The heels are a good choice. You often wear them, so learning to do this while in heels will be effective."

Caution flooded me and I slowed my pace. "Learning to do what?"

He was at the side of the room and he stripped off his shirt—which in and of itself seemed a party foul. The man was exceptionally ripped and he had an inordinate number of scars. They all did, but I never got a chance to really map his. Even if he slept without a shirt on, he *always* woke up before I did.

"To fight," he said over his shoulder.

"Excuse me?" Arms folded, I crossed the room. The clip of my heels was muffled against the different flooring.

"Self-defense, Dollface," he continued. "Come here so I can wrap your hands."

That made me stop dead. "First of all, stop giving me orders. I didn't join the army and I don't report to you."

He fixed those cool gray eyes on me. "No, but you are continuously going into dangerous situations and you have a mission you want to undertake."

A mission...

"That's just to play Am, while I fake out her boss to find out what the hell he did." That didn't seem even remotely as dangerous as the other challenges we'd faced. "I've done way harder stuff already."

"I know." Clipped. Terse. "You've handled yourself well, even if you've also been hurt."

Mouth open to argue, I blinked. The compliment threw me.

"However, there's luck, and then there's training.

Relying on luck will get you killed. You will not die on my watch. So, we need to train you."

I stared at him and it genuinely took me a moment to find my voice. "You're serious."

"Yes," he said, crossing toward me with what looked like a roll of red gauze. "Deadly serious." The man towered over me as he took my right hand in his then began to wrap it. "We don't have enough time to put you through an accelerated combat course."

That made me picture both of us in fatigues with streaks of black to keep down the glare and… This close, the muscles in his chest rippled with each movement of his hands as he wound the tape over my knuckles then across my palm.

"You're going to learn a handful of moves, then repeat them until they are second nature—until your muscle memory has you responding before you even think about it." The measured tones jerked my gaze upward to find him not looking at me but at my hands.

"And we have this kind of time?" The leads were getting colder and colder. That was one thing when we were fighting a battle for Doc and his friends. This was different.

"We're making the time," he said, checking the tautness of the tap. "Flex your hand. Now make a fist."

The manicure I'd gotten while in Braxton Harbor had grown out. So, I'd filed them and just gone for shaped at this point. The guys had picked up the polish I asked for, and the simple pink gave them the suggestion of length. Asking for another manicure so soon seemed a really bad form all things being equal.

He made some adjustment then went to taping up my left hand. "Your target has almost eighty pounds, and eight inches on you in height. Physically, you are not only smaller, you *are* weaker. If he decides to blitz you, and you don't at least know some manner of real defense—he could kill you."

It was only the hoarse note that crept into his chilly tone at the end that kept me from being a real bitch back at him. However... "Newsflash," I said softly. "I've always been small and men have *always* been a threat."

Pausing when he finished taping my left hand, he fixed those stone-gray eyes on me. "Yes, they are. While I don't think you'll ever be able to take down a fully trained combat veteran or even a lightly trained one, particularly if they outweigh you and are much taller—there are things you can do that can incapacitate and buy you time. Even a few seconds can mean the difference between them getting their hands around your throat and us getting to you."

My heart fisted for a moment, the squeeze making it kind of hard to breathe.

"You're a lot bigger than Am's boss."

A faint smile touched his lips. "So, we know if you can stop me, you can definitely stop him."

Blowing out a breath, I tilted my head. "You know, I know how to walk with my keys slotted between my fingers to create claws if I have to be on the street. I've carried mace before then pepper spray. I also know that if you kick a man in the balls, he's going to be too busy holding them to hang onto me."

"Those might be fine for a mugger, but they won't stop someone truly determined to hurt you. Sometimes, it will just piss them off."

"I've never seen a man shake off having his balls meet my knee." Honestly, the first time I slammed my knee into the balls of a guy had been behind the bleachers when I was fourteen and a senior named Hampton had gotten really friendly. He also didn't take no for an answer. The best part beyond the explosion of air he released had been him actually slamming into one of the struts as he doubled over.

Two hits for the price of one.

Not that I was going to bring that up right now. Am had always been big on self-defense and so had Eleanor—

All of my mirth dissolved. Eleanor was dead.

"Kick me in the balls," Bones said.

Wait— what?

"I'm sorry, I think I misheard you."

An actual huff of laughter left him. "You didn't." He'd finished taping my hands and tossed the roll back toward the bench. "Kick me in the balls."

Of all the things for him to say, I just stared at him. I wanted to *touch* him, not *hurt* him. "You know that might be going a bit—"

All at once, he grabbed my biceps and hauled me up off my feet. His pitiless expression arrested every single thought I had as he glared at me and put his face right up to mine.

"What would you do now?"

Since he was asking...

I kissed him.

SIX

GRACE

Something in Bones forever dared me to defy him. Even when we were cooperating, it wasn't about working together—it was about doing it *his* way. He set my body on fire, but never let me touch him. The stroke of his fingers could drive me to orgasm over and over, but not once did his lips even so much as brush mine.

Did I ask them to train me? To teach me? To help me help them? Yes, I had. But I didn't sign up to be in the military and I sure as shit didn't promise to obey every single order. That was what Bones did—he *commanded*.

He didn't ask. He didn't suggest. He said jump and expected my ass to be in the air when I asked how high. After the past few weeks of bending over backwards to be "good," I was done.

Done waiting.

Done pretending.

Done playing nice.

Of course, when he wanted to know what would I do if he dragged me off my feet and put his face in mine? I did exactly what I would do. I kissed him before I could talk myself out of it. The flex of his fingers around my biceps kept my arms trapped at my sides, but I made the most out of crashing my mouth against his.

The contact was a shock—sharp, electric, like stepping off a ledge and realizing too late you meant to fall. For a second, he didn't move, and my stomach sank. Had I made a mistake? But I didn't pull back. I pressed in harder, demanding a response.

I had to know and he could at least—but then he kissed me back and everything just *snapped*.

Anger and desire surged up, hot and tangled. I bit at his lip; he squeezed my arms. It wasn't romantic. It was messy, furious. A clash of pride and pain and everything we'd left unsaid. I wanted to bruise him with it. I wanted him to feel how long I'd held it in. His hands gripped tighter, his breath rough, matching mine beat for beat.

But something shifted—somewhere between the fury and the fire.

The kiss deepened, turned hungry, almost desperate. I wanted to slide my fingers into his hair while his hands roamed over me, but I couldn't move. We were trapped in this moment, with our mouths feasting on each other. Wildfire consumed the anger and irritation. I drowned in the want of him, and it cut all the safeties.

I devoured him—or maybe he devoured me. The whole world narrowed to where we connected. We thrust our tongues against each other's in an infuriating duel. Suddenly, he jerked his head back to stare at me. His pupils were huge, and his breathing as ragged as my own.

That was something.

"What the hell was that?" he growled in a harsh voice.

Oh, there he was. Snarly Boney Boy doused the incendiary moment with the cold reality.

"That—" I said, licking my lips, savoring the taste of him that already had me addicted, "was a distraction." I slammed my knee into his crotch—just like he'd demanded.

Shock rippled over his face, swiftly followed by pain. His hands spasmed and opened. I dropped to my feet even as he went down, gasping.

Still panting, I put my hands on my hips and met the blazing storm in his eyes. "That's how I do it—anyway. So what's my next lesson?"

Coughing once, Bones continued to glare at me. "Doll-face, you ever kiss another guy like that when he's attacking you, I'll kill him and spank you."

A little shiver went through me. That was hot. "Don't threaten me with a good time."

Irritation still raged in his eyes as he straightened. A part of me wanted to apologize, but I bit my tongue.

"Grace..."

"Don't you 'Grace,' me," I said, wagging a finger at him. "You said the objective was to kick you in the balls. I did it. How I do it is my business."

"So throwing yourself at a guy is *how* you do it?"

I shrugged, then folded my arms to contain the sudden trembling rioting through me. "It was how I survived being taken." I wouldn't apologize for *that*. "I'm not a six-foot-four badass who can kill someone with my pinky. If kissing someone means they stop hurting me, then I'll kiss them. If fucking them means I don't get beaten *and* raped, then I'll do that too. All I have to do is *survive*. You don't get to judge me for how I do it."

His frown deepened. "That was—" He cut himself off abruptly, slicing a hand through the air. "Time out. I need clarification." The emotions simmering in his stormy gaze decried the sudden calmness in his expression.

"I'm listening." My pulse continued to race as I went hot, then cold, then hot again.

"Did you have to do that when you were taken?" He held up a hand before I could answer. "Did you have to have sex with those men to prevent them from raping you?"

"If I did?" I couldn't quite quell the defensiveness. From soul-searing kiss to wild agitation, I wasn't sure I wanted to keep going. As it was, I backed up a step before I even realized I was moving.

"Dollface," Bones said, his rough voice softening. "I'm *not* angry with you."

I swallowed hard, fighting to strangle the freefall of anxiety ripping through me. "Then why do you want to know?"

"Because you're hurting." The gentleness in those three words cut the ground out from underneath me.

"I'm fine." I didn't want to focus on what hurt or why it would. At his skeptical look, I lifted my shoulders in a shrug that I just wasn't feeling. "I'm fine. I didn't get beaten or raped. Is it my favorite memory? No. But I made it in one piece."

The ground beneath my feet continued to shift as he took a step closer. Before I could stop myself, I backed up to keep the distance between us.

"You're not okay."

"It doesn't matter." I shook my head. "Look, you wanted to do some self-defense. So let's do self-defense."

His brows drew together as he studied me. I had no idea what he was looking for, but I lifted my chin even as my heart thumped more painfully.

"Come here," he said in a deceptively soft voice. Before I

could argue that he was giving me another order, he added, "Please."

Everything in me just—stopped. Like a game on freeze-frame. Then, as if he'd just turned the right piece in some knock-off Tetris mobile game, all the rows beneath my feet just broke apart and crumbled.

My feet were moving before I even registered making a decision. This time when I crashed into him, Bones wrapped his arms around me and held me tight.

The bare skin of his chest was hot as fire under my palms as I slid my hands up to wrap around his neck. A part of me wanted to run the other way, but the rest of me just held on.

"I'm fine," I repeated in a horrible, wobbling tone as my jaw trembled. The shaking hit me next, my teeth clicking and tears filming over my vision. "I'm *fine*."

"You're fine," he repeated, all but cradling me as I clung to him. I did *not* want to cry. But the damn tears wouldn't stop sliding down my face.

One of my shoes slipped off as he moved, but then he was sitting down and I was in his lap. My nose had started to run even as the tears wouldn't stop. He shifted me around like I was a doll, and then began to rub my back in slow, even circles.

I had no idea how long we sat there. Bones murmured a lot of soft words, but they all bled together into just this low hum. If not for the faint vibration of his chest, I wouldn't even have realized he was still speaking.

Swallowing hard around a lump, I tried to pull back and stop. But Bones kept his arms around me and then pressed my cheek back to his shoulder.

"I can't seem to stop," I hiccupped.

"I'm not going to melt," he continued in that same gentle voice. "I'm not that sweet."

Surprise arrowed through the misery. "You're not?"

"Not according to the chaos pixie who keeps turning everything upside down in my life, no."

Oh. I sniffled, trying to reconcile which of the guys he was talking about. But no, he wouldn't call them that. Even as I tried to sort it out, the awful hiccups kept jerking little pops of sound out of me.

"Do you have a girlfriend?" I knuckled away some of the tears as I leaned back to look at him.

That earned me a bland look as I blinked trying to focus my sore eyes. For once, I was really glad I'd skipped any kind of makeup today. Because in addition to a shiny, drippy nose, I'd have runny mascara or something to go with it.

"Apparently not," he said slowly and I frowned.

"Apparently—" Squeezing my eyes shut, I sniffled again but when I opened my eyes he was still there and his bland expression had given way to something more incredulous. "I just—who is the manic pixie?"

"Chaos pixie," he corrected even as one corner of his mouth kicked up. Then with callused fingers, he gently traced away some of the tears still tracking down my face.

"Right—oh." Then it hit me. "You think I'm a chaos pixie?"

"Think?" He shook his head. "I *know* you are."

I sniffled again. "I really hate crying."

"It looked like so much fun, too." The deadpan response had me smiling, a little. "The shiny nose—it's very attractive."

Even if the tears were still leaking a little, I stared at him in actual disbelief. "Really?"

"On you?" He nodded. "You're always attractive. Though, I would prefer you didn't hurt to do it."

"I'm not hurting." No sooner did I say it than he raised his eyebrows. "Fine. I have to be fine. I can't—"

One ragged breath.

Two ragged breaths.

Then...

"I did it to survive. If I break up about it now, then I'm admitting I let them hurt me. That *I* hurt me to do it. I—just did it so I could make it out the other side." I licked my lips, this time just tasting the salt from my tears.

"Doing something to survive doesn't mean remembering it won't hurt." The even tone held not one ounce of judgment. He'd actually moved one of his hands to my lower back and traced light circles with his thumb against my skin.

It grounded me.

"Doesn't mean you don't get to hurt over it either." Another gentle caress of his fingers against my cheek to wipe away more tears. "Hurting tells us we're alive. Even when we aren't sure we deserve to be."

I wanted to protest, but the last sentence stilled the words on my tongue.

"Survival is hard. Surviving is a little easier, but once you've survived, you have time to look back. To question. To wonder. To decide what you could have done, should have done maybe, or would have if you had known everything."

I didn't think we were talking about me anymore and I *listened.* "Hindsight is twenty-twenty and all that."

"Yes, it is. Because once you've survived, you know what happened. You have all the details, not the suppositions or the maybes or even the possibles, you *know.* But you can't know until it's over."

He rubbed his cheek gently against my forehead. The faintest rasp of his stubble seemed inordinately loud, but I held on fast to the prickly feeling of it.

"I didn't want to die," I admitted. "When I woke up in that place, I didn't want to die. I didn't want them to hurt me like they were hurting those other women." Each word seemed to break loose from the stone where I'd entombed those memories. "I didn't want to think about it. Even when I told you guys about it—"

This wasn't the first time. I'd danced around it maybe, or rushed past it.

"If you don't say it out loud, it didn't happen." He tilted his head back, watching me from beneath his lashes.

"Maybe," I said. "I wanted to be tough and strong and just—you know, get through it."

"You are tough." Straightforward. Simple. "You're also strong."

I sniffled again. "You're just saying that."

"Well, you did kick me the balls."

A smile twitched at the corners of my lips. "You told me too."

Amusement seemed to stealth into his expression. "I did."

"So do I pass?"

With care, he traced a finger down the center of my face, then gently touched my nose before he tapped it against my lips. "No."

I blinked.

"No?"

"No." He repeated.

Outrage struck a damp spark. "But I did it."

"Yes, you did. But that wasn't the lesson."

I made a face. "Oh." Then I sighed. "I distracted you."

"Dollface, you've been doing that since you showed up." The admission seemed like a lot. Then he cupped my cheek and leaned in to press his forehead to mine. "Grace—you are stubborn, infuriating, mercurial, and oftentimes, delightful. I will never *judge* you for what you did so you survived."

Relief flooded me.

"Never," he repeated. "Wounds have to be cleaned out, then stitched closed if we want them to heal. This wound, it's in there, whether you want to say it is or not."

I swallowed hard.

"It's been in your dreams. It's been pushing you to keep moving. Keep going—always forward. If you sit still for too long, it's going to catch you."

I wanted to look away.

I didn't.

"I haven't been moving that much."

"No," he said. "You've been entrenched so we could take care of things. That mission is done, we can move forward again."

Blowing out a slow breath, I nodded and let my gaze dip to where I was smoothing my hand over the hard packed muscle of his shoulder. There were dips, and dimples in the skin. Scars. Some places were smoother than others.

Burns?

I didn't want to ask.

"We have the mission specs, we can do a black bag job and scoop up the boss." He made it sound like we could swing by the grocery store.

"Get ice cream while we're at it?"

Another flicker of a smile. "If you want." Then, he tucked a finger beneath my chin and lifted my gaze back up to his. "You want to take this man on. You want to confront him yourself. Your way."

"Because——-"

"Shh." He pressed his finger to my lips. "You don't need to tell me why. I get it. Amorette is your sister. You'll burn the world down if you have to in order to get her back."

Yes.

Yes, I would.

I sucked my upper lip between my teeth as he searched my gaze.

"We will help you, but you have to train. I need you to know everything you can do to protect yourself."

"Except the kissing thing as a distraction?"

"You may kiss him if you wish," he offered, almost magnanimously. "I will kill him slowly and feed him his own intestines however."

God, that made me feel—good. Maybe I really was fucked up. "So, maybe a different plan?"

"If you'd like..."

"Bones?"

He just raised his brows.

"Why haven't you ever kissed me?"

"Because I'm not good enough for you. None of us are." That was *not* the answer I expected.

I frowned. "Shouldn't I get to decide that?"

"No," he said, not even seeming to hesitate. "We're all damaged, Grace. All of us. Some of us just hide it better. You deserve better, a lot better."

Then, paradoxically, he brushed his lips against mine.

"You confuse me."

That netted me a real smile. "Good. The feeling is mutual."

CHAPTER

SEVEN

GRACE

"*Good,*" *he'd said with a real smile. "The feeling is mutual.*"

After my utter breakdown in the gym, Bones had me wash my face, drink some water, then we started again. The next two hours had left me limp as a dishrag with spaghetti muscles, sweat soaked hair, body odor that wasn't remotely pleasant, and a nagging headache.

"Go shower. We'll have food after." He'd given my shoulder a squeeze before he'd gestured to the door.

Frankly, I was too damn tired to argue with him which might have been a first. I even ditched the heels on my way back through the house semi-aware that Bones followed.

"Hey..." Alphabet straightened from where he leaned against the breakfast bar across from where Legend was cooking. Legend frowned, worry flickering across his expression as he stared at me then turning almost thunderous as he glanced past me.

"Hey," I managed to say with a little wave. "Don't let

63

my appearance fool you. I totally managed to kick his pinky toe there at the end."

It took all my training and experience to not grimace at the stairs. My quads screamed with each step as I made my way up, but I didn't stumble. Not once.

"What the fuck…" came Alphabet's half-growled imprecation.

As tempting as it was to turn around and look at them, I didn't. Because I wasn't entirely sure I wouldn't collapse. Particularly since I seemed to be leaning in the direction I faced. If I glanced back, I had the sad realization I might fall face first down the damn stairs.

Voodoo had a phone to his ear where he stood in the center of a bedroom as I passed. At his frown, I lifted a hand to wave at him in passing. Pretty sure it came off more like a swipe of "hey" rather than the bouncier, more upbeat waggly fingers of "hello."

Fairly certain I wasn't limping only out of actual exhaustion rather than determination, I kept moving. Stopping might mean I didn't make it. I had to have some pride. At least enough to get into the shower.

After that, I could sit under the pound of hot spray. Doing a mental handshake on that deal I just offered myself, I managed to not shuffle my steps until I reached the bedroom I'd claimed for myself. Dropping the shoes on the floor, I peeled the sports bra off on my way into the bathroom.

The gross stink of my own sweat assaulted me even as my muscles screamed their objections to trying to yank it off. The tile on the bathroom floor was deliciously cool against my aching feet. I stretched into the shower to twist the knob on to get the spray going.

I almost tipped sideways but caught myself with a

ragged little laugh. Then I caught sight of myself in the mirror. Flushed cheeks, too bright eyes, and sweat gleaming off my skin even as my hair stuck as uncomfortably to me as my clothes.

Right, I needed to get the capris off and then into the shower. Leaning there, however, I wasn't sure I could push myself straight. A shuffle of step in the doorway dragged my head up to find Bones in the doorway to the bathroom with Voodoo just a few steps behind him.

"Not now," Bones said over his shoulder, then he shut the door in Voodoo's face and locked it.

Surprise rippled through me at the storm of heat in Bones' traditionally cool eyes. All my usual pithy comments seemed to vanish in the face of his steely gaze as it swept over me. I did manage a somewhat weak, "Hi."

Definitely not my best effort.

"Hi." He never had put his shirt back on and what immunity I'd developed during my emotional breakdown and subsequent self-defense "lesson" collapsed in the face of his rugged, muscular frame filling the bathroom to the brim.

Without another comment, he toed off his own shoes, then stripped the sweatpants and boxer briefs, revealing a body honed by years of physical training and combat. His muscles rippled with each movement, a testament to the hours spent in the gym and on the field.

I couldn't help but admire the way his body moved, fluid and powerful, like a predator ready to strike. His presence was overwhelming, a mix of raw strength and an almost primal energy that seemed to fill the room. It was a sight that was both intimidating and undeniably alluring, a perfect blend of power and grace that left me breathless.

"You need help?" The depth of his voice was a temptation all its own.

"Help?" I blinked slowly. Help with what? All the moisture in my mouth evaporated, however, as he closed the distance between us. The slow, deliberate pace of his steps was almost feline in intensity.

"With this," he murmured, his voice a low, velvety purr that seemed to caress every inch of my skin. The words danced over my overheated flesh, igniting a trail of goosebumps that left my body tingling with anticipation.

I could feel the heat pooling in my core, my breath catching as both of my nipples peaked, aching for his touch. The air between us crackled with tension, a silent promise of what was to come, and I found myself yearning for his hands to explore every curve and contour of my body.

The "this" as it turned out were my capris. He rolled them—and the scrap of panties I'd been wearing—down over my hips and then dragged them down my legs as he knelt in front of me. Thoughts in turmoil, I tracked his path as his thumbs skimmed along my thighs and lower until he reached my ankles. Then, and only then, did he tilt his head up to meet my gaze.

"Lift your foot Dollface."

I raised my right knee just enough that he could tug the fabric off that foot. Then I repeated the motion with my left knee. The steamier air in the bathroom offered little in the way of relief. Particularly not with the way he ate me up with his gaze.

He tossed the fabric behind him to join his sweats with a careless kind of gesture. The breath kept backing up in my lungs as he held me captive in his stare.

"How long do I have to enjoy this obedient side of you?" The edge of something devilish curled through me at his remark and I raised my eyebrows. His sudden, uncensored grin stunned me back to silence before my smart-ass remark escaped. "That long, huh?"

As he straightened, his chest brushed against mine until he reached his full height and I had to lift my chin to stare up at him. With one finger, he traced a line from my brow to my cheek, and then finally to my lips.

Torn between curiosity and need, I wet my lips even as I sucked his finger into my mouth. His pupils seemed to grow fatter as he watched me. Contact between us narrowed down to where he slowly thrust his index finger into my mouth. I ran my tongue in circles around the tip then stroked it along his finger as he pressed it all the way in.

His nostrils flared and my cunt clenched around emptiness as the idea of trading out his finger with its roughened calluses for the steel silk of his cock.

After swallowing once, I pulled off his finger to look down at him. It was the first time I'd really gotten to *see* him. Not just part of him, but all of him. His cock seemed to hang heavy, thickened with need, and it was so red that it made me think it had to hurt.

And it would hurt. None of these guys were small men, but Bones seemed larger than most. Not for the first time was I glad I could stretch. When he would have lowered his hand, I caught his wrist in a gentle grasp and pulled his finger back to my lips.

Head tilted, he watched me through lowered lashes as I sucked against each of his fingers, one at a time, then pulled three into my mouth to test the stretch. Yeah, he would reach my throat without much effort and I didn't think I'd be able to breathe around him.

Desire unfurled like a wild wind pushing the storm toward the shore. I couldn't wait to find out how it would all feel. "Shower?" Finding my voice shouldn't be so challenging that it came out husky.

"That was the plan," he said, then slid an arm around my waist and lifted me almost effortlessly. His skin was so hot against mine that a groan pushed out of me.

As he carried me into the shower, the world seemed to blur around us, the only reality being the heat of his body and the strength of his arms. He set me down gently, his hands lingering on my hips for a moment before he reached for the shower controls. It had already filled with steam, a thick, oppressive fog that clung to our skin and made everything feel even more intimate.

Bones stepped back, his eyes never leaving mine as he let the water cascade over him, the droplets clinging to his skin like a second layer of muscle. I watched, mesmerized, as the water traced paths down his chest, over his abs, and further south, highlighting the thick length of him. He was a vision, a perfect specimen of male perfection, that his scars only made that much more spectacular.

With a smile that promised sin, he held out a hand, beckoning me to join him. I didn't hesitate, stepping under the spray and into his embrace. The water was hot, almost scalding, but it was nothing compared to the heat of his body against mine. His hands roamed, exploring every curve and valley, leaving a trail of goosebumps in their wake.

I pressed against him, feeling the hard length of him against my stomach, and a shiver of anticipation ran down my spine. He was so big, so powerful, and I had the singular most primitive urge to climb him right now and sink down on that length until we were both breathless and begging for more. The thought sent a wave of wetness between my legs, and I ground against him, seeking friction, seeking relief.

Bones groaned, a deep, guttural sound that vibrated through his chest and into mine. His hands gripped my ass, then lifted me until the head of his cock nudged against my entrance. I was so ready, so wet, and I ached to feel him inside me, to be impaled on his length.

But he held back, goddammit. His self-control had bypassed impressive and tumbled right down into frustrating as hell. The only thing stilling my protests was the naked hunger burning in his eyes.

"Not yet," he murmured, his voice a low rumble. "First, I want to taste you."

With that, he spun us around, pressing me against the cool tiles of the shower wall. His mouth found mine in a searing kiss, his tongue invading, exploring, claiming. I moaned into him, my hands gripping his shoulders, my nails digging into his flesh. He tasted like sin and promise, like everything I ever wanted and more.

His mouth trailed down my neck, nipping and sucking, leaving marks that would no doubt bloom into bruises. I arched into him, offering myself up, a willing sacrifice to his desires. His hands cupped my breasts, his thumbs circling my nipples, sending jolts of pleasure straight to my core. I was a live wire, every touch sending sparks of sensation through my body, every kiss leaving me more desperate, more needy.

I had no idea if he was pushing me up the wall or he slid down, but then his mouth was on me, his tongue swirling around my nipple, sucking and nipping, and I cried out, the sound echoing off the tiles. He was relentless, his mouth and hands working in tandem, driving me higher and higher, until I was a trembling, begging mess, pleading for release.

The demand in his lips and tongue were every bit as fierce as when he stroked me to mindless pleasure in the bed, but at least this time I could touch him. I gripped his soaking wet hair as much to hang onto him as to anchor myself in the moment.

Not that it stopped him. He slid his hands down my body. Then his fingers found my clit, circling, teasing, until I was riding the edge of orgasm. The little death seemed like a great gaping chasm that I wanted to dive into. With a final, almost kind flick of his finger, he sent me tumbling over, my body convulsing, my scream of release lost in the steam and the spray of the shower.

As I came down from the high, I found Bones watching me, his eyes dark with desire, his cock throbbing against my thigh. I reached for him, my hand wrapping around his length, and he hissed, his hips jerking forward. I stroked him, my hand sliding up and down his shaft, feeling the velvety softness of his skin, the steel hardness beneath.

He was so big, so impressive, and he would fill me completely, stretch me in a way that would leave me aching and satisfied. The thought sent another wave of wetness between my legs, and I guided him to my entrance, rubbing the head of his cock against my clit, coating him in the slick release.

"I've wanted this so much," I managed to squeeze out in a hoarse whisper. "Wanted you."

"Anything you want, Dollface." Despite the declaration, he hadn't moved more than to rock against my palm. Little teasing strokes that bumped him against my clit and sent shivers of electricity through my system.

"You," I said, sliding another hand up to fist his hair. "I want *you*. Now."

Bones groaned, a primal sound that was more growl than moan. It was so fucking beautiful, just like him. Then he thrust forward, impaling me on his length in one smooth stroke. The sensation of being filled so completely, so perfectly, was almost too much to bear. It shoved all the air out of my lungs and I cried out. I wanted more and had no idea if I could take more, though neither conflicting thought was going to stop me.

My legs were around his waist, gripping as tightly to his damp skin as I could manage. The earlier muscle fatigue fled in the face of so much wild need. He held still for a moment, giving me time to adjust, and his gaze locked on mine. His breathing seemed to be coming in the same ragged explosions as mine.

"Hi," I whispered, drinking in his fierce expression and the way his eyes threatened to devour me.

"Hey," he whispered with far more control than I would ever have. "I'm going to move now."

"Oh, thank God," I swore and another genuine smile creased his face and stopped my heart. I forgot how to breathe until he began to rock his hips, thrusting, and his cock slid in and out of me in a rhythm that was both brutal and beautiful.

I wrapped my arms around his neck, holding on for dear life as he pounded into me, each thrust sending sparks of pleasure through my body. The tiles were cool against my back, a stark contrast to the heat of his body. I could feel the pressure building again, the coils of pleasure tightening. I was close, so close.

Bones must have sensed it too, for he reached between us, his fingers finding my clit, rubbing in tight, quick circles.

I cried out, my body convulsing, my inner muscles clenching around him as I came, hard and fast, my orgasm ripping through me like a storm.

He followed soon after, his body tensing, his cock pulsing as he spilled himself inside me, filling me. We stayed like that for a moment, our bodies entwined, our breaths nothing but ragged gasps.

At some point, he pulled back enough to cup my face. The stroke of his thumbs against my cheek helped me float back to the steam-filled haven we occupied. With care, he eased out of me and we both shuddered but he helped me to stand on my feet.

"Shower?" he asked, his voice a low rumble, and I laughed, filled with a savage sense of satisfaction and utter joy.

"Shower," I agreed, and together, we stepped under the spray, ready to start all over again.

CHAPTER

EIGHT

VOODOO

I stepped into the dimly lit bar, the air thick with the weight of stale cigarette smoke, old sweat, and tired secrets. The isolated location on some back highway in the middle of the desert set the stage like we were actors in some bad western.

Or worse...

Some *Sons of Anarchy* meets some Walter White knockoff. Neither were very appealing.

I was also really overdressed for any of the above. The Tom Ford suit had a cut that allowed for better weapons coverage. It also tended to soften expectations. Win-win in my book.

The bartender eyed me over a stream of blue smoke she currently exhaled. Despite the presence of air conditioning —the old condenser rattled to life noisily and the ancient fans circulating air—the bar was warm. Thankfully, it was mostly empty. There was no way either could keep up with a packed crowd in this space.

O'Rourke was already there, his silhouette framed

against the shuttered windows that barely let in any light. "Two beers, Sandy."

After stubbing out her cigarette, the bartender opened a cooler and pulled out two icy beer bottles. She set them on the bar, her flat stare sweeping from O'Rourke to me then back again.

"Thirty minutes," she said. "Not one minute longer."

She left the bar to flip the lock on the front door behind me, then she turned and headed back behind the bar and then out through what passed for their kitchen. This wasn't a place you came for food, so I was happy enough with the bottles of beer.

Retrieving the cold bottles that had already begun to sweat, I crossed to where O'Rourke had taken the chair that put his back to the wall. Nice of him to leave me all the other open spots. The tension in the room was palpable, a living thing that seemed to coil around us like a snake ready to strike.

"Voodoo," O'Rourke acknowledged with a nod, his voice a low rumble. "Glad you could make it."

I didn't respond, just stood there, my eyes locked onto his. It had been a long time, not long enough in my book, but still a long time since we were face to face, much less preparing to have a conversation.

"Why am I here, O'Rourke?" I finally asked, my voice steady despite the churning in my gut. None of the guys had been happy about this meet. Not about the fact O'Rourke wanted it or that I was going to deal with him alone.

They liked it even less when I made it clear that they could be backup only—because I wasn't a fucking idiot—so they were parked a couple of miles away. The location was too desolate and wide open so they couldn't be any closer.

With a sigh, O'Rourke dragged out his chair then popped the bottle top off before he took a long drink and sat. "To have a beer."

I just stared at him and set the unopened beer on the table. "I only drink with friends."

"You used to be more fun," O'Rourke said, an air of disappointment lingering around the words.

"Tick tock," I reminded him. "Talk or I walk."

The man paused with his beer halfway to his lips, then he shook his head with a chuckle. "Fucking poet." He took another long slug, then set the bottle down. "I've got an opportunity."

"I care, because?"

"Because," O'Rourke said, his smirk firmly in place. "The people who *hired* me are not the ones footing the bill. Unfortunately for them, I vet everyone who tries to engage my services."

"What happened? Did you manage to get a prosthesis for the conscience you amputated?"

O'Rourke chuckled at that, but it didn't reach his eyes. It never did. The man could fake warmth like the best of them, but I'd seen too many corpses and too many blown operations to ever mistake it for real. He leaned back in his chair, tilting it just slightly so the front legs left the floor. His beer hung lazily from his fingers.

"You know," he said slowly, "I almost walked away from this one. Almost."

I didn't answer. I let the silence stretch. He hated that.

"It's funny," he continued, his tone suddenly casual, light, like we were old friends reminiscing and not two men who'd tried to kill each other before breakfast a few years back. "You do a little digging, start turning over rocks, and surprise, surprise—guess whose name keeps slithering out from under them."

I said nothing. Just watched him.

He grinned like he'd scored a point. "I haven't even told you what the job is, and you're already giving me that look. The one like you're deciding whether to put a bullet in me now or wait until you've had your next cup of overpriced coffee."

The bastard sipped his beer again, long and slow.

"So?" I said flatly.

"So what?"

I leaned forward, planting my hands on the table, voice low. "You're circling something. Either say it or don't. I'm not here to play catch-up, and I don't give a damn what rocks you think you've turned over. Just tell me what you're trying to say."

His smirk widened. The bait had landed.

"I was *hired*," he said, dragging the word out, "to track a target. Isolate them. Assess threats, weaknesses. Standard gig. But then—then I ran the name through a few systems. Pulled some old files. Compared incident reports. Cross-referenced timelines."

He gave me a meaningful look.

"Care to guess who kept showing up on the periphery?" he asked.

I held his gaze. "No."

O'Rourke laughed again. "Jesus, you really *haven't* changed. Alright then, I'll skip ahead. The name they gave me? I think they were hoping I wouldn't connect it to you. Or maybe they figured I wouldn't care. But like I said, I vet my contracts. Especially the ones that stink of setup."

His eyes narrowed slightly.

"So, there I am, considering declining. Not because I

care, of course. But... let's say I've learned that when *you* or your *team* is involved, things tend to get bloody. Fast."

He paused, apparently waiting for me to respond.

I didn't care, ready to just wait him out, but he had that obstinate look about him. Tired of this dance, I exhaled slowly. "What's the job, O'Rourke?"

He leaned forward, finally dropping the chair's front legs to the ground with a dull *thud*. His smile vanished.

"They want me to bring in someone. Quietly. A ghost, off the books. No body, no trace. Someone with very specific knowledge of a very dirty operation from a few years ago."

His pause was dramatic. Fuck, I forgot how damn impressed with himself he was.

"Problem is," he said, eyes boring into mine, "the only person who fits that profile... is you."

I didn't flinch. Not when he dropped the bomb, not when he leaned in like he expected some kind of reaction. That was the game. O'Rourke was baiting, poking at old wounds, trying to get a read on whether I'd known someone was hunting me before he showed up with the warning disguised as a threat.

Arms relaxed, I just waited. Casual. Controlled.

"That's cute," I said, voice low, even. "But you're dancing around it again. Who hired you?"

O'Rourke tilted his head, running a finger along the condensation on his bottle. "You know how this works. Names cost."

"And if you were really going to decline," I said, keeping my tone steady, "you wouldn't be sitting here tossing out riddles like a Bond villain who's two minutes away from triggering his own death trap. You want something. So cut the shit."

He grinned at that, but it was all teeth now. No humor.

"Old habits, I guess."

I didn't blink. "Name."

He let the silence breathe. The air buzzed with it.

Then: "Does the name *Vega* mean anything to you?"

It did. But it could mean a lot of other things too, so I wasn't going to just jump at this first bit of bait

I just shrugged slightly. "Vega's not a name. It's a direction. Could be a hundred players."

"Could be," O'Rourke allowed with only the faintest hint of doubt, swirling his beer, "but in this case? It's not. The job came down through a third-party broker out of Santa Fe. But the funding, the chatter, the protocol? Black string budget. Not cartel, not corporate. This is deeper. Shadow-funding, limited oversight, built for total deniability. The kind of thing that makes politicians nervous and keeps internal affairs chasing their tails for years."

That tracked. The Vega I knew wasn't a person—*wasn't supposed to be*, anyway. Vega was a codename. A myth wrapped in intel that was always just out of reach. Last I heard, it had ties to an ops division that was shuttered during a clean sweep six years prior. Not shut down—shuttered. Buried. No paper trail, no accountability.

Just ghosts.

"Job specifics?" I asked. This just sounded like a lot of horseshit. For all that the government loved its shadow ops, this was just a step too far.

O'Rourke smirked again, like I'd just asked for the weather. "Surveillance. Tracking. Pattern disruption. And then extraction. Real quiet. They were very clear about *quiet*."

Which meant kill or capture. No witnesses. No heat.

My eyes scanned the room as he talked. The bar was empty, still, but too *perfectly* so. Dust on the old jukebox in the corner, sure. A stack of unread newspapers on a shelf, untouched in weeks. But the fans overhead were freshly cleaned. No dust buildup. And the cooler? Overstocked with beer that didn't match the brand signage out front. Like someone had staged the bar just enough to sell the illusion of wear without actually being in business.

Even the bartender—Sandy—had disappeared too fast. Thirty-minute window, locked door, no questions. No locals had wandered in, and no highway noise filtered through the boarded windows.

This wasn't a meet. It was a *box*.

"You chose the location?" I asked.

"I suggested it." O'Rourke arched a brow. "You agreed to it."

At my continued stare, he almost smiled.

"They secured it."

Of course they did.

"How many exits?"

"Back door through the kitchen. Side hatch behind the bar. Basement tunnel leads to the next lot over if you're feeling theatrical."

I clocked that. Marked the routes.

"And you're just handing this over?" I asked. "All this intel? For what—some warm fuzzy feeling that you're finally doing the right thing?"

He gave a short laugh, but his eyes didn't waver. "No, Voodoo. I'm telling you because if I walk, they'll just send someone else. Someone faster. Someone dumber. And because, as much as I might enjoy watching that play out, I'm also not stupid enough to get caught in the middle of it when the bodies start dropping."

He paused, then leaned forward, lowering his voice.

"They're not just trying to bury you. They want the

whole op—whatever happened in Odessa six years ago—
erased. Every name, every loose thread. And you, my old
friend... you're the last thread still out in the open."

My fingers tightened around the neck of the beer bottle,
still unopened. Odessa. It had been a bloodbath. Not just on
the ground—but in the data. Files wiped. Burn notices
issued. People ghosted or gone. And I'd walked away with a
hard drive no one knew about, a list of names that never
made it into official record.

O'Rourke watched me now, waiting to see how I'd
move.

I set the bottle down gently. "You said you were considering declining. What's stopping you?"

He smiled, but it didn't last.

"The fact that I still don't know if I'm talking to the
asset they want eliminated—or the one holding the kill
switch."

What would he prefer?

Experience and intel said he wanted *both*.

The bastard thrived in the middle—playing sides,
stacking chips no one else sees until the game's over. That's
always been his angle: don't just pick a side—*own* the
outcome.

If I was the asset they want eliminated, he got to play
the informant. The guy who tried to warn me, kept his
hands clean, maybe collect a favor down the road. or a
bounty, if things went sideways.

But if I was the one holding the kill switch?

That was leverage.

It was also the kind of insurance O'Rourke liked best.
He'd want to cozy up just enough to stay close to the fire,
without getting burned. Make himself useful. Buy time. Get

a copy of whatever I was holding, maybe sell it before I even realized it was gone.

So what would he *prefer*?

He'd prefer I *was* the kill switch—but I *didn't know it yet.*

That gave him the edge. That gave him the time to figure out how to make the most off of both sides.

But the thing about O'Rourke? He was a snake who thought he was clever enough to watch you bleed without getting his boots dirty.

Problem for him? I had thicker boots and skin now.

I also had backup which he should remember. The guys were quiet, didn't mean they weren't right there—waiting for my signal.

Then, for the first time since I walked over to the table, O'Rourke glanced over my shoulder.

I didn't move. But I recognized what it meant.

We weren't alone anymore.

Showtime.

CHAPTER

NINE

LUNCHBOX

I t started with static.

Soft, low—just a whisper in my ear. Then Alphabet's voice broke through the haze:

"You've got movement. One vehicle, blacked-out. Two klicks west. No lights. No plate. Parking near the service road."

I didn't respond. Just exhaled slow. O'Rourke was still sitting across from Voodoo like this was some fireside heart-to-heart.

Bones was already moving. I knew that before Alphabet said his name.

"Bones is in motion."

Damn right he was.

Like a ghost, I'd drifted in through the kitchen and used each external sound from the bartender talking to Voodoo walking to muffle my movements. Voodoo was more than capable of handling O'Rourke on his own. We were just here to back his plays.

Play time was over though, so I shifted my weight, slow and easy. Gliding through the door that separated the kitchen from the bar, I moved silently until I was ready to

83

let them know I was here. The cracked floorboard under my boot groaned just enough to earn O'Rourke's attention again. He blinked like he was coming out of a daydream. Like maybe he forgot he wasn't the only one in the game. Or maybe he'd just forgotten what it meant to have a real team.

I kept my voice low, calm. "How many exits you say again?"

His eyes narrowed but not before his faint jerk revealed his surprise. "Why?"

"Because," I murmured, hand slipping beneath the edge of my jacket, brushing the cool metal of the M84 flashbang tucked under my arm, "we're about to find out if you're full of shit."

"Second vehicle. Same direction. They're leapfrogging. Military pattern. This is a hit, Lunch." Alphabet's voice was tight now. Controlled. Focused.

Voodoo canted his head, enough to catch me in his periphery without ever taking his gaze off O'Rourke.

I leaned just enough to the side to glance toward the shaded windows. They gave us cover from a sniper, but not much else. Just that slow build of pressure in my chest, like the moment before a detonation.

I knew that feeling. It never lied.

"You done?" I said, lifting my chin to Voodoo. When he described O'Rourke as a theatrical asshat, he hadn't been kidding. I hated the guy but at least I'd never had to get to know him.

The smirk vanished from O'Rourke's face. His eyes flicked toward the bar, the kitchen—he was calculating. Fast. Too fast.

Voodoo had him by the front of his shirt and hauled

him up before he could finish his thought. "Tell me you didn't bring all this down on purpose."

"I didn't—"

"Tell me with your hands behind your back."

Shoving him against the wall, Voodoo caught the flex-cuff I tossed him from my belt. The fact O'Rourke didn't struggle told us a lot. Either he was innocent, or he was damn sure someone else was doing the dirty work so his hands stayed clean.

Either way, we didn't have time to play this game.

"Team of four. Two dismounting now. Kitchen and side hatch. No chatter on open comms. All tac-quiet. They're professionals."

Alphabet kept us in the loop using the drone we'd parked in a fuel station sign an hour earlier.

I dropped low and moved behind the bar. Bone-dry. No one stashed there. No surprise. Sandy never came back from her little walk.

The air shifted. I smelled it—burnt oil, sweat, friction.

"One's on the roof," Alphabet said. *"He's got overwatch on the front."*

I slipped the flashbang from my coat. Clipped. Primed.

Three seconds.

Tick. Tick. Boom.

I lobbed it toward the kitchen door just as it creaked open. The door didn't even get a chance to swing fully before the grenade hit the tiles and—

KRACK!

A pulse of white light and bone-shaking sound tore through the back half of the bar.

I moved. Hard and fast. Low. My gun was up before the echo died. The Remington 870 bucked once, the bark deafening even after the flashbang.

One down in the kitchen. Camouflage fatigues. No insignia. No name. Just a blank mask and suppressed MP7 clattering to the floor.

Not cartel.

Not mercs.

Wetwork.

Bones came in through the side door. I saw him just as he moved—a shadow moving like smoke, silent and brutal.

The second intruder barely got a shot off before Bones had him up against the cooler, elbow driving into his throat, knees snapping tendon. The man collapsed in a heap.

Not saying a word, Bones just gave me a nod, then moved toward the stairs leading to the basement tunnel. He knew better than anyone: there was always a second wave.

"*Roof's clear,*" Alphabet called in. "*Sniper's down. Looks like Bones got him from below—made him step back onto a pressure plate. Cute trick.*"

"That was mine," I muttered, jogging back to the table as Voodoo dragged O'Rourke upright again. "Little welcome mat surprise."

O'Rourke's face was pale. "You brought a kill team?"

"No," I said. "*You* did."

"*Wait,*" Alphabet cut in, voice sharp now. "*Third vehicle just rolled up. This one's different—four doors, black SUV, full tint. VIP transport pattern.*"

That stopped us. Voodoo and I both looked at O'Rourke. His lips parted slightly, but no sound came out.

He wasn't in control of this anymore.

"*One passenger. Tall. Moving with security detail but not talking. Looks... command.*"

Bones was already moving back up, gun raised, one

hand signaling silently—two fingers, wide apart. Heavy armor. Likely rear guards.

Who the hell was this?

O'Rourke stared at the window like a man watching the gallows being built. "It's Vega."

"No." I grabbed him by the collar and yanked him back. "Vega's not a person."

He shook his head, eyes wide. "They made him one."

I swore under my breath. Sure, turn a project into flesh was one way to disguise it and utilize it. Something you could move around. Something deniable. A puppet with a dozen strings leading back to places no one could follow. It was also *bullshit*. Odessa was a dead end and we were hardly in some science fiction world where you could bioengineer a program into a person.

The door banged once. Hard. Controlled.

Then again.

I turned to Bones. "Play it loud or play it quiet?"

His gaze went to the last flashbang. The shaped charge under the bar. The collapsible SMG I hadn't even drawn yet.

I glanced at O'Rourke. "You've got five seconds to tell us what they want."

He swallowed hard. "Not you. Not just Voodoo. They want the list. The drive."

Of course they did. Odessa. Six years ago. This ghost wasn't about to come back to life. We didn't just bury it. We incinerated it.

Bones keyed the mic. "Alphabet, loop the feed. Make it look like we're still inside."

"Already done. They're watching a frozen frame from two minutes ago. Whole team's ghosted."

With that, Bones was already moving again, pulling a service panel behind the bar open. Tunnel access.

I jammed the last charge under the table, synced it to remote, and kicked the chair over for good measure.

O'Rourke struggled. "Wait—what are you doing?"

"Keeping the myth alive."

Voodoo tossed him down the tunnel first then followed with Bones right behind them, silent and cold. I hesitated for half a second, glancing once more at the door.

It banged again. Harder. Louder.

"*Package on the doorstep,*" Alphabet said. "*Whatever's behind that door—doesn't knock twice.*"

Exactly.

I dropped the detonator behind the bar, and slid down into the dark.

Three seconds later, the world upstairs went white.

The blast above ground was surgical. Controlled fury. A shaped charge designed not just to destroy, but to confuse. Shrapnel laced with magnesium and thermite—no simple flash, no simple burn. It would eat through anything soft and light up the rest like hell's own fireworks show.

I landed hard in the tunnel, knees absorbing the impact as I rolled. Dirt walls. Reinforced ceiling. Stale air and narrow space, just wide enough to crawl single-file if it came to that. No one had used this exit in a decade—not until Bones found it last week during recon.

"*Confirm detonation,*" Alphabet's voice cracked through my earpiece, distorted by the sudden interference.

"Confirmed," I muttered, brushing dirt off my vest and pushing forward. "Party favors worked."

"*Thermal's useless,*" he replied. "*They're blind. All they're getting is heat bloom. You've got sixty seconds max before they fan out.*"

I could already hear the muffled scuffle of boots behind me. Bones was in motion. Always first in, last out. Voodoo was just ahead, dragging O'Rourke, who was coughing from smoke or panic—maybe both.

"Keep moving," Bones said, his voice quiet but sharp. "This way splits. I'll take the right. Loop back and converge two blocks east."

"What about our tail?" I asked.

He didn't answer right away.

Then, "I'll handle it."

I didn't like it—but I didn't argue.

Voodoo didn't either. Just kept O'Rourke moving.

We pushed down the left tunnel, the heat from the blast bleeding through the earth above us like sweat through skin. Dirt shifted underfoot. My bag was heavy with what we didn't get a chance to use—and what no one behind us could be allowed to find.

Twenty meters in, we hit the first grate. I crouched, yanked a pry tool from my belt, and wrenched it free with a sharp metallic groan.

Alphabet was back in my ear.

"They're breaching. Entering from the front. Sending drones to sweep. No heat signatures, but they've got air sniffers. You need distance."

"They see Bones?"

A pause. *"Not yet."*

That was the answer I needed.

Voodoo dropped into the storm drain below us, boots splashing in runoff and old rainwater. I followed, then reached up and pulled the grate back into place.

Metal scraped over metal. Sealed again.

O'Rourke stumbled, slipping on the wet concrete. Voodoo caught him, none too gently.

"You should've walked away," Voodoo muttered, voice quiet but dangerous.

"I tried," O'Rourke wheezed. "You think you're the only one with ghosts?"

"I buried mine," Voodoo said. "Looks like yours came back with friends."

We moved fast now, under the street, guided by old maps and old instincts. Alphabet fed us location markers from the drone uplink. Street cams were offline—fried by our EMP burst before the bar lit up.

But *they* were still up there.

Moving. Coordinating. Hunting.

And not just for us.

"*They're not pulling out,*" Alphabet warned. "*They're spreading. Staggered leapfrog. Room by room. Street by street.*"

"That's not a hit," I muttered, glancing at Voodoo. "That's a net."

"Which means we're not the only fish," he said grimly. "They're looking for the drive."

Shit. We didn't have it. I doubted they would believe us.

We rounded the next turn, ducking into an alcove of corroded pipes and graffiti-painted concrete. I keyed the mic.

"Bones. Talk to me."

Static.

Then—"*Two down. Third's armored. I'm bleeding.*"

Not a complaint. Just a fact.

"How bad?"

A pause.

"*Worse than it sounds.*"

"Worse than *your* standards or human standards?"

Bones gave a low chuckle. "*Keep going. I'll meet you back at the safehouse.*"

I glanced at Voodoo, who shook his head.

"We're not leaving you."

"*Yeah*," Bones said. "*You are.*"

And then—

Silence.

I clenched my jaw and turned back to the path. No time for sentiment. Not down here.

We moved.

Faster now. No chatter. No lights.

O'Rourke stumbled again. I didn't catch him this time.

Let him bleed.

When we finally surfaced, it was behind an abandoned garage just off the highway. Two miles from the bar, maybe more. The sun had just started its descent—drenched everything in gold and shadow.

I slammed the hatch behind us.

Alphabet's voice came back, clearer now. "*You're clean. Thermal sweep passed over. Bones bought you time.*"

I didn't respond.

Voodoo walked O'Rourke to the rusted-out SUV we'd parked the night before. Slammed him against the hood.

"Start talking," he growled.

"I told you everything," O'Rourke gasped. "Vega's a group now. They took what was left of the operation, turned it into something new. Self-regulating. Self-funding. You think someone gave the kill order?"

He looked up, eyes wide.

"No. They *are* the kill order."

That stopped us both.

A project given autonomy. Access to black string funding, legacy assets, terminal authority. No oversight. It made no damn sense and at the same time, it made sense in the worst possible way.

O'Rourke looked between us. "You think this ends here? You think burning that bar did anything but scratch the surface? Vega doesn't care about your past. It's coming for your future."

Voodoo didn't flinch.

"You know what they really want, Lunchbox?" O'Rourke asked me.

I nodded. "You said they wanted the drive."

O'Rourke shook his head. "No. That's just the key. They want what it *unlocks*."

Which meant we were already behind.

Voodoo turned away from him, muttering low. "Get us to the fallback. Now."

I opened the SUV's rear door. "You sure on taking him with us?"

He glanced back at O'Rourke—bleeding, sweaty, pale.

Then he looked at me. Cold.

"Dead men don't talk."

That meant O'Rourke still had a purpose.

But I didn't trust him. Especially not around Gracie.

Then again, if "Vega" really was coming, they weren't going to knock again. They would just break down the door next time.

CHAPTER

TEN

BONES

P ain was just a message. You could ignore it, rewrite it, push it down until it sounded like someone else's voice echoing in your head.

The hard part was remembering *why* it mattered.

I rolled my shoulder once, slow and sharp, feeling the tendon pop like overstretched wire. Armor plate caught the edge of the impact from the third operator's burst. Not enough to drop me. Enough to piss me off.

I was pinned behind an old concrete support beam in the maintenance corridor that ran parallel to the storm tunnel. Voodoo and Lunchbox were clear. That part of the op was done. Alphabet had already looped the thermal feeds—they were ghosts.

I was the distraction.

A flare of movement in my peripheral—shadow, gunmetal, movement too clean to be civilian. I pivoted hard, drove my elbow into the oncoming shape, and felt the impact crack bone. Mine or his—I didn't care.

He hit the ground with a grunt and I put two fast strikes into his throat before he could bring the rifle up.

Three down.

Still one more.

I heard the shift before I saw it—boots on concrete, the telltale rasp of a suppressed bolt sliding into battery.

I didn't think.

I moved.

Ducked low, rolled into the next alcove, and came up with the backup piece in my hand. The Glock barked once. Twice.

The corridor lit up as a flashbang hit the far end. Not mine.

Shit.

That wasn't part of the plan.

I dropped flat and covered my face just as it went off. White-hot light. Pressure wave. My ears rang like church bells in a storm.

Footsteps followed.

Heavy. Purposeful. Not like the previous crew—these weren't operators. These were *cleaners.*

I pulled my knees under me, pressed back against the wall, eyes still swimming.

Then I saw the silhouette.

Not armor.

A coat. Long, black. Military cut.

He didn't move like a soldier. He moved like a man who owned the floor under him.

A voice followed.

"Captain."

Not a question.

Not a command.

Just... acknowledgement.

I forced myself to my feet. Slow. Deliberate.

"Who the hell are you?" I asked, voice rough.

The man stepped closer. He wore gloves. No insignia. No rank. Just the coat and the weight behind his stare.

"Vega," he said.

Bullshit.

Vega wasn't a person. Wasn't a name.

That's what we'd always told ourselves. It was an operation, a protocol. A codename. Something someone could deny in court.

But this guy—he was walking like someone who didn't need court.

"You're late," I said, flexing my hand. The bleeding hadn't stopped.

He gave the faintest smile. Not warm. Not cold. Clinical.

"We're never late. We arrive when the math says we're needed."

I didn't like that phrasing. The *math*. That wasn't military talk. That was something else. Something that felt— performative.

"You going to try to take me?" I asked.

The man didn't answer. Just turned slightly—enough for me to see two more behind him.

Same coats.

Same silence.

Only one of them had blood on their gloves.

"Voodoo still breathing?" I asked.

Another pause.

"Define breathing," the man said.

That was enough.

I moved.

Fast.

Hard.

No warning.

The Glock was up—but the one with bloodied gloves

had already raised something in his hand. A square device. High-frequency pulse emitter. The second it chirped, my world flipped.

My vision crashed. My body locked.

Not pain.

Interruption.

Like my nerves weren't mine anymore. Worse goddamn taser—ever.

I dropped. Twitched. Fought for control.

The leader crouched next to me.

"You don't know what you're carrying, Captain. But you're going to lead us to it."

My teeth ground together.

"I'd rather die."

"Not your choice," he said calmly.

Then something sharp pricked the side of my neck.

Cold fire raced through my veins.

Blackness surged.

But just before it swallowed me, I heard Alphabet's voice break into my comms:

"Bones. Say something. You've got a tag. They just—Bones —talk to me—"

Too late.

Then—

Silence.

ALPHABET

Pain wasn't just physical. Sometimes it came through clean audio. A sudden cut. A heartbeat that never got its echo.

"Bones—say something—"

I stared at the waveform. Static. Spike. Then nothing.

I re-routed. Dumped signal through every dirty node I had cached on local infrastructure. Old towers, microwave backhauls, shadow-bandwidth riding shotgun on a grocery store's security net.

Still nothing.

"Goddamn it—"

The drone feed showed only black. The area where Bones had been lit up with residual infrared, but no moving shapes. No heat sig. They must have used a thermal-dampening field to extract him.

Fuck me, they were fast. Too goddamn fast.

I exhaled, leaned back in the van, and flicked through every feed we had left. Goblin leaned against my leg, his head resting on my thigh. The pressure and the presence helped me to breathe, to keep my cool. Right now, I needed to be thinking. Not reacting.

Dropping my head to Goblin's head, I scratched him between his ears both to acknowledge him and to comfort myself. It let me take a beat, to refocus—then I saw it.

Not him.

Not Bones.

The man in the coat.

No insignia. No badge. Just presence. The camera caught a half-profile as he passed beneath a flickering exit light.

I snapped a still.

Zoomed. Cleaned. Ran it against every known-face DB I had—including ones we weren't supposed to have.

Match: *Null.*

Not "unknown."

Uncatalogued.

Even the system flagged him: "Outside of available scope."

My hands froze over the keys.

Then I did what I had to do.

Rerouted signal. End-to-end encrypted the file. Then dialed a secure number.

She answered on the second ring.

"AB?" The whisper softness of her voice was a balm. I really fucking hated what I had to do next.

"Gracie," I said. "It's me. You need to sit down."

GRACE

My heart was a pulsing bruise at the tension in Alphabet's voice. "What happened?"

Despite his warning, I didn't sit. I hadn't been able to be still since they'd left three hours earlier *after* they'd walked me through the plan and *after* they'd made sure I felt like a part of it, even if I *wouldn't* be there.

All four of them were united on this, *none* of them wanted me there when they went to see O'Rourke. It didn't matter that O'Rourke wanted a private meeting with Voodoo, it was all of them or none of them.

Voodoo voted to skip it entirely, but Bones disagreed. *"We should deal with him and whatever angle he's working. I don't want to leave anything behind to ambush us."*

Legend and AB agreed with him, so Voodoo had shifted his gaze to me. *"You promise to stay here and not fight us on this?"*

Without missing a beat, I'd folded my arms and said, *"You promise to brief me so I know what's happening and when, that way I'm not sitting here paralyzed, not knowing?"*

"I will, if he won't," AB volunteered. Funnily enough, Bones' snort and rolled eyes entertained me almost as much as the one-upmanship that the guys engaged in for my briefing.

That amusement carried us—or me at least—through the briefing, then armed with the maps, the GPS, the locations, and their contingencies as well as their plotted schedule, I settled in to wait.

The safehouse was not associated with them directly. It was secured. There was a safe *room*, that was a fireproof vault if I needed it, and Bones made sure I had a taser *and* a gun. *"Taser first. Then the gun."*

I stared at him. "You want me to tase them down *then* shoot them?"

"It's easier to hit a stationary target." Honestly, I really didn't know what to do with that deadpan response. Was he serious? Teasing? Both?

Then he kissed me and I forgot about that debate. There was nothing joking about his kiss. It was fierce, breath-stealing, and burned like he was branding me. The intensity had me shaking, just a little before he strode out ahead of the others.

"Always knew he'd be the dramatic one," Voodoo told me with a wink, but he left me with his own firm kiss before he followed Bones, then Legend, and finally AB. They were all so different and yet, they fit. The four of them together were so very much a team, it was hard to picture them without each other.

That they functioned as a unit without Doc made sense to me, because I really didn't know Doc. Yet, at the same time, when he was there, he slotted right in. They had a bond I couldn't truly fathom, yet that bond didn't exclude me.

From the beginning, they'd been protective. Then they'd encircled me and wrapped me up in the shield of their team. I was still very much in the cosseted heart of the team, but I was also a *part* of the team.

"Bones is down," AB said, the grim words and tone yanking me into the brutal present.

The air pressure change that made your ears pop when bad news was coming seemed to muffle everything. Those three words played on a violent loop in my head.

No breath

No sound.

Just the walls closing in.

"He's dead?"

"No, Gracie," AB said, his tone gentling immediately. "No, he's—he was taken."

"By who?" How could they have taken him? Bones was —they were all tough, but Bones was so hard. So damn fierce. The idea that anyone could hurt him seemed impossible and at the same time, I wanted to rain fire down on whoever *had* hurt him. "What are we doing to get him back? What can *I* do?"

VOODOO

I kicked a metal crate across the floor of the garage. It hit the far wall with a crash. Lunchbox didn't flinch. Alphabet's voice still hung in the air from the comms.

They took Bones.

That phrase hadn't even finished settling into my bloodstream yet. My hands were clenched. I didn't even remember balling them. Even as I blew out a breath, I forced my hands to uncurl and focused my attention on O'Rourke.

"How much?"

"Not enough to set you up," he said, not even pretending to misunderstand my question.

"Then why the isolated meet and greet?" Lunchbox asked, his voice as cold and remote as it ever got. Of the four of us, he was probably the most human—most of the time. I played the part almost professionally. While

Alphabet seemed the more relaxed of the two, his humor hid a well of pain.

Bones was the hard ass. He was the one who knew when to break jaws and when to pull the punches. He kept us centered. And he *never* blinked even when the mission went to hell. No matter what happened, Bones would come for us and we damn well knew it.

"To let you know there was a threat," O'Rourke said flatly. "I knew you wouldn't come alone. The backup was supposed to make sure none of you got dead." His expression tightened. "To be clear, as far as I knew, they wanted *you* specifically, Voodoo. Not Bones."

I shrugged. It didn't really matter who they wanted. It mattered why. It mattered where. It mattered who the fuck they were... Those were the things that mattered.

Whatever we were chasing before—shadows, echoes, cover-ups—none of it mattered anymore. The thought scraped through me like a wipeout on asphalt. Grace mattered. That meant her sister mattered.

But they had Bones.

"How is Vega a person?" It was an operational protocol. Not an individual.

"Shifting priorities up the chain. Assignment of resources. Retasking wetwork and specialist teams. Black ops." O'Rourke shrugged. "You know how it goes."

A headache pulsed behind my eye.

"I told Grace," Alphabet said as he came back on comms. "She's holding steady, but we need to check back in with her in thirty. Where are we doing this?"

"You have eyes on him at all?" Lunchbox asked.

"Not yet." Alphabet's response was clipped. "I sent the activation code for his tracker. We'll have something in an hour."

Unless they planned for that contingency and managed to block the signal. I could practically see the same thought streaming through Lunchbox's eyes. We could only deal with it when it came. At the moment, I was in charge.

Bones was down. That left me in command.

"Pick us up," I told Alphabet. "Tell her to get ready. We'll divert if necessary."

No cutting her out. But if we got actionable intel beforehand, we were going to take it and run.

"Is he picking all of us up?" O'Rourke asked, pulling my attention back to him. His hands were still secured behind him, and his expression resolute. Still a soldier.

"You know what comes next," I told Lunchbox and he nodded once.

"Wha—" O'Rourke didn't get to finish asking the question. Lunchbox knocked him out with one hard punch. The man went down like a ton of bricks.

Shaking his hand once, Lunchbox grunted. "That felt good."

"Secure him." Because he was going. "And scan him." We weren't taking any other trouble back with us. We had one job right now.

We would get our brother back.

ELEVEN

GRACE

Sitting in the back of the van, I kept an eye on O'Rourke where he was bound with his hands behind his back, blindfolded, and sporting a pair of noise canceling headphones. He hadn't made a sound since the guys picked me up. Course, he also had duct tape over his mouth so talking wasn't really an option even if he was conscious.

The last time I'd seen him had involved fancy outfits, people shooting at us, and him biting me. I was pretty sure explosions had also been involved. It had been a few months, but I couldn't really decide what his presence here meant.

Particularly because the guys were ignoring him, even if they'd brought him with us. In the meanwhile, AB sat in the back with me, working on his laptop and Goblin lay between us while Legend drove and Voodoo was on the phone with a contact in the front. I had a dozen questions, none of which I asked.

Tension wound around the guys like electrified barbed wire. Every shift, every move, every glance drew blood and threatened to send a shock through the system. It was like playing the board game Operation with metal tweezers and we're bouncing around.

A hand stroked down my arm and pulled my attention from O'Rourke to AB. He frowned as he studied me. "We'll find him."

"I know," I said, not a doubt existed within me. These guys would burn the world down. I had seen them do it. "It's just…"

"It's Bones." Those two words summed everything up. The definition of the man, and oh, how he could irritate. At the same time, at no point when it had been just the two of us had I ever thought I was anything but safe with him.

Even when he was making me crazy, he saved my life.

"I get it," AB said. "But he's a tough son of a bitch. He'll be fine."

"How did they take him?" Because, every time I'd seen him in a fight or an "action" as they liked to call it, he was like the Terminator. He just didn't stop. How hurt would he have to have been for them to take him captive?

"Don't focus on that, Gracie." There was a request in his voice even if the words were an order. "We'd just be speculating. Speculation has a place, but right now, we need hard facts only."

I turned those words over in my head, then nodded slowly. "You need hard facts because speculating can go in wild directions and our imagination can run amok."

"More or less," Voodoo said over his shoulder and I twisted to find him glancing back at O'Rourke before he focused on me. "They had cleaners with them. Everything is gone. The bar. The location. Everything. Scrubbed like it didn't exist."

"How can they do that in a couple of hours?" That was insane.

"They had four," Legend said and I curled my fingers into my palms, digging my nails in. "It took us time to make sure we had no tails before we headed back to you."

They probably had to make sure that O'Rourke couldn't be tracked either. I sighed. "So whatever clues might have been there are gone now?"

"There wouldn't have been any," Voodoo told me, his expression gentle. "I wanted confirmation of who or what we're dealing with."

"Do you know now?"

"Some," he said, shifting to look forward. "We're about an hour out from the new safe house. Can you give us time to secure it and O'Rourke, then we'll do a full brief?"

He was asking, not telling. They were all worried. "Whatever you need." Right now, I could do just about anything. A flicker of surprise crossed his face and I caught Legend shooting me a look but I just put a hand on Goblin's head to pet him and soothe myself.

I could be difficult. I was aware. But I could also be a team player. Right now, that was what they needed me to be.

Ninety minutes later, we were in the new safe house with O'Rourke secure in an actual cell in the basement. I didn't want to know how they had a house like this set up. Nope. Some things were probably better that I didn't know.

AB showered while the guys brought his gear in, then I helped him with his thigh while Legend was in the shower. The limp was a lot more noticeable.

"Just cramps," he said as he stretched the leg out on the sofa.

"Are you overdoing it?" I needed to get baselines on

what would be overdoing it for him. Honestly, he never slowed down. Even when he was hurting, he kept going. Goblin passed out on the floor next to the sofa. Perching on the edge, I lifted the laptop off of him and set it aside so I could work my fingers into his thigh.

"Gracie..."

"Five minutes," I told him. "Set a timer. You hurting yourself won't help Bones and, based on what I've seen, he'd rather you took the time so you could move than potentially leave yourself hampered with both pain and limited mobility."

As light as I kept my tone, I didn't ease up on the pressure of the massage. The tension in his thigh, the rigid cording of the muscle and the way his jaw tightened told me he was in pain.

The damp blond of his hair settled in a wave over his forehead despite his attempts with finger combing. We locked gazes and I read all the stubborn in his blue eyes. Hopefully, he read the same in mine. I was not going to let him hurt himself if I could do something to help.

Blowing out a breath, AB reached for me and wrapped his hand around my nape. When he dragged me toward him, he was gentle but I was far from resisting. His lips parted even as our mouths crashed together. The kiss was heat and hunger, yes, and beneath it, something deeper thrummed.

A quiet vow nestled in the press of his mouth against mine, in the way his fingers tightened slightly, not possessive but certain. It wasn't just want—it was welcome. It was the kind of kiss that said, *I see you. I'm not going anywhere.* My pulse stuttered under the weight of it, all heat and tenderness braided with something that felt dangerously close to forever.

He eased up just enough for air, but his hand stayed at my nape, anchoring me there, our foreheads nearly touching. My breath came fast, shallow, but I couldn't bring myself to pull away. Not when his eyes were that close, that open. He searched my face like he was memorizing something, like maybe he'd found something he hadn't expected. Then, soft—so soft it almost undid me—he said, "Thank you for worrying about me."

I didn't know what to do with his gratitude, the raw sincerity in it. It landed somewhere deep, unsettled something that I wasn't ready to name. So I went back to what I'd already given him, what I knew to be true.

"That's what loving you means," I whispered, the words barely catching on my breath.

At least to me.

I kissed him again. It was just a brush this time, a promise of my own tucked into the moment. When I eased back, I concentrated on massaging his thigh once more. The tension was still there, knotted and tight, and I pressed into it gently like I could take some of the pain from him if I just tried hard enough.

He was quiet, and when I glanced up, his jaw was set like he wrestled with more than just his own discomfort. Maybe words. Maybe the same words I'd just said, but they didn't come.

"AB," I murmured, working both thumbs against a particularly stubborn knot. "You don't have to say anything."

"You deserve to hear it though," he argued, his voice tense and rough.

I paused, hands stilling for a beat against the firm line of muscle beneath them. That edge in his voice—it wasn't resistance. It was strain. Like he was trying to push something past a wall he hadn't let anyone near before.

"I'm not going anywhere," I said quietly, easing back into the motion, gentler this time. "Whenever it comes—if it comes—it'll mean more because it's real. Not because you felt backed into a corner."

His thigh twitched under my hands, like his body wanted to argue even if his mouth didn't know how. I looked up, and his eyes were already on me, stormy and uncertain and unbearably soft.

He opened his mouth, closed it, then gave a frustrated shake of his head. "It's not that I don't feel it. I just... haven't said it in a long time. Not like this. Not when it actually matters."

My chest ached, but I managed a small, steady smile. "Then let it matter. I'm not keeping score."

His hand found mine, fingers curling tight, like he needed the contact to hold the words steady. He looked at me—really looked—and something shifted behind his eyes, something fragile trying to take shape.

"When this is done," he said, low and steady, "when we have Bones back, when we've found your sister, when we've done all of that—" His grip tightened just a fraction. "I want you to have a reason to stay."

My breath caught, the weight of what he was saying folding over my heart like a blanket—heavy, warm, impossible to ignore.

"You already are," I said, voice barely more than a whisper. "You're the reason." All of them were.

He exhaled hard, like I'd knocked something loose in his chest, and leaned forward to press his forehead to mine again. There were still miles ahead of us—fights to win, wounds to reopen—but in that moment, between the unspoken and the not-yet-said, something *real* settled between us.

And neither of us pulled away.

A quiet beat passed, thick with everything we weren't rushing to say and Goblin's adorable snores. AB brushed over my knuckles, and I could feel the smallest tremble in it, like something in him was finally letting go.

Then, from the stairs as Voodoo descended them, "That's good to hear."

He had one brow lifted with his usual easy calm, though the corner of his mouth tugged just slightly upward. "Didn't mean to eavesdrop," he said, clearly lying, "but with all this *feelings and healing* going on, figured I should make sure nobody was dying."

AB let out a slow breath, and I could feel the warmth of a reluctant smile at my temple.

Voodoo's gaze flicked to me, and held. "Glad to know we're *all* on the same page now." He let that sentiment linger in the air as he joined us. "But unless you two are planning to kiss your way through a rescue mission, we've got a plan to finalize. I'll grab Lunchbox and food."

AB groaned under his breath, rubbing a hand down his face. "He's never going to let us live this down."

"Nope," Voodoo called over his shoulder as he walked away. "So hurry up, Romeo."

AB watched Voodoo disappear down the hall with a quiet sigh, the warmth of the moment still lingering between us like an ember we weren't ready to stamp out. He didn't say anything right away, just leaned back against the cushions with that slow, thoughtful way of his, like maybe the world was just now settling into something he could breathe in again.

I stood, reluctantly breaking the contact, and lifted his

laptop from the coffee table and returned it to him. It was closed, but it still hummed faintly.

"You left it open to the satellite map," I said softly. "Didn't want to lose your place."

"Thanks," he murmured, glancing down at it but not opening it yet. His fingers ghosted over the top, distracted. Still somewhere in the space we'd just carved out.

Before either of us could say more, the floor creaked again, and in came Voodoo and Lunchbox, both carrying plates and mugs like offerings to exhausted gods.

"Sandwiches and caffeine," Lunchbox declared, setting everything down carefully. "That's the extent of our emotional intelligence today."

"Better than nothing," I said with a grateful smile as the scent of strong coffee hit the air.

Voodoo passed AB a cup, then handed me one with an unreadable look. "Eat. Think. Then we get to work."

The moment shifted—less tender, more tactical—but no less grounded in what mattered. They were all here. Still fighting. Still pushing forward.

I took a sip of the coffee, bracing myself. Then I looked around at the faces I trusted more than most people would understand, and I asked the only question that mattered now.

"Alright, what do we know?"

CHAPTER

TWELVE

BONES

This wasn't my first time facing torture. Hell, it wasn't even my first time waking up strung up by the wrists, arms stretched high and shoulders screaming from the weight of my own body. Gravity did most of the damage—slow, relentless, unforgiving. My toes could *almost* reach the floor. Balance took effort. Bracing was nearly impossible.

But at least my legs were free.

Not that it mattered. They weren't letting me use them. Instead, they kept their distance, letting the water do the work—soaking me through, letting every drop turn my body into a live wire.

Then came the shock sticks.

They didn't get close. Just jabbed at me from arm's length like cowards, letting the current rip through the water, through me. Each strike lit up my nerves like a live circuit, my jaw snapping shut hard enough to rattle my teeth. I focused on that—just keeping my tongue clear. A small win. A fragile bit of control.

And sometimes, that's all you've got.

The shocks stopped, but the water didn't.

It kept pouring steadily soaking into my clothes, my skin, the rope biting into my wrists. Cold and constant. Like a reminder: *this is just the beginning.*

They weren't in a hurry.

One of the suits stepped into my line of sight, just far enough back that I couldn't reach him even if I got stupid and tried to swing. He looked like the others—square jaw, cropped hair, mirrored sunglasses even in this dim, cement-walled hellhole. They all looked the same. Like they'd been printed from a template. Corporate-branded cruelty.

No one said a word.

Not a single question. No threats. No posturing.

Just the occasional click of the shock stick. Just enough to warn me of the next hit.

Not their first rodeo, I thought, dragging in a slow breath through my nose. *And not amateurs.* That should've worried me more than it did.

But I wasn't dead, which meant they still wanted something. Based on what the so-called *Vega* said, they wanted information *and* leverage. Maybe not much. But enough.

The silence pressed in harder than the pain.

If they'd shouted, raged, barked orders, I could've played off that. Tuned them out. Picked a weak spot. But this? This sterile, clockwork efficiency? It was harder to fight.

I could feel my mind start to drift—just a little—toward that place where you stop caring. Where the pain becomes background noise and the body starts whispering *just let go.* My jaw clenched, and I forced myself back. No good came from checking out. That's how you missed details. Patterns. Openings.

And I needed one. Bad.

"Not gonna talk?" I rasped, voice rough as gravel. "Didn't think this was just a spa day."

No answer. Not even a flicker of amusement. One of the suits adjusted his cuffs. That was it.

Still nothing.

My ribs ached from the tension. My arms had long since gone numb. The muscles in my legs were starting to tremble with the effort of keeping me upright. I shifted my weight slightly, just enough to ease the pull on one shoulder.

Another jolt hit the water.

My back arched on instinct, a full-body spasm I couldn't control, and I let out a short, involuntary grunt. It wasn't a scream, but it wasn't nothing either.

The suit closest to me cocked his head, studying me like I was a specimen under glass. Still no questions. Still no demands. Just observation.

They're measuring me.

Not for weakness. Not for pain tolerance. For something else. *Response time. Reactions. Behavior under stress.*

They weren't trying to break me.

They were profiling me.

That realization landed harder than the last jolt. They weren't sadists. This wasn't about pleasure. They didn't *enjoy* it.

That made them dangerous in a whole different way.

I swallowed hard, working moisture back into my mouth. "Y'know," I said, breath shallow, "most people at least *pretend* to get off on this part. You guys really need to work on your bedside manner."

No response.

Of course not.

But one of them—taller than the rest—finally stepped forward, something in his hand. A towel. He draped it over the spigot above me, cutting off the water.

The silence grew heavier.

I could hear my own breathing now, uneven and tight. My heartbeat in my ears. Somewhere above, maybe through a vent or behind a door, a distant hum—machinery? Air system? It barely mattered.

They were going to start talking soon.

I wasn't sure if I was more worried of what they wanted to know—or how much they already did.

Yet, despite all of that, they still didn't ask anything. In fact, they left. No announcement. No closing remarks. No whispered threats or final looks. Just a slow retreat of footsteps. The sound of the door hissing shut.

Then the lights went out.

Total black.

Like the kind of black that isn't just absence of light, but a presence all its own. Thick. Suffocating. Heavy on the chest. I blinked reflexively, but it made no difference. I might as well have been blindfolded. Buried alive.

And the silence—

The silence was worse.

No water dripping. No buzz of overhead lights. Not even the hum of cameras. Even the earlier sounds of machinery were *gone*. Leaving nothing.

A perfect, engineered nothing leaving me alone with only the sound of my harsh breathing.

My arms burned, ropes biting into skin gone raw. My shoulders trembled with fatigue. Every nerve in my body twitched like it hadn't gotten the message that the shocks had stopped. Ghost currents. Phantom pain. I could still feel that last jolt sparking in my molars.

The silence continued to creep in through the cracks.

It got in my head.

Tick, tick, tick.

Shock, breath, twitch.

Weight, rope, sway.

Where are they?

Time slipped. Minutes? Hours? A day? Could've been five. My brain was no longer on the clock. It had flipped to survival mode.

Focus. Focus.

Tracker.

Right thigh. Subdermal. Deep enough to survive some serious shit. I hoped. Maybe the shocks didn't fry it. Maybe the signal was still clean. Maybe someone was already on their way.

Maybe.

Or maybe it was scrambled with the rest of me. Cooked from the inside out. Like my spine still felt half-lit, flickering like a busted streetlamp.

Don't think like that. *Stay sharp.*

I started counting. Prime numbers, backwards. Then forwards. Then in French. Anything to keep the brain from unraveling.

And then—Grace.

God, Grace.

I could almost see her: arms crossed, that look on her face like she was this close to calling me *Boney Boy.* That perfect, wicked sass.

"How is this a better plan than mine?"

Yeah. That tracked. She had a fantastic sense of humor, but even when she gave me shit, she didn't lose that gleam of worry in her eyes.

Fuck. The delicate fragility of hers masked that very

core of steel I'd grown to respect and adore, even when I wanted to spank her ass for risking herself.

She was probably giving the guys hell about what was the plan to get to me. But only when she wasn't keeping her head down and focused. When we'd had to cut out on the guys, she'd been more than just someone for me to protect. She'd *tried* and often succeeded in being a partner.

I could see her, hair pulled back to tame the dark curls while her blue eyes burned with her temper, and her lip gloss served as her war paint. She'd be pushing them, even as she worked to support their choices.

But she'd be counting it down, and terrified or not, she'd follow us right into hell.

We so fucking did not deserve her.

I smiled—barely—but it hurt. Everything did.

Still. Worth it.

I clung to the idea of her like a tether. Her voice. That snap in her tone when she was scared but pretending not to be. The way she said my name when she was pissed—and when she wasn't. The shock and passion burning through her expression when I sank into her and the way she exhaled my name.

From the beginning, I got it. One taste of her would never be enough. She was an addiction before I ever touched her. The memories played out like a reel of actual film, flickering as the frames traveled by just a little too slowly.

Pain raked through my insides, slicing into me.

Tracker. Focus. Grace. Light. Breathe.

Repeat.

My legs were shaking now. Cramping. I shifted, trying to keep blood moving. The rope creaked softly in the dark, but the sound was swallowed up immediately. The sound proofing was impressive. Nothing bounced. Nothing echoed.

Designed to erase a person, to strip them down until all that was left was the silence and potentially the screaming inside your skull.

Fine.

Let them wait.

Let them think they were winning.

I could hold the line.

Because somewhere out there, my team *was* coming. Grace was probably going to be with them and she would be *pissed*. It would be worth it.

I DON'T KNOW when I slipped.

One second, I was gripping onto Grace's voice like a life-line—counting, visualizing, grounding myself in memories —and the next, I was somewhere else entirely. Not uncon-scious. Not exactly dreaming either. Just... floating. Detached. Like my brain had quietly decided to step out of the room and let my body rot in peace.

It wasn't peace, though. Not even close.

Because when they came back, they *tore* me out of that void.

The lights snapped on so bright and fast it felt like a punch to the skull. A flood of sterile white burned through my eyes, blinding, searing. My head jerked back, instinctive, involuntary. A sound tore from my throat—half-snarl, half-gasp—as my vision exploded into a storm of afterimages and migraine sparks.

Then came the water.

Sudden.

Cold.

Relentless.

Like an executioner's switch had been thrown. It cascaded from above, reactivating every nerve ending. Every inch of me was drenched in seconds. My breath stuttered in my chest. The water slid down my spine, across raw skin, into open scrapes. It didn't just soak. It *penetrated*.

And just like that, the *click* came.

Electric warning. Familiar. Immediate.

I barely had time to brace.

CRACK.

The shock hit with precision. Like a conductor wielding a baton of lightning, the nameless man played me like a violent instrument. My limbs spasmed, my back bowed, and I bit down hard on the inside of my cheek to keep the scream inside. Metal on nerve. My thoughts scattered like shrapnel.

This time, however, the assholes *said* something.

"Where is the drive?"

No buildup. No soft threats. No misdirection.

Just straight to it.

"Where did Voodoo take it?"

I coughed, spit mixing with blood. "Fuck if I know," I rasped, jaw barely working.

CRACK.

A second shock. Right thigh. Too close to the tracker.

I snarled through clenched teeth, the fire racing from hip to heel, nerves lighting up in defiance.

"You were his commanding officer," the voice said—neutral, precise, clinical. "You knew the mission profile. You knew his extraction points. Where did he take it?"

CRACK.

Another jolt. This one hit the water near my feet,

coursing up through both legs and into my spine. My vision whited out. For a second, I saw stars. Maybe galaxies.

"Where is the drive?" they asked again. Calm. Measured. Like this was a goddamn debriefing and not their version of enhanced interrogation in a cement crypt.

"I don't know," I said. "He ran dark."

CRACK.

This one stole my breath. My lungs locked up. My body bucked.

"You were responsible for the asset. The data was onboard. Prototype intelligence mapping. Your *team* stole it. And you let him vanish."

"He wasn't supposed to come back," I gritted out. "He volunteered for the ghost run. He knew what that meant."

CRACK.

I screamed this time. Couldn't help it. My body betrayed me, torn between agony and defiance.

Silence again.

Water kept pouring.

"You knew the contingency plan," the voice went on, stepping closer. I could almost make out the outline now—broad-shouldered, authoritative. Not one of the suits. Someone higher. Commanding. "You had eyes on Voodoo's fallback. We know he communicated with you post-mission."

"I burned the comms," I said, panting. "No signal. No trace. That was the plan. We covered our tracks."

"*And yet,*" the voice said coolly, "you were the last person to speak with him. You *knew.* So where is the drive?"

CRACK.

Left arm. Right through the shoulder. Fire exploded up my neck, and my jaw snapped shut so fast I bit my tongue.

"I don't know," I growled through blood. "Even if I did... I wouldn't give it to *you.*"

Silence again.

The man stepped closer. I felt his presence now. A pressure in the air. This wasn't one of the suits. He didn't move like them. Didn't *feel* like them. This one was military.

It was about fucking time.

He leaned close.

"You're not dying here, Bones. You'll wish you did, but you won't. Not until we have what we came for. And we *will* get it."

CRACK.

My legs gave out. Only the ropes kept me dangling.

"You should start thinking about how much pain it's worth."

My breath was ragged. Broken. But I still smiled.

Then I spit the blood into his face.

Another *CRACK.*

The world shattered into white noise again.

THIRTEEN

ALPHABET

The signal from Bones should've pinged by now.

We had redundancy built into the redundancy—a subdermal tracker, untraceable by standard sweeps, hardwired to activate if his vitals spiked or flatlined. His phone was either in a ditch or tossed into a microwave, based on the last static-laced ping we scraped from the network. That wasn't the problem. The problem was the implant—quiet as the grave.

Which meant one of three things.

Bones was dead.

Bones had cut it out himself.

Or these so-called Vega bastards had done something I didn't fully understand.

And that... *that* was the real problem.

Vega wasn't a person *or* a team. It was a program, a protocol, a whispered myth in the darker corners of SIGINT briefings. A Cold War-style ghost supposedly mothballed after the Berlin Wall fell. Counter-intelligence wrapped into sophisticated computer programming and predictive modeling

So-called artificial intelligence on crack

A program that *never* worked. But it didn't stop their repeated investment like Charlie Brown trying to kick the ball Lucy was forever taking away. Arguing that if they didn't do it, then someone else would was about as sensical as mutually assured destruction.

The one scattered reference I dug out of a redacted archive came from a former team lead. The goal: *"Vega doesn't protect information. It erases the need for it."*

Still... Leaving the computer, I headed down to the basement. This place had a cell in it, which worked out in our favor. I didn't ask where Voodoo dug this place up from, when we needed something, he damn well found it.

O'Rourke was still inside the cell, shackled at the wrists and ankles, blindfolded, headphones snug against his ears. No sound. No light. No stimuli. A human in purgatory.

I stared at him for a long moment. Taking him along was a risk. But we'd also scanned him for trackers, he had none. That didn't mean he didn't have an inert one, but I had a radio jammer down here that would hopefully mitigate it if he did.

In the meanwhile, I unlocked the cell door and walked in. He didn't move. I peeled the headphones off first. He flinched, maybe out of reflex. Then the blindfold. His pupils tightened like they were trying to crawl back into his skull.

Sensory deprivation could really fuck with a person. He didn't speak. Just breathed. Watched me.

"Bones is gone," I said.

No reaction.

"No phone trace, no subdermal ping. Nothing. Tracker's dead."

Still nothing.

"I think your pal Vega had something to do with it."

That got him. A breath, quick and shallow. The kind you take when you realize the drop's coming, but it's too late to grab the edge.

"I told them not to use it," O'Rourke muttered. "I told them it wasn't built to end problems. It was built to *erase them*."

I stepped closer. "Erase how?"

He lifted his head. "Erase *you*. The moment you become inconvenient."

"That doesn't make any sense." Did he know something or not?

"No," he said, smiling grimly. "But it's what the program became."

I didn't respond. I didn't need to. The program didn't even *exist* anymore.

He kept talking. "You still think Vega's some smart program? Some watchdog chewing on intelligence trafficking? On isolating technological advances from other countries in order to co-op them?"

"That used to be what they said in the old files about it." The whole idea behind the protocol had been to take the lead. Part of the reason the damn thing never worked, it needed too much data to actually deliver anything. Large language models still hadn't achieved that type of sophistication.

"Intent means nothing." His eyes sharpened. "Desire, design—it responds to one thing."

"Money." Because money talked and bullshit walked.

"Exactly. In the past five years, the people in charge of Vega changed—a lot."

I frowned. "They shit-canned it." Or they were

supposed to after we moth-balled it. The job had been pretty straightforward, get the hard drives, shut the whole thing down and blow it up. We'd done that.

"Alphabet, you aren't stupid or that idealistic." O'Rourke actually sounded beyond tired. "You really aren't. It was a gambit, a political play made possible by corporate synergy." He coughed, the roughened and hoarse nature of his voice reminding me we hadn't been hydrating him.

Arms folded, I studied him for a long moment. "Educate me."

"Why?" O'Rourke just stared at me. "Information is capital. I have it. You want it. What do I get for it?"

"How about a bullet in the head if you keep wasting our fucking time?" Lunchbox prowled down the stairs to join us. His presence added weight to the moment. The normally cool, level-head he boasted in most combat situations seemed completely absent.

O'Rourke sighed. "Can I trade an answer for some water?"

"Depends," Voodoo said from above, his voice hovered around us. Didn't surprise me that they'd noticed me coming down here.

When Voodoo didn't elaborate, it forced O'Rourke to define the condition. "On?"

"On whether the answer is going to be worth the time. So far, all you've done is set me up to walk into a trap."

Despite his hands being bound behind his back—and the small matter of his survival hinging entirely on our goodwill—O'Rourke laughed.

It wasn't loud. It wasn't even particularly amused. It was the kind of laugh that echoed more of defiance than humor.

"You're the one who walked into it," he said, eyes glinting. "Could've stayed in the wind."

"Ah, so it's our fault?" I asked, more curious than angry. A flicker of amusement crept in despite myself. There was a reason we'd liked O'Rourke, once.

He stopped laughing. Just—stopped. The smile slid off his face like a mask dropped on the floor. A switch flipped.

"You made the choice to come," he said, voice flat. "You knew the odds it was a trap. You walked in anyway. So yeah, it's at least fifty percent your fault."

A soft sound drifted down the stairwell.

A snort.

Feminine.

And, I got the feeling, amused.

Explained why Voodoo hadn't descended. He stayed up there to keep Grace up there. She was right, we were never going to be okay with just walking her into some of this no matter how tough she tried to be or how fierce her determination.

"Fine," I said, unwilling to argue this point. "It's fifty percent our fault, but that makes the other fifty yours. So, time to pay up."

O'Rourke just stared at me. "Doesn't sound like much of an incentive." He tilted his head from left to right and then back again. "Have Grace ask me."

Have. Grace. Ask. Me.

Those four words echoed against a cool darkness inside of me.

"This isn't a game," I reminded him. "Even if it was, she's a civilian. A noncombatant. Don't talk about her."

The skeptical look he wore just shouted bullshit. "She is in this. She's hardly a civilian. You want answers. I want to see her. Quid. Pro. Quo."

Lunchbox answered him with a hard left across O'Rourke's face. Honestly, I hadn't even seen him move. One minute Lunchbox prowled the room, the next he was punching the asshole in the mouth.

The sound of flesh striking flesh was a meaty *thunk* in the downstairs quiet. Undeterred, O'Rourke turned his head to the right and spit out blood before he looked back at me.

"I thought this was your interrogation." O'Rourke raised both of his eyebrows. "You need them to hold your dick for you too when you take a leak?" The blatant challenge just begged for us to beat the shit out of him.

"I let my friends do lots of things." I shrugged. "Friendship doesn't come with conditions."

Despite how incensed he was—as demonstrated by how hard and fast he'd hit O'Rourke—Lunchbox didn't react. At least not visibly to the taunt from the other man. Give it five minutes, at this rate, however and O'Rourke might get his wish.

"But it came with an expiration date."

"We are not debating your choices or your betrayal. Either answer the question or we stuff you back down here and leave you." It made no difference to me at the moment —except that he had answers that could get us to Bones a fuckload faster since we had zero to work with at the moment.

"I'll answer Grace," O'Rourke said. "In fact, she's the only one I'll answer now."

Lunchbox popped him again, sending another wad of crimson-laced spittle to strike the wall. Grin bloody, O'Rourke just straightened himself and waited. I could almost feel Lunchbox processing the man's request, actions, and our response.

Did we let Grace down here to talk to him?

Did we just say fuck it, and go?

Did we take the time to break him down?

We could do it. Anyone could be broken. It was all a matter of time and effort. Just because we could, didn't mean we should on any front. It also didn't mean what we got would be successful. Most intelligence obtained through torture wasn't as actionable as the information coaxed from a prisoner.

When all you wanted was for the pain to stop, you'd say just about anything. Promise anything. Do anything.

A low whistle cut through the silence. One. Sharp. Sound. Voodoo made the call. He'd assumed command. That was how it worked, particularly right now. A shuffle of step, then soft little bumps as she descended the stairs.

Her feet didn't add any additional sound, but the stairs had a light creak to them and she wasn't trying to be quiet. Lunchbox melted back a few steps. It wasn't so much a retreat as he posted himself next to the cell "bars" and leaned against them.

The way he folded his arms suggested relaxation, but he was far from it. Hell, so was I. But as Grace made it to me, I moved ahead of her and stationed myself firmly between them, but not blocking her view.

Shackles didn't mean O'Rourke was helpless.

When she was five feet away from him, Voodoo said, "Far enough."

Dressed in loose sleep pants and a tank top, she'd layered a hoodie over it but her feet were bare. The incongruity of her pale pink toenails on her delicate feet irked me. Really irked me.

She was made for softness, for laughter, and for music and fun. Instead, she was down in this dusty basement with this bottom feeding asshole who was more interested in negotiation than making peace. O'Rourke shifted his full attention to her, a faint glint in his eye and a half-smile on his bloodied lips.

Unimpressed, Grace folded her arms and actually stood with one hip jutted slightly. "Where is Bones?"

"Prisoner, would be my guess. Probably being interrogated."

"That's a supposition," Grace said. "Do you know where he is or not?"

Good girl. Direct questions. No wiggle room.

"Not." Another shrug, or as much as O'Rourke could manage in his current condition.

"Do you know who has him or not?"

"Vega."

I didn't growl, but irritation at O'Rourke's words grew.

"Is Vega real or not?" Impatience crept in Grace's voice. The sleepy doe-eyed look she had when she came in had vanished to something far crisper and intent as she watched O'Rourke.

"Vega is real enough," O'Rourke said. "What you want to know is who is *using* Vega and why."

"Do you know who is using it and why they are using it?" Sharpness punctuated the question, and she threw it down like a challenge.

"I do." He smiled, despite the reddening bruises on his face from the pair of hits he'd taken. "I would be happy to tell you all about it."

"But?" Voodoo prompted from behind her. I didn't jolt, but O'Rourke did. He'd forgotten Voodoo was there.

If he added more fucking terms to this questioning, I might consider extreme measures.

"But I want out of here," O'Rourke said, his attention

lasering onto Grace. "If you tell me I will be let go and I'll survive this, then I'll believe you."

What?

"Why?" The sheer volume of *what the fuck* in Grace's voice almost made me laugh.

"Because these assholes won't want to disappoint you or make you cry. That means if you promise me I'll be fine, then I will be."

Lunchbox cut a glance to me and our gazes locked briefly. I shrugged. I had no idea what game he was playing either.

"That might be hard for you because I'm not promising you anything." Oh, there she was, fire in her eyes and flames in her voice. "I don't owe you a damn thing. If I've learned anything over the past few months, we can and will get what we need done. We want to find Bones, we will find him."

Absolute confidence. Zero doubts.

"Ouch," O'Rourke said. "So harsh, pretty girl. I thought we bonded."

Rolling her eyes, Grace looked at me. "Is there a point to continuing this?"

Excellent question.

"The point—" O'Rourke began, but Grace snapped her gaze back to him so fast, I swore I heard the crack of it striking him like a blow.

"I wasn't asking you. You want to play games, I do not. So—shut up." Then she looked at me again, her expression gentling from that fierce almost Ripley-esque badass she'd assumed when speaking to O'Rourke. "Thoughts, AB?"

Oh, I had plenty of ideas. But there was one I needed to test.

I held out my hand. She came to me like a tide pulled to

shore—effortless, inevitable. Her fingers slipped into mine, warm and sure. I tugged her close, one arm sliding around her waist as I dipped my head and kissed her.

It was supposed to be a tease. Just a brush of lips—something light, something curious.

But Gracie had other plans.

Her hand found the back of my neck, fingers threading into my hair as she rose on her toes, pressing into me like she'd been waiting for this—like she'd decided this kiss would answer every question I hadn't dared to ask.

At the first flicker of my tongue, her mouth parted.

That was all the invitation I needed.

The kiss deepened, sharpened. Slow turned to seeking. Seeking to claiming. She tasted like something I couldn't name—something I'd been starving for and hadn't realized until now. Sweet heat and something wild, something that made my knees threaten betrayal.

She pressed herself closer, no space left between us, her breath hitching against my mouth like she needed this just as much. My hand slid up her spine, anchoring her to me, and still—still—it wasn't enough.

From butterfly wings to a hurricane, she blew me away with the ferocity of it.

And I let her.

Hell, I fell into it.

Lifting my head took serious effort, but I managed and ran my tongue over my lips to savor the taste of her. O'Rourke made a grunting sound and I caught sight of the violent desire on his face.

Desire.

And anger.

Someone was jealous.

Too. Fucking. Bad.

I tucked Grace closer to me, and wrapped an arm around her shoulders.

"You have five minutes left with Grace," I said, making a tactical decision. "Answer the questions, be fucking helpful, and we'll have room to discuss your survival. Don't answer, keep making deals, and you can be buried down here. It won't even take that long."

FOURTEEN

GRACE

O'Rourke glared at AB like he'd kicked him in the nuts. Oh, there was an idea. Maybe I should kick him in the nuts. Then the man transferred that gaze to me. Gone was the smug, entitled jackass who'd played games during the ball. It wasn't the bruises on his face, the blood marring his mouth, or even the way he sat, almost defiant in his restraints.

It was his eyes.

A chestnut color, he seemed almost—lost. No, that wasn't the right word for it. But he wasn't as in control or as arrogant as he was playing it. I leaned into AB, my lips still tingling from the kiss. As performative as that caress had been, he'd also meant it and I'd damn well enjoyed it.

"Human trafficking and corporate scum," O'Rourke said finally, his voice flat and his expression going flatter.

The air seemed thinner abruptly and I blinked. "What?"

"Human trafficking and corporate scum. The ties between the two are inextricably linked. They have been for as long as there has been an elite class."

Images of Maurizio Gallo's grabby hands and laughing

demands. The aristocrats at the party in France. More at a party in New York. Yachting invites. Corporate introductions and offers…

"Vega was a cover, a story to get it past the pencil pushers and budget appropriation committees at least here." He rolled his head from side to side, the faint cracking of his bones seeming to echo inside of me.

I fisted the back of AB's shirt as I kept my gaze fixed on O'Rourke. "Are you saying this is all related to me?"

"In a manner of speaking—yes." It was a straightforward and as direct an answer as he'd ever given. "A few years ago, these guys took a job to shut down Odessa. It was where Vega was stored."

He spared a glance at Voodoo and I followed his gaze. Voodoo's expression remained neutral, but he neither confirmed nor denied anything.

"In Ukraine?" I asked finally. Odessa was in Ukraine.

"Odessa was the name of the program that housed the tracking units for the mobile station," Voodoo said. "Not the city."

Oh.

"Operation Vega staged out of Odessa. On the move, never spending time in the same port."

"It was on a ship," I said abruptly.

O'Rourke flashed a smile at me. A small one before his expression turned to a grimace. "Yes."

Tension threaded through AB's arm where he held me. I wasn't sure if it was my imagination or not, but all three of them were buzzed with everything they weren't saying. Anger licked the air between pulses. As confident as O'Rourke sounded, he avoided any egotistical displays.

"They raided Odessa, took the drives, and fucked off to

who knows where. The last person we know for certain who had the information was Voodoo."

"We'll come back to that in a minute," I said, shifting forward to stop leaning on AB.

When I would have moved away, he flexed that arm and I found myself being tugged to stand with my back against his chest and his arms—both of them—loosely around me.

Rather than argue, I just went with it. "Who is *we*?"

"We refers to my team," O'Rourke said. "Freelance specialists. A lot like these guys. We also had a bid in on the job, we didn't get it." The lack of care about the result suggested it was in the past, but if that were the case… "Just pocketed the information and filed it away for future reference. You never know when it's going to come in handy."

"So how did you end up in bed with Vega or whoever is currently roleplaying as them?" Voodoo asked, sober, intent, and focused.

"Got snared in a net after the raid in France." Self-deprecation peppered his tone. "Caught some of the blame for that one going sideways." He flicked a look at me. "Thanks for that."

"You're welcome?" Did he want sympathy from me? He wasn't going to get it. "When you trade in people and sell them, you can get fucked as far as I'm concerned."

Another hint of a smile. "I do like you, Gracie."

"Grace." Legend, Voodoo, and AB all said in one voice. It was almost funny.

Almost.

"So you got snared…" I said, motioning for him to continue.

"Yes, I got picked up. They knew I'd worked with you before, they made me an offer." He shrugged, but his insouciance seemed feigned. "I accepted the offer. I made the call." He nodded to Voodoo. "You showed up. Chaos ensued. Bones was taken. That pretty much sums it up."

"Except you still haven't said who *they* are?" Did that come out at all screechy? I did *not* want to still be standing here in a week trying to puzzle through this man's alternately cryptic and direct responses.

"No," he said softly. "I didn't."

"You don't know," Voodoo said and I jerked my gaze to him then back to O'Rourke.

"Not precisely, no."

A scream worked its way up my throat. "Then why did you play this *game*?"

"Did I?" O'Rourke said, shifting his attention back to me. "Sweet Gracie—"

"Grace," came the stern reprimand from three voices once again and I almost rolled my eyes. My name was not the important thing here.

"Or am I merely leveraging what I have to ensure I survive this interrogation?"

I wanted to throw my hands in the air. "Is this at all helpful?" I asked, glancing from Legend to Voodoo then back up AB. They were all staring at O'Rourke, their expressions unreadable. The tension in the room seemed to swell and expand.

Voodoo started forward without a word. The knife he suddenly had in his hands worried me, but AB tightened his embrace to keep me in place. Over the past few months, I'd seen the guys do what they had to do with and without weapons.

Could they be violent? Absolutely. Deadly? Without a doubt. Had I seen them kill? Yes. But not once had I seen evidence of a cruel maliciousness in their actions or witnessed anything like joy when it came to the often brutal decisions they'd had to make.

No, they weren't psychopaths. They may not be pure as driven snow, but their actions and their choices spoke volumes for them. I'd back them in whatever they decided here. O'Rourke might not be the villain, but he'd definitely participated in the setup and he *had* been at the auction.

Voodoo stood over O'Rourke for an inordinate amount of time, his gaze locked on the other man. O'Rourke didn't beg. He didn't offer up excuses. He didn't even *ask* what Voodoo planned to do.

The stare off seemed to last forever but it was really only a few seconds. Voodoo slid around O'Rourke and released him.

"Damn," AB said. "I just lost fifty."

I blinked and cut my gaze up at him. "What?"

"I bet Lunchbox that he'd be the one who let the asshole go."

The "asshole" in question snorted at AB's grumble. It didn't take long for Voodoo to make short work of the zip ties and O'Rourke sat forward with a slow groan as he began to rub his wrists.

"What was on that drive that we took from Odessa?" Voodoo didn't wait for O'Rourke to recover before he asked.

"Files. Client files. Human trafficking. Predators. Those with strong political ties. Others with strong financial incentives. A comprehensive list built by one of the main suppliers over three decades."

With care, O'Rourke stood and popped his back.

"It started out as a CIA side project spotting irregularities, flagging patterns, locating networks, then making connections. Get the inside look. Human trafficking is a web of trade across the world and the volume of money funneled through it is enormous."

Ice shivered through my veins even with AB holding me.

"They had to train their analysts on what to look for, then it narrowed down to a couple of guys who were really good at it. Eventually, they tried to build it into a machine to do the work for them. Someone that wouldn't have the ability to blackmail them, but offered them what they needed to keep their finger on the pulse."

Legend held out a bottle of water to O'Rourke, and then another to Voodoo. We were all still *in* the cell, so I guessed this was where we were going to finish this conversation.

"The problems weren't with the program. They were really good at uncovering the patterns, finding the links, and identifying possible traffickers." He paused to down about half the bottle. "The problem began when someone saw a way to monetize Vega."

"Is it a program or a person?" Because it sounded like both.

"Yes," O'Rourke said, glancing at me. "It's a consortium of disparate but compatible groups. They were brought together to monetize Vega and they began to make power moves using the proof on the drive."

"But they don't have the drive anymore," I said, verifying with a glance at Voodoo then Legend before looking back at O'Rourke.

"No, they don't," Voodoo confirmed. "But that's why they took Bones."

"Likely. They wanted you." He motioned to Voodoo with his bottle. "You are the last one they have on surveillance with the drives before you destroyed the rest of their servers. But the captain is a good second choice, because chances are, he knows exactly what you did with it."

The pressure in my chest shifted, the air backing up in my lungs. "If it has all the things on it you're saying it does... they are going to want it back." Obviously. "That's what they'll want for Bones."

"The programs that were originally designed to help in enforcing the law and saving people now curate it. I don't know who gave you that job to take it, but Vega has been out of play since then." O'Rourke began to walk in slow circles, each step indicating he was pained after the enforced inactivity.

"Someone is playing a massive game of chicken relying on the information on that drive." Voodoo stared into the middle distance. Rarely did he ever look so *remote*.

"That's my guess," O'Rourke said. "They leveraged me to get to you. They want to leverage you to get to the drive or leverage Bones for it."

"He'll never give it to them," Legend said, zero doubt in his voice.

"No," Voodoo said softly and AB sighed. "He won't. Which means tracking them is going to be paramount." Slanting a look at O'Rourke, he continued, "Are you going to be helpful or continue to be a vague prick about everything?"

The other man glanced over at me again. "Feel like asking me to stay and help, Gracie?"

Legend slugged him. The man was on his feet then he was down. "Call her that again," he suggested. "I fucking dare you."

"Won that fifty," AB murmured in my ear and I cut a look at him again.

"Why are you betting on all of this?"

"Morbid humor. Helps me get through the bad days." Deadpan and utterly serious, but I got it.

With a sigh, I said, "If you will stop baiting them, then yes, I am asking you to help us find Bones. To be useful. To not be a prick."

Slowly, O'Rourke climbed to his feet. Fresh blood decorated his now split lip and the redness of the bruising on his jaw had deepened. He really wasn't going to be pretty when that came out.

"Then I'll help." He popped his back. "We can start by having you backtrace my own locator. They took me somewhere to put the screws to me, but I couldn't see shit or hear much over the sound of the tires on the road and running water."

"Son of a bitch," AB said abruptly, then gave me a squeeze before he pressed a kiss to the top of my head. He shifted to put himself between me and O'Rourke. "We scanned you for trackers."

"It's not active currently," he said. "Give me *some* credit here. I deactivated it with my phone. But I can get you into the—"

"Let's go," AB said, pointing him to the stairs.

"I'm going," O'Rourke chuckled as he eased past Voodoo and kept a wary distance from Legend. "I don't suppose you'd care to join us, Grace?"

"I'm good," I said, then AB got O'Rourke up the stairs. Once up there, AB gave Goblin a command in German. Pretty sure it was guard, but as muffled as it was, it could have been a variant on it.

"Are we seriously trusting him?" Legend asked Voodoo.

"No," Voodoo said. "Firecracker, can you stay away from him up there?"

"Where do you want me to go? Hide in my room?" Because that wasn't really fair.

"No," Legend said. "Stay with me." When Voodoo looked like he would object, Legend cut a hand through the air. "No, you back up Alphabet. I'm more likely to break his jaw if he keeps looking at Gracie like she's his favorite snack."

"He's just doing it to fuck with you," I told them and that snared both of their attention. At their semi-blank looks, I raised my hands. "I know when a man is interested. He just wants to yank your chain and he's figured out that you will respond to his taunts if he uses me to do it."

"I still want you to keep your distance," Voodoo said. "And before you ask, yes, whatever we find out, you will also know and whatever we plan, you will also hear."

Relief spilled through me at that. "Thank you."

Voodoo cupped my face then dropped a kiss on my lips. "We'll take care of things, Firecracker."

It wasn't quite a promise, but I'd take it. He headed up the stairs and Legend held out a hand to me. His battered and bruised hand. I was careful as I took it, I didn't want to hurt him anymore than he already was. But he didn't seem to care, pulling me into him and wrapping me up in a hug.

"We're going to find Bones, Gracie," Legend said. "I promise. We never leave *anyone* behind."

FIFTEEN

GRACE

Legend spread one large hand against my back, the weight of it offered comfort even as I rubbed my face against his shirt. The distinctly masculine scent of him was sweetened by a hint of maple and confectioner's sugar.

"Were you baking?" When did he have time to do that?

"Not yet. I was debating setting things up for it, then broke it back down. We need to be ready to move." There was an element of disappointment in his voice.

He flexed one arm around me as he rubbed a slow circle on my back. The warmth of his body enveloped me, and I leaned into him, trusting that he wouldn't let me fall. He didn't. He never did.

"Talk to me, Gracie. You look sad."

I turned his words over in my mind, trying to find the right way to express the turmoil inside me. "I'm not really sad," I started, my voice barely above a whisper. "I am, but —it's hard to explain."

He wrapped both arms around me again, his embrace

turning possessive and protective. "Let's try it this way, then. What are you thinking about?"

The steady thump of his heart helped to ease some of the tension that had knotted itself inside me. "It's so normal outside," I said, my thoughts seemed almost as distant as my emotions.

The drive here had been intense, but also—not. It was weird. The new safe house was in a brand new, upscale subdivision. Made me kind of wonder if any of the other houses boasted a jail cell in the basement or if we were just lucky. The weirdest part had been seeing others outside their houses, kids playing, cars coming and going—life.

"People going to work, going to school, just—going about their lives. That feels like a million years ago to me. It's only been a few months, but even that feels a lot longer." I blew out a breath. "In the middle of all of this 'oddness' there's this knowledge that Bones is missing. He could be hurt. He could be de—" No, I didn't want to invite that thought. "And as terrible as that is, his being missing isn't as weird as that normal life out there."

He didn't say anything for a long moment, just held me, his presence alone a silent support. A part of me wanted to be one of those people out there, to return to normalcy. But I was never going to be normal again. How could I? After everything? At the same time, what was normal except the typical every day events?

So was this "normal" for Legend and the guys? Was this what they'd had to get used to over the years? Had they ever tried to change it? Did they want to? So many things I didn't know. It made my head hurt almost as much as my heart.

The thought slipped into my mind, unwelcome but

undeniable. Wouldn't even try to deny it. At the end of the day, they weren't normal. How could I want normal if they weren't a part of it?

"Gracie?" His voice was gentle, but there was an undercurrent of something else. Concern, maybe. Or something more. I tilted my head back to look up at him, my eyes meeting his. The more I thought about it, the more I realized how often I saw that concern reflected in the depths

"Come with me for a little while?"

"Anywhere," I replied, the word slipping out before I could even think about it. He scooped me up, his movements swift and sure. "I can walk," I reminded him, again, even as he strode across the basement and toward the stairs.

"I know you can," he said, his voice a low rumble as he climbed them two at a time. "This is faster."

I snorted a laugh, then frowned. "Why do you guys keep calling me slow?"

His eyes twinkled, the light returning to them, brightening the dark shadows filling them since he'd descended the stairs to follow AB. "We're not. Or at least I'm not, I just like holding you."

On the first floor, he bypassed the dining room that AB had taken over with O'Rourke and Voodoo to do their research. Once we were on the second floor, Legend strode to the end of the hall where he opened the door, then stepped inside and locked it behind us. The whole time, his gaze never left mine. The room was dim, the blinds closed, but there was enough light to see by.

"Would now be the time to remind you that I have had a *lot* of rest lately?" I teased, these men undid me with their absolute focus on my care. Sometimes it frustrated me, other times it delighted me. Yet, nothing I said ever seemed to stifle their need to swath me in safety. Did they see it? Or was it just natural to them? I studied his expressions, trying to read the emotions playing across his face. I really had plenty of downtime while we'd been in Braxton Harbor. So. Much. Downtime.

"If you want," he said, walking toward the bed while still cradling me. My heart did a little flip in my chest. "Or you can just let me look after you the way I want to." He'd said that to me before, and it squeezed my heart now every bit as much as it had then.

At the bed, he set me down, his movements efficient and sure. Wreathed in shadow, he glanced up at me from his crouch. "Have I told you how magnificent you've been?"

"No..." I said slowly, my mind raced, but I couldn't resist. "At least not today."

He laughed. "So I shouldn't tell you now?"

"I did not say that," I assured him, I touched my fingers to his cheek. I loved these men so much it tied me up in knots.

"I told you before, you're a grenade with the pin half out, Gracie."

I loved that description so much. It told me how he felt so much more clearly than diamonds or flowers.

"You are always so fierce, so protective, so dangerous—and you always take my breath away."

That was such a wild compliment. Was it a compliment? I liked it but communication was important. He slid his boots off one at a time. "Is dangerous a good thing?" I frowned even if I wanted to grin. "I don't think anyone has ever labeled me as dangerous before."

"It's an amazing thing," he murmured, then gripped the hem of my shirt and tugged it upward. I raised my arms obediently, letting him peel the fabric off. Tension coiled in my belly and my nipples went taut. "I told you…"

He paused to nip the side of one breast and my muscles clenched at the hint of teeth. I was already soaking my panties and squirming.

"I have a thing for explosives."

"That explains so much," I said on a snort of laughter. It came out undignified, and I resisted the urge to cover my mouth. Legend's grin widened.

"Does it?"

"Oh, it does." I assured him and reached for him. When he leaned in, I kissed him, then nibbled a path to his ear. "Boom."

His laughter was magical and it smoothed over the rough places in my soul, paving over the cracks, and detonated the doubts that always tried to creep in.

"Beautiful," he said, wrapping a hand around my nape. "Petite." A biting kiss. "Delicate." A soft lick of his tongue over the sting. "Wicked temper." He kissed me fiercely then, the sweep of his tongue so damn tantalizing. Then he pulled back, the hot contact leaving me gasping. "Perfect."

He stripped me of my clothes as he talked, his movements so assured that I didn't object as he folded them neatly as naturally as if it didn't take any extra time. If only he got his own clothes off. Another few seconds and I'd help, but I was entranced by his attention and savored the way he seemed to so damn focused on me. I loved the way his eyes darkened when he looked at me, even more when he drank in the sight of my body.

With them, my body wasn't a tool or a source of income. I'd divorced myself from my looks a long time ago —beauty was so subjective. But in his eyes? In all of their eyes? I felt… glorious.

"I'm particularly fond of your aim."

Another inelegant snort escaped me.

"I'll remember that when we fight." Not if. When. I'd had my struggles with all of them.

"See," he said, his smile turning slow and devastating. "Wicked temper."

"Some people might worry that you get turned on when I'm mad."

"Some?" He shrugged that off like it didn't matter. "Not me. I love a challenge."

Nude now, I shivered but more from the caress of his words even if the chillier air sent goosebumps rippling over my skin. My heart kicked at my ribs. "Am I a challenge, Legend?"

"Do you remember when I said glass breaks, but you don't?"

I nodded slowly, as he peeled off his pants and we never lost eye contact.

He seduced me with his words, his gaze, his food—hell, everything about him was catnip to me. Heat swept through me as his cock appeared, heavy, thick, and already beaded with pre-cum. Fresh hunger ignited in my belly and I ached for him like it had been forever since the last time he touched me and not just seconds.

"You *don't* break," he said, falling forward to hover of me, his hands catching his weight where he pressed them against the bed on either side of me. When I would have objected, he didn't let me get past parting my lips. He just kissed the argument out of me. The massage of his lips on mine devastated me, plowing through every possible objection even as he settled his weight against the cradle of my thighs.

The hard length of his cock slid against the slickness of

my cunt and my hips arched to stroke against him. I sank my fingers into his hair and clung to him as he kissed me. Desperation edged every stroke of his tongue and nip of his teeth. He was so hard, his tense muscles like sculpted rock. Everywhere he pressed against me, I burned. His chest was a rough caress against my nipples.

"Gracie..." It came out ragged, a harsh punctuation to his kisses. "I need—"

I reached between us, wrapping my hand around the erect length of him. His sucked in breath buoyed me. He was not immune to this wildfire between us and I adored that he didn't even try to pretend he was.

Teasing his tip against my slit, I ramped us both up. This couldn't last, neither of us would survive and I didn't want to torment him. Instead, I just angled him at my entrance and bit at his lower lip.

"Yes," I said, answering every unspoken question between us. I wanted him. He wanted me. He slammed home and it pushed a cry out of me that he caught on his mouth. Over and over, he powered into me, all that strength and heat stretching me until I thought I might burst, and still we rocked together.

When I wrapped my legs around him, it adjusted the angle and he slid even deeper. This tine when I let out a low scream, he increased his pace. His hands were everywhere, stroking, pulling and angling me. He moved me like I was his personal salvation and I arched upwards into the contact, desperate for every single stroke.

The crispness of the hair around his base rasped against me. The bite of his teeth against my throat had me writhing. When the first ripple of an orgasm stole through me, I gasped. One moment, it had been building and the next it blew through me like a firestorm. But Legend was far from done, he kept moving as I thrashed and clenched down on him.

"Again," he said in a voice made harsh with need. I forgot how to breathe because when he said again, he meant another orgasm. He pushed and pulled, bit down, stroked and caressed, and then I was coming all over again. The world shattered and his hips stuttered before he gave a shout of his own.

We lay there trembling. Sweat slicked my skin and he had his face buried against my throat. The hot weight of him blanketed me and my cunt flexed and fluttered with reaction. He kept giving these little jerks.

"Legend?" I whispered when I found my voice again.

"Hmm?" A kiss to my throat, then a soft stroke of his tongue as he lapped at my skin. He was like a cat, except he didn't purr. The idea of that made me smile. With a trembling hand, I stroked his back. I wanted to touch and kiss him everywhere. To explore and learn his body until I had him memorized utterly.

Legend sucked a bite against my throat. The hickey making my toes curl and I clenched against him. It was a sexy torment for both of us.

"Gracie?"

It was my turn to rub against him. "Hmm?"

"You were saying?"

I blinked slowly. I was? Oh... Laughing softly, I shifted my pets to his hair, threading my fingers through it. "Boom."

Silence.

Then he began to shake as laughter rippled through him. Another bite, this one tender before he raised his head and gazed down at me. The shadows were still there but pushed back and his eyes were so heated, I swore he branded me with them.

"Now," he said, so serious, my lower abdomen tightened as I braced. "We go for the boom-boom."

I was still laughing when he swooped in to kiss.

And yes, the man really did have a thing for explosives.

Boom.

CHAPTER

SIXTEEN

VOODOO

I caught the movement from the corner of my eye as O'Rourke focused on the screen where Alphabet worked. Shifting my position, I blocked any view O'Rourke might have of the hall or the stairs. Lunchbox stole away with Grace and that worked for me.

She needed the distraction—her stress etched in every furrow of her brow, tension cinched tight around her eyes —and for Lunchbox, it was more than a break; it was a lifeline. His fury at O'Rourke seeped into every exchange, volatile and suffocating, like cloth drenched in gasoline.

Their complicated history painted a target on every goal that we neither had the time or the patience for. As long as O'Rourke could be useful, Lunchbox would suck it up. He never let his own feelings dictate the mission execution.

When we were done with O'Rourke, though?

Well, his survival might be the only thing he could ask for, particularly because he'd burned so many damn bridges. His focus on our firecracker was doing him no favors.

"Where did they grab you again?" Alphabet asked as he

reviewed CCTV footage, scanning forward in ten-to-fifteen-minute increments.

"Hotel lobby," O'Rourke stated. "The New Rothschild."

"Time?"

"Just after midnight." There was some improvement in O'Rourke's lack of playing coy. He kept his answers short and to the point.

Tabbing through the various screens, Alphabet's jaw tensed. The lobby appeared to be a dazzling homage to the opulence of the Gilded Age from the grand double doors to the marble floors veined with gold. The wainscoted walls wrapped in a rich brocade wallpaper dressed up the space as much as the staff in their crisp livery. The towering Corinthian columns rose like guardians on watch over the space.

"Betrayal must pay really fucking well," Alphabet commented. "Let me guess, their toilet lids are done in gold too?"

"Be hard to clean," O'Rourke deadpanned.

I almost snorted, but buried the reaction to keep it all business. "Why were you staying at a place like this?"

Enjoying luxury wasn't a problem. I *liked* luxury. That said, this place was not just luxury, it was a lifestyle. The massive crystal chandelier was easily twenty feet across and it cascaded from the coffered ceiling and seemed to give the impression that it was made from diamonds.

Alphabet located O'Rourke strolling inside, dressed in a tux and *tails*.

"The fuck is this?" Alphabet asked, glancing up at the other man.

"Class and style. Focus."

Everything about the decadent location seemed drenched in indulgence. This was not the ideal setting for a soldier, but O'Rourke was playing a very different role based on his current presence on the screen.

He was halfway across the lobby, strolling over the rich Persian rug in its deep burgundy not glancing at the oil paintings that decorated the alcoves along the mezzanine with their heavy gilt frames. It looked like he was on his way toward a sweeping staircase, with its balustrade wrought in intricate bronze filigree.

The place probably *smelled* like money.

It wasn't until he was five steps from that staircase when two men rose from the pair Louis XVI sofas. They were dressed in black-on-black suits and sported military precise haircuts. They looked like clones from a do-it-your-self Men in Black catalog.

One stepped in front of O'Rourke while the other moved behind him. O'Rourke barely slowed. But two more descended the stairs from the mezzanine level and another came from the left somewhere.

"Five-man team," Alphabet stated, using the mouse to manipulate the view.

"There's a sixth one you can't see, but he's upstairs. I'd wager there was another five-man team ready to back these guys up, but they didn't step into frame anywhere I could make them." The swelling of O'Rourke's lip and the bruising of his jaw added some thickness to the words and distorted his dismissive attitude.

"Brief us on what they are saying," I instructed. The fact O'Rourke actually gave the faintest of jerks amused me. He'd forgotten I was here.

Sloppy.

Very sloppy.

"I've been 'requested' to join their employer in a suite upstairs for an appointment." O'Rourke folded his arms.

His shoulders drooped slightly, weariness showing up in his posture. "They're all armed. They all move like they know what they're doing. I could agree to see where we were going with it, or I could start an incident down there. Based on what I could see? Resistance would end with a bullet in my head."

I didn't disagree.

The conversation didn't take as long as O'Rourke's explanation and he joined four of the five in an elevator. The fifth one returned to the sofa to sit and he pulled out his phone. Probably alerting their employer to the imminent arrival.

"Keep an eye on that one," I said, but Alphabet had already tabbed the image over to a secondary screen as he switched the view to the elevator.

It took a minute to get into the right feed but the image cut out as soon as the doors closed and it went to static.

"Eighteenth floor," O'Rourke said before Alphabet could ask. I had my suspicions—a sharp cry drifted from upstairs, muffled by the closed doors but not quite enough to silence it entirely.

My dick went hard at the very vocal evidence of our firecracker getting off with Lunchbox. Lucky bastard.

"Got it," Alphabet said almost on the heels of the sound reaching us. O'Rourke started to shift but Alphabet slapped something on the keyboard.

There was a clear view of the elevator until the hall indicator illuminated for going up, then it also cut to static.

"How long were you with them?" Alphabet asked, his fingers flying.

"Less than an hour. I had an escort to go back down too. They stuck with me until I lost them in Queens."

For one long moment, Alphabet and O'Rourke seemed

to freeze as though someone hit pause on a video. The look the two men shared in any other context would probably have made me laugh.

Then O'Rourke shifted to grab a chair and dragged it over. The moment he sat, Goblin settled right beneath the table next to Alphabet. The dog had been on watch since I got here, likely responding to the tension and on guard.

Goblin relaxing eased some of the rigidness locking up my own spine. Still, I wasn't going off my watch. O'Rourke had not earned much trust. Right now, he was in the position of forced ally. We would use him, but we weren't going to stretch it much further.

Burn us once, shame on you.

Burn us twice, you will never get to thrice.

The poetic dialogue popped up from some vague memory, but I couldn't place it. Probably a movie.

"Got it," Alphabet said and pulled my attention back to the screen. "Come on, show us how fucking cocky you bastards are..."

"There," O'Rourke said, leaning forward like he could make their tracking happen faster by force of will. "You're going to lose them."

"Excuse you, I don't lose my targets," Alphabet stated, his fingers all but flying over the keys before he switched one hand to a track ball and the other on the keyboard. The images snapped as he began to rotate his view.

"You already have, they went *south*," O'Rourke argued. "You're tracking me."

"Hmm." Alphabet's noncommittal sound just seemed to aggravate the other man. "Is that what I'm doing?"

Before he could respond, however, another vehicle popped on the screen and Alphabet paused the view, snapped a screenshot, then ran a facial rec in the corner.

It matched by 88% the man who had been following earlier. A little grainy, but good enough.

"Son of a bitch," O'Rourke swore.

"Don't talk about my mother that way." The half-distant comment carried no heat or really any of Alphabet's attention. Instead, he'd switched from following O'Rourke to the car—not the man he identified in the car—the *car*.

"Holy shit..." The low exhaled curse from O'Rourke had me almost leaning forward.

"Not so fucking clever now, are they?" The deep sense of satisfaction apparent in voice said everything it needed to convince me we had a lead.

Exhaling slowly, I relied on sniper breathing to keep my reactions under control. No rushing. No ordering. No directing. No pretending we could force a speedier answer by hovering. Alphabet knew exactly what he was doing. He was our resident expert for a reason.

The minutes trickled past as the screen reflected Alphabet's manipulations of the system. He tracked the car out of Queens, through Manhattan, then onto Jersey via the tunnel. From there, he picked up the vehicle on the other side—new license plate.

An hour later—based on the timestamp—they traded the car for an SUV and got on the turnpike. They continued almost relentlessly south for the next several leaps. Not once did Alphabet try to rush ahead, he verified and when his next snap didn't reveal the car, he backtracked.

"Fuck," O'Rourke half-whispered the word, his hands flexing against his thighs. Impatience swarmed over the man, but like me, he kept his comments to a minimum. It took almost two brutally painstaking hours, and two hot coffees—I made O'Rourke accompany me while Alphabet worked—before Alphabet fist pumped in the air.

"Got them."

All I needed to hear to surge forward. "Show me."

"At the risk of minimizing your admiration of my genius," Alphabet said. "I'll skip the details on just how many systems I had to hack to do this, but I tracked two of our identified goons to a location just outside of Alexandria, Virginia. According to land titles, it's owned by a private corporation that is in turn a subsidiary of a subsidiary ad infinitum. Beneath the shell game is Patriot Exports, a division of a cover company once used by the alphabet agencies to move large cargo around the world."

"Government ties," I muttered. "Check."

"I think co-opted ties, because the location itself is not a warehouse or a corporate building. In fact, it's not much of anything other than a house, a barn, and some fields with cows grazing." He shifted our view to a satellite overview.

"But?" I prompted.

"But," Alphabet said with a grin as he rolled his head from side to side and cracked his neck from side to side. "What it does have is an underground bunker, complete with low level access *and*..." He wiggled his fingers like a magician preparing to do a show and hit a key on his keyboard. "CCTV."

I wasn't the only one gaping at the screen. Even O'Rourke looked stunned.

"Why the fuck would someone running all those secrets have a network accessible surveillance system that can be hacked into?" His expression sobered abruptly. "Wait—"

"To bait someone like me into a trap," Alphabet answered, smug smile firmly in place. "Too bad for them that I always ghost my intrusions so I can send their bots off on wild goose chases."

"In about fifteen minutes, we're going to know everything they do, specifically, the operatives working on it, who they are in bed with, is it actually a government operation or is it government adjacent…"

He rose slowly, stretching as he went. His back cracked lightly, then his shoulders before he began to move. The limp was there for one step, but then he exerted force of will and erased it from his posture. Goblin rose, stretching as he went and moved to join Alphabet on his slow pace around the room.

"Don't touch it," he said without glancing back and O'Rourke pushed out of his own chair.

"I wasn't planning on it." The edge of defensiveness in his voice betrayed him, however, and Alphabet just shot him a look. For his part, O'Rourke didn't deny but he did throw his hands in the air before pacing away. Neither left the room fully and I shifted my stance to keep an eye on both of them *and* the computer.

The map to the location was still up on the screen so I took a beat to study it. I didn't know the place, but that didn't mean anything. We had a number of bolt holes across the country and overseas.

Forward planning meant you had the place ready to go so it was there when you needed it whether it was tomorrow, next week, next month, or even next year. Government facilities had to have a certain amount of transparency, but you didn't give shadow ops their name for fun.

"Once we have the information locked down," I said. "You need rack time."

Alphabet scowled at me, but it was more the expression of a man who wanted to get a thousand other things done and none of them had anything to do with sleep. He could and would go without sleep. All of us did when the mission called for it. Right now, we were on a limited clock, but we were also down a very vital part of our team.

We couldn't afford fuckups on any level. Rather than argue, Alphabet just nodded once but flicked a look at O'Rourke.

"He has a bed downstairs," I reminded him and O'Rourke scowled.

"You still don't trust me." He actually sounded irked.

"Clearly," I told him. "Don't push your luck."

Cause we could just as easily solve the problem of him with a bullet. I didn't want to execute him on a whim, but I also have very little patience for a prolonged argument of any kind.

"Fine." The capitulation came almost too easily and I narrowed my eyes as I studied him as he cracked his knuckles, then his neck, before he popped each of his shoulders.

While he didn't relax after the release of tension, he did seem to settle. I wasn't the only one shooting him a skeptical look. Goblin sat in the middle of the room, between Alphabet and O'Rourke, but his hackles weren't up.

Good sign.

"Wondering why I'm not arguing?" O'Rourke asked and I shrugged.

"Not particularly." It was a lie, but honestly, I didn't even care what his truth behind the action was as long as he did as he was told. "We don't have time for bullshit."

"Agreed," O'Rourke stated. "Trust has to be earned. I can cooperate."

I didn't snort or make any other sound of disagreement, nor did Alphabet. But when O'Rourke paced away from us again, I met Alphabet's eyes and raised my brows.

He shook his head.

Nope, we didn't have a bead on O'Rourke's game—yet.

We would though.

His game.

Bones' location.

Who took Bones.

We'd have a nice little checklist that we would then make our way down and cross off all the problems.

One. By. Fucking. One.

CHAPTER
SEVENTEEN
GRACE

The first thing I felt was warmth—solid and steady, wrapped around me like a second skin.

I blinked against the soft light bleeding through the curtains, golden and slow, casting long shadows across the bed. For a second, I didn't move. I just breathed, letting the moment stretch around me, quiet and unfamiliar in its comfort.

Legend's arm was slung across my waist, his body pressed tight against my back. He was heat and muscle, all steady breath and sleeping weight, like he'd anchored himself to me sometime in the night and refused to let go.

I didn't realize I was smiling until I felt it—something softer than warmth, cooler than breath. Fingers. A thumb brushing the line of my cheekbone with the kind of gentleness I wasn't used to. Not anymore.

I opened my eyes, turning just enough to see Voodoo sitting on the edge of the bed. His eyes met mine—dark, unreadable, but softened by something quiet. Something real. He was tracing my face like it was sacred, like the smallest part of me deserved to be memorized.

163

"Morning, Grace," he murmured, voice low and rough with sleep. "You dreaming, or just pretending to ignore me?"

I tried to speak, but the words caught somewhere behind my breath. Maybe it was the way his touch didn't ask for anything. Or maybe it was Legend still wrapped around me like I was something worth protecting.

Reality caught up to me, Bones was still missing and the guys had been working on O'Rourke's info when Legend and I slipped away to head up here. Voodoo being here offered me bittersweet comfort. The comfort of waking up between him and Legend—I didn't know how much I needed to just *be* with them—but the bittersweet part came knowing that it meant Bones was still a prisoner somewhere.

As much as I hated the idea of him being a captive, I refused to contemplate the idea that Bones wouldn't survive.

No, I absolutely refused to accept that idea.

Period.

The man was too damn onery to die.

Voodoo's fingers trailed down to my jaw, lingering just beneath my chin. His touch was still gentle, but there was a spark behind it now—mischief creeping in behind that quiet calm.

"You gonna keep pretending to sleep," he said, thumb brushing the corner of my mouth, "or are you gonna get up and shower with me before he realizes we're missing?"

I huffed a breath, not quite a laugh. "You're the one waking me up like a dream, and now you want me vertical?"

"Didn't say anything about staying vertical," he murmured, voice dipping lower.

My cheeks warmed before the rest of me caught up. His grin widened, lazy and crooked, like he already knew what I was thinking. Like he'd planted the thought there himself.

Legend shifted behind me, letting out a low, content sound as he burrowed closer. His arm tightened around my waist instinctively, and for a second, I hesitated. Legend needing me like he had the night before was something I didn't want to disrupt. Something rare.

Voodoo must've seen it in my eyes because he leaned in, pressing a slow kiss to my temple. "He'll still be here when we get back. You need a minute for yourself. We both do."

I let the silence stretch for a beat before nodding. "Alright," I said, my voice a little rough from sleep, a little too honest. "But if the water's cold, I'm walking out."

Voodoo laughed, low and smooth. "You think I'd pull you out of bed just to freeze you? Firecracker, baby—when I convince you to get wet, I *make* it worth it."

I rolled my eyes, but I was already reaching for the sheet, peeling myself away from Legend's hold as carefully as I could. He barely stirred, just mumbled something that sounded like my name and let me go. Voodoo helped me slide out, easing the sheet up.

As he rose, he offered his hand and I slid my palm across his. The lightness of his touch belied the inherent strength he housed. They were all so much bigger and stronger and they were all so damn careful with me.

And just like that, I let him lead me—bare feet across cool floors, heart ticking a little faster than it should—as if walking into the shower with him was just another way of waking up.

Another way of letting go.

He wasn't wrong, I liked showering with Voodoo even more now than our very first time when I'd been such a mess. Then, he'd been all gentleness and sensuality—two things I'd needed so badly. Once in the bathroom, he closed the door then stripped out of his clothes with an economy of motion.

Once he was naked, he turned on the water, his movements unhurried, practiced. He didn't look at me right away, just stood there with one hand under the stream, waiting for the temperature to settle. The muscles in his back shifted beneath his tattoos, the ink catching light when he moved.

I watched him—watched the way his jaw tightened like he was holding something in. Something he didn't trust with words yet.

When he finally looked at me, his expression had softened. "Come here," he said, and it wasn't a command—it was a request. Quiet. Needing.

I stepped into his space without hesitation.

His hands came to my hips, slow and warm, and he guided me into the shower with him like he was afraid I'd vanish if he moved too fast. The water hit my skin in a soft cascade, and I let out a slow breath savoring both the warmth of the water sliding over me and the weight of his hands on me.

He didn't pounce. Didn't press me against the wall or reach for more than I was ready to give. Voodoo just... held me. One hand at the back of my neck, the other splayed low on my spine, and his forehead resting against mine while the water poured down around us.

"I didn't pull you in here just to feel you naked," he murmured after a beat, voice quiet against the sound of the water. "Though, don't get me wrong—it's a hell of a bonus."

I smiled, small but real. "You're stalling."

His lips curved, but his eyes stayed serious. "Maybe. Or maybe I needed a minute with you before the noise starts again." He pulled back just enough to meet my gaze. "Everyone's looking at me for answers, Grace. For decisions. And I'm not gonna make them when my head's full of static."

His thumb brushed a strand of wet hair from my cheek. "But with you... it goes quiet. Just for a little while."

I leaned into his touch, chest tightening. "You don't have to carry it all alone."

"I know," he said, pressing a soft kiss to the corner of my mouth. "But I need to figure out how to carry it at all. And right now, I just need this."

He kissed me then—slow and deliberate, like he was choosing to be here in this exact second with no one else pulling on him. His hands never moved lower, never demanded more than I gave. He wasn't asking for my body.

He was asking for peace.

Understanding his desire and needing to fill it, I gave it to him. I pressed my hands to his chest, steady and open, and kissed him back like I understood.

Because I did.

We stayed there in the water, lips brushing, foreheads pressed together, the rest of the world shut out.

And for a little while, it was enough.

I pulled back slowly, my eyes searching his. The water beaded on his skin, tracing the lines of his tattoos and highlighting the sharp planes of his face. There was something in his eyes—an intensity that made my heart race.

"Voodoo," I whispered, "you don't have to do this alone. You have me. You have Legend and AB. We have *Bones* too.

We're in this together." I refused to think of it any other way.

He nodded, a small, almost imperceptible movement. "I know," he murmured. "But sometimes, I just need to feel you. To know you're real."

His hands tightened on my hips, pulling me closer. I could feel the heat of his body, the solid strength of him, and it made me ache in a way that was both familiar and new. I reached up, cupping his face, my thumbs brushing his cheekbones. "I'm real," I said softly. "And I'm here."

He closed his eyes, leaning into my touch. When he opened them again, there was a fire burning in their depths. "I want you, Grace," he said, his voice rough with need. "I want to feel you wrapped around me, to lose myself in you."

I shivered, the words sending a thrill through me. "Then take me," I whispered. "I'm yours."

He growled low in his throat, a sound that was pure possession. His hands moved to my ass, lifting me effort-lessly. I wrapped my legs around his waist, feeling the hard length of him press against me. He turned, pinning me against the shower wall, and I gasped at the sudden contact.

"You feel that?" he murmured, his lips brushing my ear. "That's how much I want you. How much I need you."

I nodded, my breath coming in short gasps. "I feel it," I managed to say. "I feel you."

He kissed me then, hard and demanding, his tongue exploring my mouth with a ferocity that left me breathless. I clung to him, my nails digging into his shoulders as he ground against me, the friction sending sparks of pleasure through my body.

He broke the kiss, his breath ragged. "I need to be inside you," he growled. "I need to feel you come apart around me."

"Yes," I gasped. "Please, Voodoo. I need you too."

He reached between us, positioning himself at my entrance. I was already wet, my body aching for him, and he slid in with a single, smooth thrust. I cried out, the sensation of being filled so completely overwhelming.

As slick and ready as I was, it was still a hard stretch to accommodate him. I could spend every single night in one of their beds and I'd never be totally ready for how they felt when they filled me.

I hoped I never would. I craved the pain of the stretch as much as the pleasure of the way they glided against me. Voodoo's clever fingers and silken voice were as devastating to my senses as his focused attention.

He started to move, his hips thrusting against mine in a rhythm that was both urgent and slow. Each stroke was deliberate, designed to build the pleasure until it was almost unbearable. I clung to him, my body meeting his thrusts, the water cascading down around us.

"You're so beautiful," he murmured, his eyes locked on mine. "So perfect. So mine."

I whimpered, the words sending a wave of pleasure through me. "Yours," I agreed. "Always yours."

He kissed me again, his tongue mimicking the movements of his hips. I could feel the pressure building, the pleasure coiling tight in my core. I was close, so close, and I knew he was too.

"Come for me, Firecracker," he commanded, his voice a low growl. "Let me feel you fall apart."

Coming on command wasn't always in my wheelhouse,

but when he paired the order with sensuous caresses, and bold thrusts, I shattered. My body convulsed around him as waves of pleasure washed through me. He followed soon after, his own release triggering another round of spasms in my sensitive flesh.

We stayed like that for a moment, our bodies entwined, our breaths mingling. The water continued to fall around us, but it was distant, unimportant. All that mattered was this—us, together, in this perfect moment of connection.

Voodoo finally pulled back, his eyes soft as he looked at me. "Thank you," he said quietly. "For being here. For being you."

I smiled, my heart full. "Always," I promised. "I'll always be here for you." Committed as fuck, I didn't avoid the words that would have turned me inside out upon a time. I adored these men. Was adored by them. The words didn't matter as much as the actions.

They felt things so damn deeply and I was one of those things that slipped under their guard. Being there for them was not so impossible, even in my darkest moments, this was where I wanted to be.

He kissed me one last time, a soft, lingering press of lips. Then, with a sigh, he set me down, his hands lingering on my hips for a moment longer than necessary.

"Ready to face the world again?" he asked, a hint of a smile playing at the corners of his mouth.

"Yes," I said as I worked to get my breathing under control. "I need to wash my hair."

A light knock on the door pulled my attention and even Voodoo shot a look over his shoulder at the very naked, and aroused Legend stood there palming his dick.

"Can we make you filthier first?" The question sent a wild quiver through my system and Voodoo shut off the water abruptly. His cock stirred at my thigh, growing harder by the moment.

Dark eyes dipping to lock onto mine, Voodoo said, "Say yes." It was as much a request as a command and a shiver raced through me. My cunt clenched and even my ass went tight as anticipation raced through me.

"Do we have time?"

Voodoo had come in here for a reason.

"Not as much as I'd like," AB said from the other room and another shudder went through me. "But we can make it work if you're willing, Gracie."

Running a tongue over my lower lip, I wrapped my hand around Voodoo's nape and dragged him down. His mouth collided with mine in a kiss that was all tongue, teeth, and hot possession. His cock was hard as stone where it poked at my belly.

"Where and how?"

Even with the slickness of his release still sticky on my thighs and water dripping down my breasts. I wanted *more*.

I *wanted* them.

Legend moved, pulling the curtain back and lifting me away from Voodoo. The handoff was so smooth, I barely realized he was moving. The cold air was a rush against my skin but Legend carried me right out to the bed where AB sat, waiting. He wasn't naked... not yet.

But the raw want in his blue eyes set me on my fire. Bones' absence was a bruise that expanded when Voodoo followed us out. Before I could say a word though, Legend kissed me. His tongue sweeping in to duel mine as fingers cupped my cunt from behind and three fingers pressed inside.

Then AB must have risen because his lips were on my shoulder and when Legend lifted his head, it was AB who slid his hand into my wet hair and dragged my mouth to his. Fire kindled in my blood and my body went up in flames.

"I need you," I whispered, longing punctuating every breath in between AB's demanding kisses. "All of you."

CHAPTER

EIGHTEEN

GRACE

AB's lips curved into a wicked smile against mine. "We're all yours, Gracie," he murmured, his voice a low rumble. "Every inch of us."

He deepened the kiss, his tongue exploring my mouth with a hunger that matched my own. Behind me, Legend's fingers continued to work their magic, stroking and circling, building the fire within me. I moaned into AB's mouth, the sound muffled by his lips.

AB broke the kiss, his breath ragged. "Get on your knees, Grace," he commanded, his eyes dark with desire. "Show us how much you want us."

I complied without hesitation, lowering myself to my knees in front of him. His cock was hard and ready, straining against the fabric of his pants. I reached up, my hands trembling slightly as I undid his belt and zipper, freeing him.

He was thick and long, the head already glistening with pre-cum. I leaned in, my tongue flicking out to taste him, and he let out a low groan. I took him into my mouth, my lips stretching wide as I sucked him deep. He tasted salty and musky, and I loved every second of it.

Behind me, Legend's hands were everywhere, exploring my body, teasing my nipples, and sliding between my thighs. I moaned around AB's cock, the vibrations making him curse under his breath. Voodoo moved to stand beside AB, his own cock hard and ready again, and I reached out a hand to stroke him as I continued to suck AB.

Voodoo's hand came to rest on the back of my head, guiding my movements, urging me to take AB deeper. I did, relaxing my throat as I took him in, feeling him hit the back on the next thrust. He groaned, his hips bucking slightly, and I swallowed around him, making him curse.

AB's hand fisted in my hair, pulling me off his cock with a wet pop. "Enough," he growled. "I need to be inside you."

He pulled me to my feet, spinning me around so that I was facing Legend. AB's hands were on my hips, positioning me as he pressed the head of his cock against my entrance. I was still wet from both the shower and Voodoo. There was something electric as AB slid into me, gliding through the heat of cum still leaking down my legs. The first thrust rocked me forward, but he didn't let me go far, dragging me back so that his pelvis slapped against my ass.

I gasped, my head falling back against his shoulder as he began to move, his hips thrusting against mine in a steady rhythm. Legend's hands were on my breasts, teasing my nipples, rolling them between his fingers, sending jolts of pleasure straight to my core.

Voodoo moved in front of me easing onto the bed as AB rocked me forward, at this angle, it put Voodoo's cock level with my mouth. I opened obediently, letting him stretch my already tired lips and cheeks. I didn't care how much effort it took, it felt so good to taste him even if he still wore the musk of my own release.

I licked and sucked as I bobbed my head, trying to match the rhythm AB set as he fucked me intensely from behind. Every stroke of his cock against my insides lit me up. When Voodoo fisted my wet hair and thrust all the way into my throat, I choked on him but swallowed hard to take him even deeper.

The hands on my breasts were suddenly replaced by a mouth. Legend nipped and tugged, the scrape of his teeth threatening to leave bruises and marks even as he suckled my breast like it was his favorite treat. He divided his attention between each breast with a kind of abrupt delight that kept me off balance.

It was like floating between them. My feet weren't even on the floor. Hands caressed my hips, then my breasts, in between biting and sucking against them. Another hand worked against my ass as two fingers added pressure to spear into me there.

The pressure was unbearable—too much and not enough. "Fuck," AB swore as someone rubbed their thumb against my clit. I lost track of what hands were where entirely. I was one vibrating nerve of pleasure.

I moaned around Voodoo's cock in time with AB's thrusts and then I was shifting as AB pulled out and Voodoo eased my mouth off of him. My jaw ached from the stretch and my vision blurred. The change in position brought me down almost face to face with Legend as he thrust upward and impaled me on his cock.

Little sounds escaped me that might have been vowel sounds but my thoughts were shredding before I could fully form them. Hands locked over my breasts as another hand wrapped on my throat, tilting my head back and then

Voodoo filled my mouth again. Another cock pressed against my ass, and I was and wasn't loose enough.

"More lube," Legend ordered in a harsh breath. "She's too gone to tell us…"

"On it." AB accompanied the grunted words with liquid heat pouring over my crack, then he was pushing in. The relentless thrust took me right to the edge of pain and all three men just stilled once he bottomed out and my eyes were dazed as I found Voodoo holding my hair and staring down at me.

My neck ached, my mouth was stretched, and tears gathered in the corners of my eyes.

"You still with us, Firecracker?" The demand hummed through me as he held my gaze. Tears spilled out of the corners of my eyes and I was pretty sure I was drooling. But none of it mattered, I was suspended between all of them and the only thing that could have made it more perfect was if Bones was there.

His absence was a gouge in my soul.

"Squeeze my hand, Gracie," Legend said. "If you're ready for us to move, squeeze my hand." The words reached me as if from a million miles away. I shifted my gaze almost too slowly to where he pressed his palm to mine, raising our hands together. AB reached from behind me to cover his hand and mine with his and then Voodoo also gripped our hands.

I dug my nails in, squeezing and holding on.

"Hell yeah," one of them, maybe all of them, said and then they were moving. Legend pushed up as AB drew back and then AB thrust in as Legend rocked me upward. All the while, Voodoo dragged my attention back to him as he fucked my mouth.

Sparks of pleasure ignited all over me. Every inch of

discomfort only fed the rapture spasming through me. The teasing of my breasts and my clit triggered reactions I couldn't control. Voodoo cursed as a steady stream of groans wrapped his cock up in a fist of vibration that as my throat.

When Legend bit down on my shoulder, I came. I shattered, the waves of pleasure drowned me even as Voodoo came in the same rush, his release choking me as he pulsed in my throat. I swallowed him down even as another wave of incoherent delight speared me as AB pushed deep and came.

The last was Legend, though he still had me impaled on him as I floated on the battering ripples of ecstasy. When Voodoo pulled out of my mouth, I cough, then swallowed before AB groaned as he eased back.

"Good girl, Gracie," Legend growled before he kissed me. The thrust of his tongue into my mouth matched the cadence set by his hips as he used his hands on my hips to guide me up and down.

Ragged breathing punctuated our kiss and I wanted to sob when someone reached between us and teased my clit. Too much, too sensitive and I screamed. The clamp of my pussy spasming on Legend's dick had his hips stuttering and then he came in a rush.

Liquid heat spilled through my whole system, I drowned in the feel of them and then Legend sank back against the bed, I draped across him while someone ran a gentle hand along my back and someone else stroked my wet hair.

I had no idea how long I floated there, my ass hurt. My face hurt. Even my cunt hurt. But it was the kind of pain that reminded me of just how much I'd enjoyed myself.

Even my nipples ached where they pressed against Legend's chest.

"Hey," Voodoo said softly as he shifted to lay next to Legend and I, his face now in my line of sight. He was so beautiful. All gorgeous lines, sexy eyes, and a voice to die for. His ability to pet me to orgasm was not bad either.

"Hi," I whispered, and it came out a croak like I'd forgotten how to speak.

"There she is," AB murmured. "Sweet Gracie... your ass is spectacular. "

A laugh escaped me.

"Just my ass?"

"Pretty fucking fond of that mouth," Voodoo said, stroking his thumb over my lower lip.

"Your pussy is magic," Legend said without missing a beat and for some reason, that just sent a dazzling shock of laughter through me. One by one the guys joined in and then Voodoo kissed me, when he let me go, Legend took another but only released me to let AB capture my lips for a kiss.

The room reeked of sex, release, and sweat. It was— delirious and decadent.

"You okay, Firecracker?" Voodoo murmured as I tried to get my last two braincells on board with moving. Though all I wanted to do was sink into these guys.

"More than okay," I said softly. "I'm perfect." Another little bubble of laughter escaped me. "Only one real complaint."

Stillness wound through the guys and it gave me a moment to work out how to push myself up on my forearms. Legend was a beautiful bed to sprawl against but I wasn't sure I could do much more than that. My legs were just too loose to do more than stay right where they were.

"Report," AB said, his brilliant blue eyes fixed on mine. "If there's a complaint, we want to fix it."

"Immediately," Voodoo concurred.

"Without hesitation," Legend tacked on.

They were so damn serious. It—it filled my heart to the brim and squeezed it like a vise at the same time.

"It's morning and we have to get up and move," I admitted. "Pretty sure you guys broke me."

A slow smile lifted the corners of Legend's mouth and Voodoo began to laugh. AB nodded solemnly. "Don't worry, Gracie. We're going to get you showered, fed, and even make your coffee."

"I'm not worried." I was too sated, too content, and far too much in love. "But I think calories would be good before we go again. Not sure I can handle more just yet."

Legend had gradually softened through the whole interlude and as he slipped free, I shuddered.

Yeah, I was too damn sensitive.

"Come on, Firecracker," Voodoo peeled me off Legend and rose. "Back in the shower. You two get your own shower and get food started."

The real world was out there waiting, but for this moment, I let them take care of me so I could take care of them.

Then we were going to get Bones if it was the last thing I did.

CHAPTER
NINETEEN
GRACE

The kitchen seemed far too quiet after the tempest in the bedroom just—wow, was it really only thirty minutes earlier? My whole body was one long, sensual ache and my ass was definitely far more tender than I expected. Though it was a toss-up about what was more: sore, my jaw or my butt.

A little giggle tried to escape and I almost choked on my coffee as I swallowed at the same time. Voodoo sent me an amused look.

"No, it's not thicker than you," I told him after I successfully avoided snorting coffee up my nose. "But it is hotter."

AB barked a laugh as he set Goblin's food bowl down for him. They had just gotten back from Goblin's walk and AB's recon of the subdivision we were currently hiding in. A recon in suburbia just seemed weird, but it fit the level of strange we'd been existing in.

As I cradled the cup between my palms, I kept my focus on hoping the caffeine would chase away the anxiety trying to claw its way past the haze of aftershocks that lingered everywhere they'd touched me, filled me, petted me, and sated me.

The worry had teeth and it sank them into my spine even as I tried to keep my mind off all the things we hadn't discussed yet. Especially while Legend was cooking at the stove. With his sleeves pushed up and his hair damp, he seemed perfectly at ease as he fried bacon, sautéed onions, and cracked eggs into a bowl to mix them up.

It smelled like home. That thought settled into my hind brain and I had to turn it over. It really did smell like home in here. I was surrounded in them, the ghost imprint of their touches remained on my skin. It wasn't even a challenge to summon the memory of their cocks filling me, each of them so different, so—beautiful and thick and just them.

Maybe this new life was a little twisted, and bullet-ridden, but the feeling of home they wrapped around me was one I savored. Each time I thought about returning to the life I'd had before, I really couldn't imagine it. Not if it meant leaving them.

Leaving us.

Dismissing the concept of abandoning them left me with other questions. How did we make this work, long-term? What did it look like? Did they want a forever? Did *I* want a forever?

Did I even know how to handle a forever?

No sooner did those thoughts alight, then they were racing off again because no decisions could be made until we retrieved Bones. We needed him.

I needed him.

"I still think we should've killed him," Legend muttered, tossing something in the pan with a little too much aggression. "Would've saved us time."

"Can't kill someone if they might still be useful,"

Voodoo commented without looking up. "And O'Rourke might be a bastard, but he's a useful bastard for now."

"Still a bastard," AB added as he sipped his coffee, his laptop set up to his left and one hand on it as he tabbed through data. They were always working, always finding an angle, always looking for where best to take their shot.

Despite Voodoo's words of uncertainty in our earlier shower, he radiated a kind of quiet confidence. Maybe he didn't know everything, but he could absolutely fake it until we made it.

After another long drink of coffee, I studied them one at time then cleared my throat. "Are we gonna talk about what you found or just keep grumbling like someone spiked your Wheaties?"

AB's gaze flicked to mine. "You want it all or the short version?"

"Start with the short one, work your way up to the part where someone's blood pressure explodes." That sounded reasonable, right?

Spinning his laptop around, AB tapped the top of it. On screen: maps, code fragments, and red-flagged documents. "They're not government. At least, not officially. No agency logos, no paper trail, no black ops stamp. Just opportunists with government clearance that expired around the same time Blockbuster went out of business."

"Damn you're old," I muttered, because I'd been a kid when that happened.

"Don't remind us, Firecracker," Voodoo said dryly but the humor was still present in his eyes. They weren't *that* much older than me. Definitely older, by ten years at least on all of them, but at the same time—I would not use Blockbuster's closing as a time reference.

Particularly because I couldn't remember exactly *when* that was.

"The point is, these guys aren't some highly skilled wetwork team or specialists. What they are is clever as fuck, invested, and they have very little to lose at this point. Particularly because if you consider that they are playing a long con, they have to know leaving any of us alive will cost them in the end."

Legend whistled low. "Damn."

My heart sank even as my stomach bottomed out. Not leaving anyone to come after them made sense, but I didn't want any of it to "make sense" if that meant that Bones might already be dead.

"They're using holes in oversight," Voodoo continued. "Dead spots. Places where the CIA or NSA or whoever used to run ops and now—"

"No one's watching," I finished.

"Exactly," AB said. "It's like a back door someone forgot to close. These guys built a whole empire out of it. No one's looking, so they made sure to look out for themselves."

The knot in my chest tightened. "And Bones?"

"They took him because he's leverage," Voodoo said. "Not just to get to us. They think he knows where the drive is. Might even think he *has* it."

"He doesn't," I said, though my voice wavered more than I liked. "Right?"

"He does," AB confirmed. "We destroyed it, but they don't know that. Or they don't believe it. They think they can squeeze him hard enough, they'll get what they want."

"What about O'Rourke?"

That was the part that still itched at the base of my skull. Like I missed a piece of the puzzle and it was slicing me from the inside out.

AB and Voodoo traded a look.

"Spill it," I snapped, but then held up a hand as I took a deep breath and forced it out. Going for a far more even tone, I focused on them again. "Please. I'm not the girl you need to coddle. Say it straight."

After cracking his neck, AB reached down to stroke Goblin who'd come over to rest his head on AB's thigh. "We don't think he was in deep with them, not like boots-on-the-ground deep. Did he know *something?* Absolutely. More than he's told us? Fairly solid bet." AB leaned back as Legend started setting plates on the table. "He got into bed with these people rather than get left out in the cold. Did he know what all he was getting in to? I don't really care. But he's playing that card to get our help."

The certainty in their voices didn't offer me a lot of comfort, but I asked for the truth not comfort. I asked to be a part of this and to read me in, not to soften it for me.

"We need your help with him," Voodoo added and surprise expanded through me.

"Me?" Not even twenty-four hours earlier, they wanted me *away* from him. Not talking to him and not sticking around when he was out.

Legend slid a plate in front of me. Toast, eggs, bacon. He gave me a soft smile. "Eat first."

"I'm not—"

"Grace." One word, firm and unbending.

So I took a bite. Because I was starving. Because I'd fight better with food in my system. Because I wasn't going to fall apart now—not when Bones was still out there.

Once I started my meal, Legend turned that scowl on the guys. "You want to explain what it is you need her to do and I want you to be explicit. Because a bullet in his head is still the best option in my opinion."

AB blew out a breath. "We could terminate him. We have enough reasons to do that."

"But?" Legend asked as he returned to the stove and I stuffed more food in my mouth in order to hold my questions to myself until they resolved this. I wasn't entirely sure what I could do to "help" with O'Rourke, but I certainly was on board to try.

"But," Voodoo said as Legend filled another plate and set it in front of him. "We can't be one hundred percent certain we won't need him to get Bones out. That's the sticking point. With him, we have a fourth man—"

"Cannon fodder," AB said, before he took a bite of bacon.

"That too," Voodoo agreed with a wave of his hand in AB's direction. "If he's holding anything back, his presence might be the crucial ingredient in whether we get everything we want or not."

"By that logic," Legend countered, "his presence could also be the factor that fucks us over."

No one disputed that and I sighed. Into the silence, I asked, "So we're fucked if we do and we're fucked if we don't?" Then after washing down another bite with a swallow of coffee, I added, "and not even in a nice way."

That earned a faint huff of laughter from Legend. He shut off the stove and carried his plate over to where we were eating. "That is why I don't like the plan. Taking him is a risk that I don't think offers enough reward to cover the danger he poses."

"Okay," I said, then used a napkin to wipe my mouth. I had to pause on the eating because my stomach had gone too taut and soured over the choice we were going to have to make. "What do you need me to do with him?"

AB and Voodoo split another look and I kept my impatience to myself at the silent conversation that seemed to fill the air between them. It was Legend who put down his cup abruptly and scowled.

"No," he said aloud and earned both of their attention.

"Hear us out," AB said slowly.

"How about fuck no?" Legend scowled. "We're not tasking her with *handling* him. Not when he's made it clear he wants her."

"That's part of why she would be good *at* handling him." Voodoo cut a look to me. "You would be. You handled him in France. I've seen you do it with others along the way —including us."

I wasn't arguing. Handling men definitely fell within my wheelhouse. "Define handling for me. Bones made it clear if I kissed someone to distract them, he was going to be killing people."

The summary of his actual words didn't include the fact that he would spank me, but I didn't mind that part so much. He had to be here to spank me so that would be worth it.

All three of them stared at me for a long moment and Goblin let out a low whine that snapped first AB out of it and then Voodoo.

"Handle him in that you'll be distracting him, yes," Voodoo said slowly, his whole expression darkening. "But not with sex or kissing or touching of *any* kind. In fact, I'll add that I'll cut his dick off if he tries to touch you."

"While he's breathing," Legend said, spinning a knife between his fingers. "If he passes out, we will wake him up."

"Then we can cauterize the wound," AB joined in the threat. "So we can chop up the rest of him."

I paused for a beat, glancing at each of them in turn.

"Well, that's one plan." But it didn't answer... "What *do* you want *me* to do?"

Not one of them answered immediately. In fact, for one almost too long moment, I thought they'd engaged in a severe change of heart.

"As much as we all dislike the idea, we need her to do this." Voodoo wasn't talking to me right now, he was focused on AB and Legend. "We need her to do this and we need to *trust* her to do this."

"You need to tell me what it is so I can let you know whether I can do it or not." To be fair, I was pretty open to everything, but I also wanted to have some idea if I could be successful or if I needed to work out a backup plan.

Like poison.

Or drugs.

Maybe poison and drugs.

"You can do this," Voodoo said, his attention wholly on me. "There's not a doubt in my mind, Firecracker. But I'm not giving you a shit job or an easy task. You may have to take him down, but he won't be expecting it from you."

I blew out a breath. "What is he going to be expecting?"

"That we're putting him in charge of protecting you."

I had the coffee cup halfway to my mouth then lowered it again as his words sank in. Protecting me.

"He's going to be armed."

A nod.

"He's going to be part of the extraction as well."

Another nod.

"I'm bait."

A last nod.

"Still on board to do it?" Voodoo asked, his expression sober. "If you don't want to, we'll find another way. No questions asked."

My pulse rabbited and sweat prickled along the back of my neck. I really didn't want to screw this up.

Ever.

"Can you walk me through everything like I'm an idiot?" To be fair, right now with a fresh layer of panic bubbling through my system like a kettle on the boil, I felt a little bit like one. "Each step, so I can be as prepared as possible?"

All the spit in my mouth dried up.

"Alphabet?" Voodoo said and I shifted my attention to him. AB's blue eyes seemed almost painfully blue this morning.

"Right, our target..." He began as he pulled up more information on his screen and started walking us through the plan.

Even before he started speaking, though, I knew I would do it. I would do anything to get Bones back and these guys—they wouldn't ask me if they really thought I couldn't do it.

They were trusting me to do this, therefore, I *would* do it. I would be worthy of their trust.

We would get this done.

TWENTY

GRACE

"You ready for this?" O'Rourke asked as he offered me his arm. I stared at him for a beat then at the crowd beyond. We were going in "undercover" which in and of itself meant we went for the fancier clothes. He was in a standard tuxedo that looked like it had been cut for him. Not that I didn't appreciate a good suit, but he'd had that ready to go and easily accessible.

My dress was strapless, a deep sapphire that clung just enough to pass for haute couture but left room for movement. I hated it. No holsters, no wires—nothing but static cling and a pair of heels. I felt almost naked compared to how much I'd gotten used to at least having my taser with me.

I debated taking his arm or just moving alongside him. Really, it wasn't much of a debate. I didn't want to touch him. "We should keep our hands free."

As if to illustrate my point, I gestured with the clutch purse I carried. It was lined, and if we had to x-ray it, should clear fine. If they hand-searched it, well, that would be fun too.

"If you insist," O'Rourke said just before he cupped my right elbow with his left hand.

"Take your hand off her, or I will remove it with a rusty knife," AB said via our comms. His tone was gravel, sober, and dead serious. "She said 'no,' asshole, listen to her."

The corners of O'Rourke's mouth tightened, but his hand fell away from me smoothly. I grinned, my mood definitely buoyed by that backup. We were at the stairs, following a line of other arrivals slowly, one step at a time.

The museum glowed like a Fabergé egg cracked open—light spilled from the marble arches, violin music floated out, and beneath it all was the buzz of money trying to look bored.

I'd gone for a more sedate, if sophisticated look by having my hair braided into a crown. It dramatically changed the lines of my face to have the hair drawn back so snugly.

I'd actually made an appointment with a salon to get my hair, cosmetics, and nails done. It had taken a little over two hours and that was with me paying them extra for more staff to get it done. A necessary investment because I needed to both standout and blend in at the same time. Arm candy needed to have a certain vibe. Tonight, I was definitely winning a prize in that pretty enough to be here, but not so attractive as to turn heads.

A fine line, but I knew what I had to work with and I focused on it, right down to strapping my breasts until they appeared even smaller than they actually were. The number of guys who were boob men and would overlook me without the sign of curves might have been staggering if I hadn't modeled on the runways more than a few times.

At the top of the steps, we slowed further to hand off

our invitation, then pass through security. The metal detector was definitely a chokepoint.

"Excuse me, miss," a suited security guard said to me. "If you'll just come this way, you can join your date on the other side."

"See you soon," I murmured to O'Rourke as I followed the guard to where a line of other women, dressed in similarly sprayed on clothing were being admitted and bypassing the metal detectors.

Some were having their purses go through an x-ray machine. Others were just handing them over to be searched. When it was my turn, I gave up the clutch without argument. The man flicked it open, gave it a cursory glance in between long studying looks at the crowd behind me.

When he finished closing it and handing it back, I flashed him another smile. "Thank you so much."

I didn't even merit a grunt of acknowledgment. If anything, he'd barely looked at me. I drifted past, my heels clicking on the stone as I moved to stand near the doors but not in the direct path. O'Rourke hadn't made it quite through his line yet.

"You were right, Firecracker," Voodoo murmured. "The idea that some of these men are that blind is just sad for them."

I didn't laugh, nor did I respond verbally. Talking to myself while I was standing there alone was more likely to net me the kind of attention we didn't want.

It took O'Rourke time, but he finally made it through and strode over to meet me. "That took longer than expected." His tone was more bored than irritated. "Thank you for waiting."

"I'd say you're welcome," I answered, shifting my attention forward as I pivoted to accompany him inside. "But I don't like you, so you're not."

"Oh," he murmured in a tone dry as the desert. "Ouch. I'm wounded."

"Keep it up," I told him with a wider grin before we stepped inside, "and you will be."

There was a huff of laughter over the comms. "Focus, Gracie," Legend said. "You can ignore the asshole. If there's any need to evacuate him, I'll take care of it."

"You're all hilarious," O'Rourke said as he adjusted his cufflinks before taking two glasses of champagne from a waiter passing by. Rather than argue with him again, I accepted the flute he offered but I didn't bother to drink.

The temperature inside the wider galleries seemed to drop. What created a crowded atmosphere in the vestibule and main entry, decreased significantly as we "wandered" away. I wasn't familiar with the museum, though AB had gone over the plans with me until I could recite how many steps I needed to take to get to our first destination.

"You want it to be automatic so that when the pressure is on, you don't have to think about it."

"Have you considered what you're going to do once all of this is over?" O'Rourke asked as he caught my arm but only long enough to detour me around another couple who'd planted themselves in front of a painting that took up most of the wall. As soon as we were clear, he released me again.

"Not particularly," I told him before I passed him the flute. "Could you hold this for me for a moment?"

"Of course, sweetheart." He flashed me a toothy smile and it took everything I had to not roll my eyes.

"You really want them to beat you up, don't you?" I

pitched my voice low as I opened the clutch to pull out a tissue even as I popped a few of the beads off the top of the clutch. With the tissue, I made a show of dabbing at the corners of my mouth before I drifted toward a refuse and dropped the tissue and a couple of the beads in there.

"They're going to do it anyway," O'Rourke said with a shrug as he returned the champagne flute to me and I handed him two beads in a pass that was almost smooth.

"Ah," I said. "So baiting them to make sure it hurts more is the goal."

"He doesn't have to bait me," Legend said easily. "I'm happy to just do it."

"Focus," Voodoo said with a faint click in my ear. "Keep the chatter to a minimum. We have to be able to hear."

I was pretty sure the chatter was for them, but I wouldn't mind ignoring O'Rourke. Unfortunately, that wasn't in the cards for this. We drifted from gallery to gallery, shifting so that we were always with another group of people. I dropped beads in more than a few pockets, on trays, and even on benches near the paintings.

There were two kinds of beads—one for the cameras, and one for mobility. O'Rourke was better at the second, though I felt pretty damn good about my part.

"Darling..." O'Rourke threaded an arm around my waist and pulled me to him. The only thing that saved him from me tossing the champagne in his face was how he angled himself toward the work on the wall rather than me.

"Hmm?" I tilted my head like I was being flirty as he motioned to the hunting scene above. At least, I was almost eighty percent certain it was a hunting scene. There were dogs, horses, and a bunch of aristocracy all done up in their red coats and finery.

"Target one is here and acquired," O'Rourke said, leaning his head down toward me so that his lips brushed my ear but not quite looking at me. "Seven o'clock, muddy brown hair, square jaw."

"Got him," AB said in my ear. "He's moving. Get ready to follow."

My pulse jumped and I twisted away from O'Rourke abruptly to put my champagne flute on a passing waiter's tray of empties that he was bussing to remove from the venue.

"If you don't mind," I said with a genuine smile. The waiter gave me a quick nod and was already gone.

"What we really want to see," O'Rourke was saying as he caught my hand and motioned ahead, "is the next wing."

"You're clear," AB said following a click. "I've got him heading for an exit at the rear of that next gallery."

My heels clicked along the marble floor as O'Rourke and I made the most indirect, direct beeline after the target. I motioned as if to sneeze and flicked another bead off the bag so it bounced to slide right under a map that told us where we were in the museum.

"Bugs are live." AB continued. "I'm accessing their system. Standby. We may have to make some noise."

"Better if we don't have to," O'Rourke commented, then he dragged me to him and swung us around so my back was to the wall. Dipping his head as though he were about to kiss me, he murmured, "Don't kill me." The words were a whisper across my lips.

"You have three seconds to explain," I warned him.

"Target two is also here and he was waiting for target one." O'Rourke didn't look at all bothered as he slid his hand to my throat—

"Stop. Fucking. Touching. Her." Legend's words were a snarl and the hand O'Rourke had been about to touch me with only hovered. For all that he loomed over me, nothing of him was actually touching me.

"They know what I look like," O'Rourke responded easily enough, as though utterly unperturbed by the threat. "This way we can avoid an ambush of our own."

"Hmm." I leaned against the wall, head tilted so I could keep an eye on him. Unfortunately, with his height and bulk, it made keeping an eye on the others a challenge. "Let us know when we're clear, AB?"

"Got you, Gracie." AB promised. "Security cycle shifting in ninety seconds. Hold tight."

Despite the order, O'Rourke was already moving and he had my hand in his. If I didn't follow, I'd end up on my ass or worse. He walked like a man who didn't care about orders—straight to the staff hallway near the Roman gallery. He glanced once over his shoulder.

I followed. I had to.

"O'Rourke," I hissed under my breath. "AB said hold."

"And I damn near died to get this code," he retorted as he keyed in a code to the staff entrance.

The keypad blinked green. The door clicked open.

"O'Rourke—"

He didn't wait. His hand closed around my wrist—not rough, but firm—and he pulled me through before I could argue.

"This wasn't the plan," I said in a low hiss.

"Plans change, sweetheart. Get used to it." He tugged his tie free then opened a button at his throat. "Now stay close. I'll get you out of here, but you have to stay with me. I'm not slowing down and I'm not back tracking."

The door shut behind us with a soft *thunk*.

We were in.
The comms went dead.
Because of course they did.

198

TWENTY-ONE

BONES

I'd learned to rest with my feet off the ground.

Hanging from your wrists long enough, your body figures it out—how to go slack just enough that the fire in your shoulders becomes background noise, not a screaming siren. Let go, float inside your skull, try not to think. That's what they hadn't broken. Not yet.

Then the silence cracked.

A distant *thump*. Something falling upstairs. Then again —louder. A crash, like a statue hitting marble. Raised voices, just barely audible through the vents. Muffled shouting. And—was that an alarm?

I lifted my head, slowly, every muscle complaining. Blood ran down my arms in tired rivers. The concrete around me was still the same: damp, cold, and lit by a single grimy bulb that buzzed like it hated its job. Same tools on the tray. Same dark stains.

But the noise was getting closer. Boots. Scuffling. *Gunfire.*

Gunfire.

Something flipped in me—hope, or adrenaline, or

whatever sad little survival instinct I had left. My breath caught in my throat. I twisted, trying to see past the door. Chains rattled, weak as I was.

Then she appeared.

She came through the shadowed hallway like a hallucination. Like a goddamn painting. Grace—*Grace*—in a strapless blue dress that clung to her like silk on fire. Hair up. Something glittering at her ears. And heels, the kind that should've echoed on a ballroom floor, not this blood-stained concrete.

She shouldn't have been real. Not here. Not now.

I blinked, once. Twice.

Still there.

She stepped over a body—*someone*—didn't look down, didn't even break stride. The weapon—was that a club?—in her hand didn't match the dress, but the way she held it sure as hell matched the woman I remembered. Confident. Furious. Ready to raise hell.

She saw me. And smiled.

"Jesus, Bones," she said, like she'd just found me napping somewhere stupid. The warmth there "You look like hell."

My throat tried to work. Nothing came out.

She crossed the room, heels clicking now though there was still chaos behind her based on the sounds. What was she *doing* here? The only thing that slowed her down was grabbing a metal folding chair on her way to me. I blinked slowly—there were chairs in here?

My situational awareness was at an all-time low. The clunk of the chair next to me jolted me back to the present. I had to stop drifting. Grace was here.

"Dollface, you shouldn't be here," I croaked, or I thought I did. It sounded more like gravel being ground under a boot. Abruptly, between one pained breath and the next, she seemed to have grown a foot and a half.

Wait. No. She was standing on the chair, wearing next to nothing.

"It's not safe," I warned her and then tried to blink the sweat and blood from my eyes to look past her. Why was she here alone? Where the fuck were the guys? Reality trickled into the cracks left behind from the last "interrogation."

"Shh." Without any sign of rejection, she whispered a kiss to my bruised and bloodied cheek. I was filthy, she shouldn't have to —

Before I could pull away, she touched my face gently with a cool, soft hand like I wasn't swinging half-conscious in this basement hell.

"You're lucky I like you," she said on a soft sigh that carried some notes of impatience and... worry? "Or I'd have to let you rot in this damn museum."

Museum?

It was a museum?

I was still chewing on that nugget when she said, "Yes, I found him. He's a mess, but in one piece." A pause. "Mostly." More worry. The sadness drenching that last word had me trying to shift. "I don't know why they cut out, I'm just glad they're back on."

"Keys," a masculine voice called and then Grace twisted to catch the keys that sailed through the air. Not Alphabet.

Nor Lunchbox.

Adrenaline spiked in my system as she reached above me with the keys rattling against the shackles holding me in place.

"Who?" The word came out raw, rough, and I coughed.

Flecks of blood hit the smooth skin of her shoulder and I scowled.

"Hang on, Boney Boy," she half-hummed the words. "I'm almost there." A little snap. "Fuck." I blinked, the sweat stinging my eyes and blurring my vision. "No, I'm fine, I just broke a nail," she muttered.

"Want me to help?" The masculine voice was back—not Voodoo either.

The man circled her and then I shifted, wrapping my hands on the chains even if I could barely feel my fingers. Then I locked my legs around the guy who was too close to her and jerked him off his feet.

"No! No!" Grace said, the keys falling as she caught my face in her hands. "It's O'Rourke—he's with us…"

What? O'Rourke?

Hell—

"Bones," Alphabet was suddenly there, his voice clear and crisp. Grace had pressed an ear comm in. "Listen to me. Echo echo one two one. Goblin doesn't need any scattered bones right now."

It was an old code but still a viable one. Somewhat nonsensical, but tied together with a warning that said while it wasn't all clear, we weren't under live fire.

O'Rourke wasn't a friend.

But right now, he wasn't an enemy either.

"We'll talk about that later," I managed to push the words out as I shoved O'Rourke away. The man stumbled, one hand at his throat as he coughed. I could have choked him unconscious.

I could have snapped his neck.

The boys better be right about this.

"Especially why he's here with Grace." The fact Grace

was here at all was actively scraping over me like a cheese grater.

"You'll get a full debrief *after* we're out," Grace said, her fingers still achingly soft where she touched my cheek and at the same time her grip was steel. She didn't let me look away. "Are you with us again?"

Alphabet didn't comment. Probably wise. Anger fueled my adrenaline as I tracked O'Rourke's stumbling steps. The man straightened, his hair mussed and his expression a grimace.

"You're welcome," he muttered.

"Shut up," Grace said, and I felt the absence of her touch far too keenly. She'd retrieved the keys and she was rattling them around my wrists.

The cuffs snapped open and my arms gave out. I would have fallen but Grace caught me, arms coming around me as she stepped off the chair and went down with me as I landed on my knees.

It wasn't as hard of a crash landing as it could have been, but I was now bleeding all over her. "I've got you," she said. "I've got you."

"We need to go," O'Rourke was suddenly next to us and even with my head swimming, I had a fist ready to strike. He narrowly avoided the blow. "Fine, fucking crawl then."

He retreated once more, but I couldn't follow his movements. Not when Grace was just there, cradling my face in her hands and keeping my gaze on her.

"I don't get it," I whispered, trying to focus. "How are you even—?"

"Shh." She ghosted a kiss to my lips, then looked me in the eye. That smile again. It was so damn sinful and filled with warmth. "You're a mess. Probably have broken ribs, a concussion, and your wrists are a disaster. I can't count the cuts and the burns…" Her voice darkened on the last. "But we have a plan. If you can walk, we're leaving right now."

"I might be hallucinating you," I muttered. I didn't want to know what the plan was if I couldn't walk. O'Rourke was there, a blurry movement behind her.

She leaned closer, voice like velvet over razors.

"Then hallucinate faster. We have less than a minute before the guys set off the alarms."

Hallucinate faster?

A rough laugh escaped me. "You make me crazy, Dollface," I told her.

"I know," she said, another whisper of a kiss as she rose, then she held out her hand to me. "That's why you like me."

Everything hurt.

Fucking. Everything.

But I clasped her hand and let her help me to my feet. I swayed, but she wrapped one of my arms over her bare shoulders. "God help me," I said. "It is."

Her laughter was a balm to soothe the raw wounds in my soul. "Don't sound so mad about it."

O'Rourke was in front of us and I curled my arm a little tighter over her shoulder to keep her with me. He had no business being here with her.

"Thirty seconds," Alphabet warned. "You guys ready to go?"

"We are," Grace said, tipping her head back as O'Rourke shook his head. He didn't argue, however, just moved ahead of us. "Right, Captain Boney Boy?"

"Dollface, you remember what I said about spanking you?"

Her smile was sunshine. "Now now, don't promise me a good time until you're ready to deliver it."

"Ten seconds," Alphabet said.

"Let's go," she murmured. "One foot in front of the other."

The floor was blessedly cold against the bottoms of my abused feet. Oh, I was bare foot. That barely even registered. Did I have on pants? Took a moment, but yes there they were.

I stumbled, but caught the rhythm. She was still in heels, I did not want to knock her off her feet.

"Five seconds." The countdown galvanized me.

"How far?" I lifted my chin, tried to look ahead. An escape meant resistance. I had to be ready to handle...

"Three..."

"Oh, let's talk about that later."

"Two..."

Before I could ask why, the sound of alarms erupting everywhere drowned out Alphabet's "one."

Then all hell broke loose.

TWENTY-TWO

GRACE

The alarms were shrieking—red strobes pulsing across the concrete corridor, splashing over Bones' skin like blood. He was half-naked, torn to hell, covered in bruises, burns, and cuts that looked like they'd been made just for pain. But he was upright. He was moving.

Barefoot. Shirtless. A wreck.

But moving.

I had one arm around him as we stumbled along the basement hall of the museum, passing crates of artifacts and shattered security doors. My strapless dress stuck to my side with sweat, and every step in these goddamn heels was a death wish. The only weapon I had was the baton O'Rourke had yanked off a guard and shoved into my hand like it was enough.

Ahead, O'Rourke motioned with a closed fist—stop. Then a silent point. Hostiles up front. *Thank you, Legend and Voodoo, for the tactical shorthand lesson.*

Heavy boots. Movement. At least three or four, probably

more, coming at us from the opposite hall. It was hard to count with the screaming alarms.

"Left side—tango team, suppressing fire," Legend's voice crackled in my ear.

"Two more flanking from service stairs," AB added.

"Don't stop moving, Firecracker," Voodoo said. "They're trying to trap you."

Too late.

The hallway behind us erupted far footsteps loud enough to carry past the yowling siren of the alarm. Shouting. Light beams slicing through the shadows.

"Shit!" I hissed, spinning.

Three—no, five—men in black combat gear were charging down the rear corridor toward us. We were pinned. No exits. No cover.

"Take front," O'Rourke barked, stepping toward the advancing squad. "I've got them."

Before I could say anything, Bones tore himself out of my grip.

"Bones—"

He didn't look at me. Just pivoted—barefoot on cold concrete—and stared down the oncoming men behind us.

And then he *moved*.

Not staggered. Not limped.

He moved like a damn weapon finally unsheathed.

The first man raised a gun—too slow. Bones was already inside his guard, one arm slamming the barrel away as his elbow cracked the guy's nose. A flash of blood sprayed. He spun the man into the wall like a puppet and drove a knee straight into his spine. He dropped like dead weight.

Two more came in from the sides. Bones ducked under a swinging baton, caught the second man's wrist and *twisted*—a sickening snap, then used the man's own body as a shield. Gunfire erupted. Muzzle flashes lit up the corridor. Bones shoved the shield into the next attacker and disarmed the one behind him with a precise, brutal strike to the throat.

Another one grabbed for him—he pivoted, dropped low, swept the legs, and brought the baton down on the man's head with a *crack* like a hammer on bone.

I stood frozen, breath caught in my lungs, watching this broken, barefoot man move like something out of a nightmare—precise, fast, merciless. Blood streaked his face and chest, but he didn't hesitate, didn't flinch.

He *flowed* from one attacker to the next, never wasting a move. Each strike was lethal, clean, surgical. He wasn't just surviving.

He was *erasing* them.

I shook myself and raised the baton just as one of the stunned guards staggered toward me, half-conscious. I cracked the stick across his jaw with a grunt, then brought it down on the back of his head. He collapsed at my feet.

Bones turned toward me—blood dripping from his knuckles, chest heaving. His face was stone.

"Still with me?" he rasped.

"Yeah," I said, breathless. "You?"

He gave me a crooked smile—barely there. "Let's go."

O'Rourke's voice cut through the cacophony like a scalpel. "Hallway clear. We've got maybe ninety seconds before the next patrol sweeps back around. Move now."

I nodded instinctively. "Coming," I said, grabbing Bones by the hand. His skin was hot under my fingers—fever-hot—and slick with blood, but he didn't flinch. Just moved with me.

We jogged down the corridor, shoes slapping against

concrete—well, *my* shoes. Bones ran barefoot, silent. Every step had to be agony, but he didn't make a sound.

"Three hostiles coming up on your two o'clock," AB warned in my ear. "I'll draw 'em off. Wait for the cue."

A thundering bang echoed from somewhere above us—explosives, maybe, or a breaching charge. Real human screams joined the racket from the security system. Then gunfire. I'd never realized just how distinctive that sound was. I'd never mistake fireworks for it again.

The feed in my comms flared with updates—Voodoo's voice sharp and low, Legend barking orders. They were tearing through the hidden compound and the museum like a storm.

Distraction successful.

Too successful. O'Rourke was *gone.*

"Come on," I hissed, dragging Bones into a side alcove. He pressed back against the wall, sweat and blood glistening under the flickering emergency lights. His eyes were wild—flicking down the hall, up at the ceiling, then back to me. He was scanning for threats even now.

I wanted to stop. I wanted to *look* at him, take in what they'd done. The lashes across his ribs. The mottled bruises. The burns that peeled in places, raw and angry. But we didn't have time.

"Can you keep going?" I asked.

"I'm already gone," he said, voice like broken glass. Any other time, he might have deadpanned it. Right now, he was just breaking my heart. "You just haven't caught up yet."

O'Rourke reappeared in the corridor like a ghost—no warning, just *there.* His tuxedo was splashed with someone else's blood, and his expression was ferocious. Far angrier than I'd ever seen him. His glare seemed fixed on me.

"I said *ninety seconds*," he snapped, glancing past us. "You're down to thirty."

I met his eyes. Cold. Calculating. And yet—still here. Seriously, I didn't know what to make of him much less what to do with him.

I didn't trust him. Somehow, I doubted I ever would. The animosity between him and the guys was just too palpable. No matter what decisions he was making at the moment, he'd *betrayed* them in the past. Forgiveness, much less trust, seemed like a real stretch. Thankfully, right now, I didn't have to rely on him for much. We just had to use him.

After looping Bones' arm over my shoulder again, we moved. He leaned on me more than before, though he didn't want to. I felt the tremble in his arm, the slip of his foot when the concrete turned slick. I tightened my grip.

Frankly, I'd never been so glad for all the runways I'd walked in ankle breaker heels. I could keep us both balanced.

Mostly.

Another corner, another stretch of hallway. Lights flickered—some shattered from the blast above, others barely holding on. Overhead, the ceiling groaned with weight and movement.

"Stairwell ahead," AB said via comms. "Two contacts. I can give you ten seconds. No more."

"We'll take it," O'Rourke said and was already moving before he finished speaking—knife out, fast and low. No hesitation. No mercy. He flowed from one guard to the next, a blur of precision. One throat slit, one temple stabbed. No wasted motion. No sound, either.

Like Bones earlier, he wasn't just clearing opposition, he was exterminating it. The wet slices and meaty *thunks* were enough to penetrate the tumult. My stomach rolled, but I focused on moving again. The smell of sweat and blood that clung to Bones was overpowering, but breathing through my mouth helped.

We pushed past the bodies and hit the stairwell. Bones staggered against me, and for a split second I thought we were both going down. I shifted to use the wall to brace us both. His grunt shivered with pain and I grimaced.

"*Look at me.*" My voice was sharper than I meant it to be, but I needed him *here.*

A harsh exhale.

A second one.

Then his eyes locked on mine. Bloodshot. Too wide.

"Don't you leave me now," I said. "We didn't come this far to die in a stairwell." My heart sank at the very idea.

That ghost of a smile flickered again. "Dollface," he said on a wisp of a pained chuckle. "Always so romantic."

Tears burned in my eyes and I sucked in a deep breath to keep from crying. We so did not have time for me to cry right now. "Look, Boney Boy." I tried to inject as much snark as I could into my voice. We were good at the sarcasm and the picking on each other. Really good. I leaned on that heavily right now. "I broke a nail for this escape already. Don't push your luck."

A ghost of a smile creased his mouth and his eyes actually seemed to soften. "You really have a problem with keeping your nails done. Maybe you should just cut them short and keep it them that way."

The roughness of his voice robbed the flip comment of its impact, but I made a face at him anyway. "No one asked you," I muttered, then shoved his arm over my shoulders again.

"Are you two going to make out or get the hell out of

here?" O'Rourke reappeared in the stairwell door and I glared at him.

"Get out of our way," I ordered and the other man just shook his head before he took the stairs two at a time. Bones and I were a hell of a lot slower, but he gripped the railing with his bloodied hand to help stabilize himself as he climbed.

We were leaving his blood everywhere.

I really hoped the guys were right about this *not* being a real government operation.

Because we were leaving DNA and fingerprints behind, and Bones was *not* light on his feet despite his spectacular show of physical prowess downstairs. Still, we kept moving. I was hot, sweaty, *and* panting by the time we made it to the ground level.

We were gonna make it out. We had to.

Or we were going to burn this place to the ground trying.

Once we made it to the ground floor of the museum's grand storage area, the damage was—catastrophic. Smoke thickened in the air. Scorch marks blackened one of the walls. A door that had been there earlier was literally blown off its hinges.

The alarm changed, it shifted from the siren force to a ring that reminded me of old school bells. A hiss of sound had me looking up, but there was no water dumping on us. That was good, right?

My panting increased. "Guys…"

I hadn't heard from AB, Legend, or Voodoo in a few minutes. I swung my head around to scan the area. O'Rourke was gone too. Shouting came from the hall, but I waited another ten seconds.

Bones rested more and more of his weight on me. His

head listed forward as he wavered. It seemed to grow progressively more challenging for him to lean on me considering how hard it was getting just to *breathe*.

My lungs burned like I'd been sprinting uphill for miles, and every inhale felt thinner than the last. It wasn't smoke—there was no smell, no sting. Just this creeping weight in the air. Invisible. Insidious.

Something hissed again overhead.

I looked up and saw the nozzles—dozens of them—lined across the ceiling like a silent army. The suppression system. Not foam. Not water.

Gas.

My stomach dropped.

"Bones," I choked out, tightening my grip on him. "We gotta move. Now."

He didn't answer. His head dipped again, then jerked like he was trying to shake it off. But his knees buckled, and his whole body seemed to list and fall. There was nothing close enough to lean against and I went down with him as carefully as I could to keep him from hitting his head.

Or anything else for that matter.

"No, no, no—*damn it.*" I dropped into a half-crouch, dragging his arm over my shoulder again. He was damn near a dead weight. My legs screamed in protest, but I didn't care.

We couldn't stop. Not here.

"Come on, Bones," I muttered, half-dragging, half-hauling him toward the blown-out door. "You survived your time in the torture spa, you don't get to die in a museum. You might be old, but you are *not* that old." I grunted, growled, and groaned as I fought for every inch of space we achieved. "You stubborn bastard."

The hiss grew louder—more vents kicking in. The air

thinned further, my head swam, and my knees felt watery. I stumbled, slammed my shoulder into a shelf—when did that get there?—and nearly sent both of us back to the floor.

He groaned. That sound vibrated against my skin and lit a fire along my spine. He was still with me. Still breathing. Still fighting. If he could do it...

Then dammit, so would I.

I gritted my teeth and pushed us forward, one foot after another. I didn't know where O'Rourke had gone. Didn't know where *anyone* was. Comms were *dead silent*—like we were sealed in our own little hell, cut off from the world.

It was really hard to get a deep breath. The more I tried, the more my vision seemed to swim. Oh, and wasn't that just great. Now I was seeing stars. I didn't want to think about how low the oxygen had to be for me to feel it.

Pushing away from the shelves, I guided us across the room, following the path they'd made me memorize. Only, I wasn't so sure about it at the moment.

The hallway stretched ahead—long, dark, scattered with debris. I didn't know the museum had this many back corridors. I didn't know where they went.

I saw light at the end of one. Flickering. Smoke-diffused.

Good enough for me.

Angling toward it, I stagger-walked with Bones like he weighed nothing and everything at the same time.

A burst of static hit my comm and I jerked, half stopping before I made myself keep going. Bones was trying to walk. We needed the momentum.

Then—finally—Legend's voice.

"—exit north-side loading dock—repeat, Grace, do you copy?—"

I had no hand free, but hopefully if I was receiving, it was transmitting again. "Legend, I copy—barely. We're moving. Bones is moving, but barely. Suppression system's dumping gas, we're getting lightheaded."

"Gas is non-toxic, but oxygen levels are being sucked out to kill the fire. Keep moving. You've got four minutes tops before you both black out."

What was I supposed to say to that? Thank you? I wasn't a damn soldier.

Four minutes.

How much time had we already lost? Bones had gone limp again, and my own legs were trembling like a newborn foal trying to stand for the first time.

"Bones," I whispered. "Don't you dare quit on me now."

Nothing. Just his weight pressing into me.

I pushed forward.

Another corner. Another hallway.

I could see the loading dock now—bright halogen lights stuttering on through the haze. The doors were cracked open, smoke pouring out into the night beyond.

Fresh air. Just a little further.

Another step.

Then another.

And then—O'Rourke emerged from the smoke near the loading bay, dragging a fire ax behind him like he'd just walked out of a war zone.

"You two lovebirds planning on dying dramatically or getting in the damn truck?"

I blinked at him, wheezing too hard to throw a comeback.

Instead, I stumbled the last few feet. "If you can't help —shut up."

O'Rourke surprised me then, he dropped the axe and

moved right to us. Without hesitation, he hauled Bones away from me and over his shoulders in a fireman carry.

"C'mon, beautiful," he said over his shoulder as he carried Bones out into the night like a rag doll.

I followed, lungs hitching, head pounding.

The air outside hit me like a fist—*cold, fresh, real.* I stumbled, my balance truly wobbling for the first time and I sat down rather than fall when the loading dock seemed ready to rush up to meet me. In between brutal coughs, the likes of which scraped my throat raw, I sucked in bigger gasps of air. Oh, it hurt to breathe, but I could breathe.

We made it.

We made it.

O'Rourke was suddenly in front of me again, sans Bones this time, and he slid a hand under my legs and around my back before lifting me. I wanted to demand what the hell he was doing, but I kept coughing.

Ground eating strides carried us along the dock and then down to where a catering truck was parked. There was something about the truck, but my mind seemed almost as blurry as my vision at the moment.

"Give her to me," Voodoo was just there, he pulled me away from O'Rourke and the tension threading all of my muscles just fell away.

"Get her in here," Legend said from ahead and then he was there too. I was in the back of the catering truck and there was a mask over my face. The cold, pure air helped. But I was still coughing.

Bones sat, collapsed next to me and the engine was already running. As soon as the rear door slid down with a rasp of metal, we were moving. I shifted to look at Bones, searching for his pulse, breath—something.

He looked even worse in here than he had inside. Blood

covered half of his face, but he was still here. With us. Someone had slipped a mask over his face and there was a faint fogging on mouth piece.

"Next time," I rasped, glancing at the guys as I leaned my head back. Goblin licked my cheek. Oh, he was here too. Good boy.

"Next time?" Voodoo prompted.

Honestly, I didn't really have it in me to say anything at this point so I just waved it off for now.

"You did good, Firecracker," Voodoo said, running a hand over my hair before he returned his attention to Bones. AB was probably up front with Legend. The plan had gone exactly as they wanted it too.

And precisely how they'd mapped it out.

Save for one thing.

As I leaned back, I met O'Rourke's stare where he leaned against the other side of the van. His tie was gone, so was his suit jacket, and blood, soot, and more stained his white shirt.

He just shook his head. "Don't thank me."

I pulled the mask away from my face for a moment to say, "I wasn't planning on it."

His smirk said he didn't believe me, but I really didn't care. Voodoo reached over to secure my oxygen mask again. Hopefully their part of the plan went as well as mine.

Though, I did have a next time thought now as I pulled off my shoes.

Next time I didn't want to do this in heels.

Behind us, the museum burned.

TWENTY-THREE

ALPHABET

THIRTY-SIX HOURS EARLIER...

LOCATION: SUBURBAN SAFE HOUSE

"Explain it to me again," Lunchbox said from where he stood by the now cleaned counter and sink. Breakfast was done and we'd gone over the intelligence that I'd been able to run through the night before.

O'Rourke gave me enough information to pierce the veil of secrecy these guys were operating under. I wasn't sure whether to be more amused or irritated at the simplicity of their plan. Covert only worked as long as no one knew what to look for. Once you pulled apart one string, the rest began to gradually unravel.

Finding the *right* thread to pull had been the key.

Not that I planned on thanking O'Rourke. Not today. Not tomorrow. Not ever. That dick was part of the reason we were in this particular fight.

"From the top…" Lunchbox continued and I didn't sigh. Too much coffee, too little sleep, and worry for Bones had me on edge. Or it had… until our morning play with Gracie. She made everything better.

"Do you have a specific issue you want to review?" Voodoo asked before I could kick it off. "Or do you really want a repeat of what we already discussed?"

Not an unfair question.

Lunchbox shifted his gaze to where Gracie sat with her hands wrapped around the fresh cup of coffee.

"He wants to know why you guys are letting me run part of this solo." Oh, she definitely got it. "Or at least participating in the op."

"Actually," Lunchbox said through a tight jaw where he wasn't quite grinding his teeth. "What I want to know is why we're trusting O'Rourke to be your backup."

"We're not trusting him." I kept my voice flat, even, unemotional. Goblin leaned against my leg, where he'd pretty much planted himself since we started the briefing. "I don't like him any more than you do. I am trusting Gracie."

For her part, she tilted her head to glance between us. After the first part of the briefing, she hadn't said much. Instead, she seemed to be mulling it over.

"If Gracie isn't up to it," I said, raising a hand to stave off any response from her at the moment. "Example only, I told her." Then I refocused on Lunchbox. "If *she* isn't up for it, or if we find too many holes, then we don't do it."

"What is she supposed to do if O'Rourke flips on her?" The only reason he wasn't pissing me off at the moment was I was right there with him.

"She can tase him. She can scream and out him to the security there…or we'll shoot him." Voodoo shrugged. "Currently, O'Rourke thinks he can win her over. If we give a little in his direction, he's going to think he can get a lot. That makes him play a little nicer. I want him there as a meat shield."

"And we're damn certain he hasn't told us everything," I finished.

Pinching the bridge of his nose, Lunchbox blew out a long breath. Then like us, he focused on Gracie. "What do you think of the plan?"

"I think I need to get my hair and nails done." She glanced down at her hands. "This manicure is more than a month old and if we want me to blend in as arm candy, then I need a little help."

"Gracie, you would look like a billion dollars in a burlap sack." And I meant it. She was—everything.

Her nose wrinkled up adorably as she made a face. "You do not get to make the fashion choices."

Grinning, I made a mock obeisance bow by rolling my hand and dipping my chin.

"Firecracker." Voodoo didn't raise his voice or snap a command, but it was enough to snare all of our attention. "Are you up for this?"

"Weirdly," she said slowly. "I think so. Not I know so, I think so. But only because I don't think you'd make this suggestion or even use me in this plan like this if you weren't dead certain it would work."

She had a point. Lips pursed, Lunchbox shook his head. "I still don't like it. I'd rather just shoot him."

"Me too," I said in chorus with Voodoo, then continued, "However, we can't—yet. Not ever, just not right now. He's useful and we want to get Bones back."

Rising, Gracie carried her empty cup over to the counter where Lunchbox stood. After setting the cup aside, she pressed her hands to his chest. It was damn hard to hold onto stoic when she looked at me like that, so I wasn't remotely surprised when some of the rigid tension in his shoulders relaxed.

"I can do this," she said. "I also know, if anything happens, you guys will be there. But if anyone cuts anything off of him...I want to pick the first part. That's my deal."

"Bloodthirsty." Lunchbox said with a faint chuckle. "I like it." He wrapped his arms around her, then shot a look at Voodoo and then me. I nodded. So did Voodoo.

She could do this and we would make sure she was fine.

"Right..." Voodoo glanced at me. "Let's get moving..."

VOODOO

TWENTY-FOUR HOURS EARLIER...

LOCATION: ARCADIA MUSEUM OF CULTURAL HISTORY

I'd seen a lot of fronts in my time—strip malls that covered bunkers, churches that funneled weapons, even a suburban daycare that ran a listening post out of the nursery. But this? A high-tech, freshly minted museum in the middle of the city... this was almost elegant.

From the outside, the Arcadia Museum of Cultural History looked clean, expensive, and just *off* enough to draw attention but not scrutiny. New concrete, shining glass, and some overly abstract modern sculpture of a phoenix in the courtyard. Not subtle. Not trying to be. That's the trick with these kinds of operations—don't *hide.* Just fit in loud enough that no one wants to look closer.

I'd parked a block away, took a slow circuit on foot, no gear that would get flagged by their facial rec. Black jeans, battered jacket, camera hanging off my neck like any other out-of-towner soaking in the sights before the museum closed for a private event. Baseball cap and sunglasses helped sell the tourist angle.

Private events happened every third night, apparently. According to the schedule, that frequency wasn't listed online. But the frequency showed up in their power usage logs. Dumb move.

People lied. Data didn't.

There were four main entrances: public, staff, deliveries, and fire exits. Two side alleys. One underground tunnel that *wasn't* on city records but definitely existed—thermal scan had picked it up when we did the drive-by recon. That one would need more investigation. Probably part of the emergency egress or a VIP escape route. Whatever it was, they cared enough to keep it quiet.

The loading docks though? Perfect. Isolated. Cameras easy to loop—primitive system there, not even cloud synced. Big mistake. Alphabet had been incensed by the setup. It was almost funny. Still, the wobbly security might just be a cover. Distract by appearing unimpressive. It was a choice.

Trucks came in twice a week for exhibit rotation, and if we believed that I would be investing in a bridge that was already located in Arizona. The delivery manifests and weight scans didn't match—not even close. They had been moving cargo in and out that didn't get logged.

My kind of backdoor.

I took a stroll past the public lobby, made note of the

security guards. Overdressed, undertrained. They scanned people's tickets like TSA LARPing agents and didn't notice half the tells they should've. One of them kept scratching his wrist where a wrist tattoo was clearly trying to peek out from beneath his uniform. Real pros they had here.

The museum *looked* new, but too much of it was smoke and mirrors. Corners of the façade still smelled like freshly cured resin. But other sections—like the west wing—felt older, hidden beneath cosmetic upgrades. Reinforced walls. Vibration sensors tucked under the molding near the display cases. High-end tech, but only in select zones.

This place was built to *look* like a museum. And maybe some of it *was*—but the rest? Storage. Staging. Something deeper.

Every piece of information confirmed our supposition. This was most likely where they were holding Bones.

I finished my loop, ended up back near the side alley that fed toward the loading dock. Looked like a blind corner —no camera angle covered it fully. That was intentional. Could make for a clean extraction route if we had to go loud. Not preferred, but good to know.

It was well past sundown by the time I finished my last circuit of the area and headed back to the parked van. My gear bag was still where I left it, tucked in the hidden compartment beneath the false floor. Slid it out, ran a quick check—drones, thermal imager, EMP disruptor, snake cam. Good. Grabbed the burner phone and sent the signal to Alphabet.

"Ingredients acquired along with the recipe. Heading back now."

I took one last look back at the museum, then slipped into the driver's seat. The engine purred low as I pulled away, merging into the flow of evening traffic.

Bones was in there. I could feel it. And if I was right about the setup, getting in would be easier than getting out.

And we were sending Gracie in, but if everything went according to plan—we would take all the fire while she got out.

LUNCHBOX

FIVE HOURS EARLIER...

LOCATION: UNDISCLOSED LOCATION NOT FAR FROM THE VENUE

She stepped out of the guest room and it hit me like a goddamn bomb going off.

Grace was already huge in spirit—fierce, fast with her mouth, quicker with her mind—but the heels made her 5'2" frame feel like 6'2", and the dress? That strapless blue number looked like it had been airbrushed on. Seamless, molded to her like a second skin. She looked dangerous, the kind of dangerous that didn't need a weapon. The kind of dangerous men underestimated, but never made the same mistake twice.

I didn't say anything right away. Just stared. Blinking like a jackass.

"Well?" she asked, raising a single brow, lips painted just enough to be taken seriously.

"You look..." I trailed off, tried again. "You look like something people start wars over."

"Not helpful, Lunchbox," she said, but her smirk told me it *was*.

Still, I didn't like this.

Not just the dress. Not just the heels. Not even O'Rourke, who I trusted about as far as I could throw him—and considering the guy was built like a water heater filled with bad decisions, that wasn't far.

It was the whole damn setup.

There wasn't much room for a weapon in that dress. This wasn't *that* kind of mission. She couldn't go in armored to the teeth. She needed to play the part: arm candy, not assassin. Which meant her only weapons were what she could say, how she could move, and the hope that O'Rourke didn't screw us all sideways for whatever price someone had whispered in his ear.

Grace could handle herself. I didn't doubt that. But I hated the idea of sending her in alone—like this.

"Turn," I said, motioning with two fingers.

She gave me a look, but spun slowly, her movements smooth even in those ridiculous heels. I scanned the length of her back, waist, hips, ankles. Nowhere to stash anything heavier than a lip gloss tube.

"You're stalling," she said.

"Damn right I am." I scrubbed a hand through my beard, brain working overtime. "You don't have any way to protect yourself if things go sideways."

She patted the small clutch in her hand. "No taser, but I have all the bugs and the little pellets Alphabet wants me to drop. Just like we agreed."

I really hated the lack of a weapon for her.

Like—despised it.

"I'll talk my way through it," she said, easy. Confident. But I still caught the flicker of nerves behind her eyes.

That sealed it.

"Stay here. Ten minutes."

I didn't wait for her to argue. Just turned and headed for my gear. It was new, most of it repurposed, but Voodoo had done a full supply run. We didn't have everything here, so we made do with what we had. I had enough to cobble together a decent bench, and enough tools to build or break damn near anything in a pinch.

What I needed was small. Concealable. Something we could use to keep O'Rourke in line. Something that didn't look like a weapon, but *was* one.

I found the casing for a magnetic RFID patch—a leftover from something—and started modifying it. Stripped out the original tracker guts, replaced them with a micro-shock circuit, not enough to kill, but plenty to get someone's attention. Especially if it was placed near the base of the spine. Added a remote trigger, paired it to one of our encrypted comms channels.

Took longer to solder than I liked, but it needed to work, not win awards.

By the time I came back out, Grace was sitting on the edge of the couch, scrolling through her phone like she wasn't about to walk into a lion's den. She looked up as I held out the patch.

"Another tracker?" she asked.

"Better." I motioned for her to stand. "Turn around."

She hesitated a beat, but complied. I peeled back the top layer of the dress just enough to press the patch to the inside, at the base of her back, right above the zipper. It held fast—good. Seamless. Invisible. I smoothed the dress back over it and stepped away.

"What does it do?"

"If O'Rourke even *thinks* about turning on you, I hit this button—" I held up the trigger "—and he's on the ground, pissing himself. Doesn't knock him out. But it hurts like hell."

Her mouth curved. "You turned me into a remote-controlled cattle prod?"

"Think of it as a shock collar," I said. "Except it's for the asshole walking you in. Don't worry, it won't hurt you. Probably only good for one or two uses, but that should be enough."

"I love it," she said, with real warmth. "And I love that you're paranoid enough to think of it."

"Not paranoid. Just prepared." I hesitated, then added quietly, "You get in trouble, you stall. Long enough for us to get to you."

"I know."

I nodded, jaw tight. "I still don't like this."

"You don't have to," she said gently. "You just have to let me do it."

I looked at her again—really looked. She'd taken a couple of hours and gone to a salon. Voodoo had covered her while she got her hair, cosmetics, and nails done. She'd said something about her eyebrows and lashes, but she was just—stunning.

"Gracie?"

"Hmm?"

"When we get a free night, feel like getting all dressed up and let me take you out? Like for a real date?" I hadn't really done anything like that with her and... I wanted to know more about what she liked.

Fuck, I just wanted her.

"Yes." No prevarication, no caveats, and no conditions. Just a simple acceptance.

"You come back in one piece," I ordered. "I mean it, no scratches or bruises. Hell, I don't want even one hair out of place." Damn, I was starting to sound like Bones.

She leaned up on her toes and kissed my cheek. "You'll all be there to make sure I do."

Damn right I would.

BONES

NOW

LOCATION: VAN ON THE INTERSTATE

Everything hurt, but a soft hand held mine and it was the first thing that registered as awareness snapped through me. There was a trick to waking without alerting any potential observers, but my last memory was Grace giving me hell, so I just opened my eyes.

Voodoo was right there and he had a hand on my shoulder before I could move. It was dark, we were in a vehicle, and on the road. Voices carried from the front— Alphabet and Lunchbox. Where was...? Voodoo cut his gaze to my left and I turned my head.

She was curled up right next to me and it was her hand in mine. Hair disheveled with wisps tangling everywhere, she was stunning.

"She's fine. You're out. That operation is shut down. I'll brief you on the particulars later."

"O'Rourke?" I asked in a rough voice, but I kept my gaze on Grace. She'd walked in there to rescue me in a goddamn sexy dress and pair of stiletto heels I wasn't sure whether to kiss her or spank her. Probably both.

"We dumped him... alive. For the moment. We can

change that if we decide otherwise, but we wanted him gone."

Acceptable. For now.

"I want a full debrief."

"You'll get it," Voodoo said, his tone implacable. "*After* you rest. We're heading back to base. We all need the break to retrench and get ready."

Grace.

Grace needed to get ready for the next part and I lifted her soft hand up to rest it against my chest and held it there. Everything hurt, even my palms. But I wasn't letting her go.

Wild thing had walked in there like she was badass on a mission.

"Bryant," I said in a low voice.

He sighed.

"You can kick my ass as soon as you've healed up. I made the call. She handled it."

I nodded. Good to know he understood.

But at the same time. "Thanks." Then I raised my voice. "Thanks for coming for me."

"Always."

TWENTY-FOUR

GRACE

The next few days were an exercise in patience, frustration, and at times, hilarity. It ran the full gamut of emotions, and I wasn't quite sure what to do with all of it—or them for that matter. Goblin, AB, and I took a lot of long walks in the snow.

Oddly, when AB first invited me to go out in the snow, I said I didn't have enough warm weather gear. Voodoo disabused me of that swiftly. Apparently, a whole *wardrobe* had come in while we were away and the guys had found time to collect it. Included in this wardrobe was an adorable purple and blue ski suit, insulated leggings, and warm, water proof boots. Everything fit.

Like fit almost exactly. He was so pleased with himself so I kept my creepy stalker teases to myself. But seriously, how did he nail my size so accurately? I liked the outfit, it was comfortable and made the walks fun. It wasn't so deep we had to wade through it, but it had been a long time since I'd been anywhere with snow quite this pristine.

Yes, I'd been to Banff, Zermatt, and St. Moritz. I liked skiing, though I was a better snowboarder. But there were always people and this... This place was magic in the snow. The crisp air and the blanket of hush that lay over everything, made it easy to forget the bloody madness we'd been dealing with on and off for...

Months.

All at once, my mood plummeted and I retreated from the window where I'd stared out at the snow. Flames licked over the wood in the fireplace merrily crackling. With a sigh, I turned away to head to the kitchen.

I'd made it exactly nine steps into the kitchen. Nine. That's how far I got before Voodoo, perched like some unholy gremlin on top of the fridge, shot me in the neck with a Nerf dart.

"Holy shit—why?!" I hissed, rubbing the welt like it was a real bullet wound.

"Situational awareness," he said, grinning like the devil. "You've got the instincts of a day-old kitten, Firecracker."

He tried to hand me a little plastic pistol. I stared at it like one of us had lost our damn minds. "Don't you want me to learn to fire a real one?"

"Not with that reflex time. Maybe once you master the nerf, we'll take you to the real thing."

"You're not funny," I deadpanned.

Then he shot me again and took off with a whoop, after he leapt down from the top of the fridge and I chased him. I had no idea what Bones had said to them, but *every* single one of them was in on my training now.

THE NEXT TIME IT HAPPENED, I was working on laundry. *My* laundry. I'd been innocently folding sports bras—*bras*—when Bones materialized behind me like a damn poltergeist and wrapped me up in a surprise wrestling hold.

"What the hell?!" I squawked, flailing.

"Get out of it," he grunted, amused, as I elbowed him in the ribs. "If I were a hostile, you'd be in a van already."

"If you were a hostile," I gasped, still struggling, "I'd never have helped rescue you."

"Too late now," he practically purred against my ear. "Now get free, Dollface. The clock is ticking."

Why did I love these guys again?

LEGEND GOT CREATIVE. *Subtle.*

I was standing by the mudroom door, boots soaked and fingers numb, just trying to knock the snow off my coat and feel something like human again. The house was quiet. Peaceful. Suspiciously so.

Then a blast of *freezing* water smacked me right in the side of the head.

I shrieked like a horror movie extra and spun around, slipping slightly on the mat. There he was—Legend—standing inside the kitchen with a gleaming stainless steel sink sprayer in one hand and the world's smuggest grin on his face.

"Why—why are you like this?" I sputtered, wiping icy droplets from my ear.

"Water is a weapon," he said, deadpan. "Never let your guard down near plumbing."

He sauntered off like that was a normal thing to say.

Later, I tried to wash a mug and got blasted *again*. Turns out he'd rigged the sink nozzle to trigger when anyone touched the handle.

I was starting to think he missed his calling in psychological warfare.

AT LEAST ONCE A DAY—*ONCE a day*—someone snuck up behind me just to whisper "boo" in my ear like a six-year-old gremlin. I never caught who did it. I'd turn, heart pounding, and there'd be no one. Just air. Or a door swinging slightly. One time, a hastily discarded hoodie.

They *insisted* it wasn't any of them.

Bones swore on his life. Voodoo said I was developing paranoia. Legend suggested I install a motion detector.

I was going to find out, one way or the other. My reaction time was getting faster, and when I did find out—well they were going to need a new set of teeth.

AB and I took Goblin out one morning. It was a beautiful day, cold but not so biting. The snow fell lightly against the already white painted landscape. It was almost holiday postcard perfect. Instead of the usual, we were debating movies. AB, it turned out, was a huge fan of old black and white classics and was determined to "educate" me. I was actually enjoying myself.

Then something smacked me square in the back just hard enough, I stumbled forward.

I turned slowly. Legend was a couple of yards behind us, holding another snowball, looking very pleased with himself.

I turned to AB, aghast. "Are there *no rules*?"

He shrugged. "Snow's a gray area."

"Does that mean you can help me?"

With a grin, he said, "Yep."

As it turned out, despite growing up in Southern California, AB had a killer arm and I discovered what they meant about leading the target much to Legend's chagrin.

∽

AB NEVER AMBUSHED ME. Never jumped out of a closet. Never wrestled me into submission.

What he *did* do was sit me down in front of a fake ATM—I had no idea where the hell they got this thing—and said, "Try to get this card reader to accept a blank card."

"Why would I ever need to do this?" I asked, holding up a rubbery decoy card like it was radioactive.

"You wouldn't," he said, calmly. "Unless someone else needed you to. Or you needed to spoof access in a locked building. Or they hand you a decoy."

"Oh. Right. Perfectly normal, everyday scenarios."

He nodded, utterly serious. Then we spent hours like it was the toughest game of Operation I'd ever played. I did manage to spoof it once though.

Another time, he slid a thumb drive across the table. "That one just lights up. Don't use it on your actual laptop."

I blinked at him. "Where am I supposed to use it?"

With an innocent shrug, he said, "The guys have their own laptops."

They did...

Since Voodoo started it, he was the one I nailed with the flash drive. Apparently he earned a pornado. His yelling at AB was epic. AB *never* ratted me out.

The best part of all: it *was* kind of fun.

AFTER THE EIGHTH or ninth ambush of the week—I'd lost count—I almost had an epic meltdown. Even on shoots that took hours with the grittiest and most irritating photographers that stripped your soul of any kind of feeling, I'd never had a diva meltdown.

No, that came when *Legend*, of all people, rigged the hallway to spray shaving cream all over me when I opened my bedroom door. It was creative, I'd give him that. I rarely slept in my room or slept in there alone, last night had been an anomaly. But there I was, wanting coffee and hosed down in shaving cream that smelled minty fucking fresh.

A big plop of it dropped from my cheek to my shoulder, then slid down my bare arm to hit the floor. Bones frowned at me from the doorway to his room. I wasn't sure if he was on his way back in there or on his way out.

"We have a workout this morning," he said. The bruises that had littered his face had diminished from ugly blue-black to yellow-green. The ones on his body were still a little closer to the purple-green. Unfortunately, his burns were likely to scar in the handful of places he'd gotten them.

Not that he cared.

"You don't say," I said in a voice so calm, I barely recognized it. Ignoring the shaving cream that continued to drip off me, I passed Bones and then descended the steps. The quiet hum of conversation in the kitchen cut off abruptly at my arrival.

Legend's eyes actually widened and Voodoo struggled to not spit out his coffee. Ignoring all of them, I headed for the espresso machine to make my own coffee.

"Gracie?"

"Yes, Legend?" I asked before starting the grinder to turn the beans into grounds.

He didn't say anything until I had finished and tamped it into place. "You're dripping... stuff."

"Really?" I glanced at him over my shoulder and maintained a straight face as another glop rolled down my forehead, then along my nose to drip off onto the floor. "Wonder what happened?"

AB coughed. "You want one of us to make that while you...?"

When I shifted to look at him, he mimed zipping his lips. Satisfied, I returned to making my coffee. I didn't say anything when Legend set the oat milk next to me. I maintained my silence while the guys shuffled, and shared looks, and whatever secret communications they could manage while I had my back turned.

When my coffee was ready, I took a long drink with my eyes closed. The magic of caffeine, it was real. Another sip, then I took a breath before I pivoted to face them.

"Gentlemen," I began and AB mouthed "oh shit" even as Voodoo straightened and Bones instantly went wary. I couldn't see Legend from this angle. There was more foam melting down that side of my face. "Would one of you care to explain what exactly it is you think Mark Sinclair is going to do in that meeting that requires just this much *preparation?*"

I was extremely proud of myself.

I. Did. Not. Yell.

Not a single one of them answered, though all three of my four culprits focused on Legend. His trap, so his explanation. Fine.

I turned to look at him as well.

"Well," he said, almost too casually. "We don't know

what he might be hiding or what skills he hasn't advertised. Maybe he is a five-thousand-dollar stuffed suit and maybe he's a whackjob in Armani, we don't know. With that in mind, we want to keep you sharp."

"I'm not a scalpel," I said, well snapped. Another deep breath. "I'm a model."

"Not anymore," AB murmured from behind me.

"You need to be ready for anything," Bones said. "When we're sure, then we'll continue with the plan for you to see him."

At this rate, I would never be judged "ready" at least not by them. No, they were back to AB digging. I got that. Bones definitely needed time to heal, but the mission appeared to be delay, delay, delay.

Time to change their minds or at least their plans.

IT STARTED WITH A POST-IT NOTE. Small, neon pink, stuck to the inside of Bones' protein tub. I'd written just four words:

You missed leg day.

It was childish, yes. Petty? Absolutely. But the next morning, Bones stood there, spoon halfway to his mouth, staring into the powder like he'd just found out the container was full of arsenic. He looked up. I smiled over my coffee. Said nothing.

One point for me.

LEGEND WAS HARDER.

He was *always* watching. Doors, corners, mirrors—*my*

face. But I found his blind spot. More specifically, I found his *snow boots.*

Most of his shoes he kept almost obsessively neat and stored away. He polished them, kept them in perfect shape, the whole nine yards. His snow boots, however, had to stay in the mudroom like all of ours after being outside.

So I may have, possibly, filled them with frozen peas.

Later that afternoon while working on AB's latest mental puzzle of plug and play, I heard a shout from the hallway, followed by something that sounded like, "What the fuck?"

Two points for me.

When AB glanced at me, I just grinned and kept on working.

VOODOO GOT ME BACK.

He replaced the sugar in the ceramic jar with salt. And not just "oops, a dash" levels. He went full *Dead Sea.* I took one sip of my morning flat white and just—froze.

Slowly, deliberately, I set the cup down.

His smirk was adorable even if that one hurt.

Back to one point.

BONES HAD this thing about control.

Everything in the gym had to be perfect. Gear lined up. Mats cleaned. Shoes off the mat. No phones, no gum, no water breaks until *he* called them.

So naturally, I decided that was the best place for my next act of sabotage. It began with his training sweats.

They kept spares in the laundry room. Big, bulky things that could double as body bags. He had a few that he traded out regularly, so late into the night after the boys were all asleep, I crept downstairs to sew the bottom hem of each of the pant legs together. It was a lot easier than I expected, but I had picked up a few skills during all those fashion fittings.

The next morning, he stalked into the gym like a drill sergeant in a snowstorm. Cold, cranky, and five minutes behind schedule. I was already there, stretching. So innocent.

"Grace," he said in a terse voice.

"I'm here, all stretching and everything." I kept it sweet and upbeat, even gave him a smile.

"Good, let's get started." We squared off on the mat. He went easy at first. He always did. Not a lot of movement from him, feet always together and mostly just making me work for it. The man had talent. Then I landed a hip toss that surprised us both.

"Again," he snapped.

This time, he came in harder, and then it happened.

He shifted his weight, tried to step wide to catch my leg in some kind of trip—and his feet stopped short.

He stumbled.

Hard.

The tangled hem yanked his legs together mid-move, and down he went like a redwood in slow motion. I didn't even touch him.

The sound when he hit the mat? Music.

Bones just lay there a second, staring at the ceiling like he was calculating how much dignity he had left. Then, slowly, he sat up. Pulled at the hem of his pants. Realized.

He looked at me. I smiled.

"Oh no," I said. "Did someone sabotage your gear? That must be so frustrating."

He didn't say a word.

Just got up, walked off the mat, and went to change, passing Voodoo who stood laughing his ass off just inside the doorway. When Bones was gone though, he gave me a slow clap.

"He'll get you back," he warned, and I shrugged.

"You guys already said you were going to keep doing it until I figured it out, so... what have I got to lose?" I wasn't sure if it was my sweet smile or my words that stymied him, but Voodoo actually looked less amused and more worried.

Three points for me.

OF COURSE, my success was short-lived. Legend retaliated by hiding a motion-activated soundbox under my bed. Fortunately, I wasn't alone when I discovered it at midnight. Voodoo was in bed with me and when a creepy child's voice whispered, "I see you" into the darkness as he thrust into me, we both froze.

I didn't scream or throw anything. I just stared up at Voodoo and he stared down at me, then he dipped his head, kissed me fiercely and pulled out and off. A moment later, he sat up from where he removed it from under the bed.

"I'll be back."

The thumping that came next was definitely nowhere near as fun as the thumping I'd been about to engage in. When he was done, Voodoo and I went to his room. Mine now officially creeped me out.

I wasn't sure if that was the reason the "training war" began to die off or if it was because AB found me in the kitchen quietly unscrewing the battery case on one of Legend's old motion sensors.

"Good," he said, pulling up a chair. "Now let me show you how to clone a phone off a dummy SIM."

Because *obviously*, that was the logical next step after surviving shaving cream, haunted beds, and salted coffee. I still don't know what exactly they think Mark Sinclair is going to *do* at that meeting.

If I needed to wrestle him to the ground, I was about 60% confident I could land an elbow now. If he pulled a gun, I'd at least learned not to freeze. And if he tried to talk circles around me?

Please.

He didn't stand a chance.

Because no way would I fail after all of this. The boys would *never* let me live it down, even if they killed Sinclair first.

CHAPTER

TWENTY-FIVE

GRACE

Virginia.

It seemed almost surreal when Legend landed the plane at the private airport in Loudoun County. The distance from here to Alexandria where Am's law firm was seemed as far as Am herself. After all these months, I still couldn't wrap my mind around the idea of not seeing her again.

We'd never gone this long without talking. The aching open wound of her absence tore open. The new damage split the scar tissue that had formed over the intervening time. While I could never forget her, the struggle to survive both the search and the time after while the guys helped their friends—it had numbed me.

A little.

The jagged swipes tearing down the walls and reconnecting me to those emotions *hurt*. Like a limb that had gone to sleep, the pins and needles were brutal in their assault.

"Hey," Bones said and it roused me to the fact the guys

had all deplaned and it was just me still in my seat, and Bones crouched next to me. "You good?"

"No," I admitted. "Not really." I didn't have a lot more than that to offer.

While I could have made something up or just faked it until I made it, I didn't. One thing had become almost second nature over the past few months with all of them, though it was the most true with Bones. Maybe because he aggravated me so much and didn't retreat even when I snapped back.

They didn't need me to pretend. I didn't have to be sunshine or bright. I didn't have to fake cheer I didn't feel or be upbeat when all I wanted to do was wallow.

"You still good to do this?" The phrasing of the question was careful, even if his voice was matter-of-fact.

"I will be." I sucked in a deep breath. Even though he didn't ask, I added, "It just hit me all over again how long it has been. I've been so distracted that—" I hadn't forgotten. That was the wrong word. Not to mention what a betrayal that would have been.

"That you let it slide to the back of your mind while you focused on what is in front of you." Bones nodded. "Take a minute, catch your breath, and then we'll go. Voodoo and Lunchbox are going to recon the firm and Sinclair's house. Once we have all the data, we'll work out the insertion."

I nodded once.

"My turn," I said, and when he would have risen, he sank back into the crouch. "You still mad that I want to do this?"

"I was never mad." No matter how flat the statement, he couldn't fool me.

"Liar."

One corner of his mouth curved upward. "I don't like it.

I will never like having you go into danger. You have scars now, Dollface. Scars you didn't have before you met us." He touched a finger to high on my cheekbone. There was a small one there, I'd seen it. From when I'd gotten a cut. Honestly, I barely remembered the injury, much less when I got it.

"They aren't so bad," I told him. "If they really bother me, there's creams and stuff." Things I probably should have thought about before now, but I hadn't. Bruises, scars... who cared when Am was out there?

When he cupped my chin, I focused on his gaze. There was just something so compelling when he looked at me like that. It was as though he could stare right into my soul, weigh it, then make a choice based on what he discovered.

"You will be wired when you go in," he said, his tone utterly uncompromising.

"Okay."

"You will have a receiver on here," he continued, curving his hand over my ear before stroking his fingers against the skin.

"Visible or hidden?" Just because he was stroking the soft, vulnerable flesh behind my ear—when the hell did that become an erogenous zone—didn't mean it was going to be there.

"Flesh-colored ear bud." He paused, considering me for a beat. "Can you wear your hair down?"

I considered it. When it came to work, Amorette was buttoned-down and professional. "I can make it work." Containing her sexuality was as much a weapon for Amorette as it was for me to use mine to get my way.

"Good." His touch on my face remained feather light. "We'll have eyes and ears on you at all times, if I call abort

—you get up, you walk out and you keep going. Do you understand?"

While it wasn't phrased as an order, it was still very much a command. Previously, my kneejerk reaction would be to balk. But that was before...

"I don't like it," I admitted. "But I'll do it."

The fact something like real relief shivered through his eyes made the breath back up in my lungs. Bones could be such a hardheaded asshole, but he *cared* and he was *worried*. He brushed a kiss to my lips, then another to my forehead. The ghost like touch was barely there before he rose.

"Thank you, by the way," I said, standing to grab my small backpack that also doubled as a purse at the moment. Bones took it right out of my hands.

"For?" He ducked at the hatch and walked down the two steps before turning to offer me his hand.

"For not suggesting she might be dead, and that all of this won't net any real answers or even... where she is." I had to swallow around a hard lump at the end of that. "I know it's a possibility." One I hated so damn much. "But..."

"You need hope." The words were so soft, I wasn't sure I'd heard them right but his expression matched the soft sentiment. "If I ever truly think that we're on a fool's errand, I will tell you. I promise."

That offered me an odd kind of comfort.

"But until then, we keep looking and we fight." He handed off my bag to Legend as he rejoined us.

"And maybe we pick up someone to torture along the way. Maybe more than one." His quicksilver smile helped settle the jumble of debris that had been crushing my heart since reality sank in that we were officially back on the hunt.

"You guys know how to show a girl a good time." The teasing remark earned me another grin from Legend and a stroke of a hand down my arm from Bones. "Right. No more time for my sulking." I summoned the smile.

While it was cold here in Virginia and there was snow on the ground, it was nowhere near as cold as it had been back at base. Didn't make it that warm, a fact that Voodoo seemed concerned about when he tugged my knit cap lower to cover my ears. We had two big SUVs waiting, and they were fully loaded with gear.

"Will you guys tell me one day how you have so much stuff *everywhere* we go?" At this point, I was more curious than anything else. The sun chose that moment to slide out from behind the clouds, even if it was already late in the afternoon.

"Maybe if you're a very good girl," Voodoo said with a wink.

"Or a bad girl," AB countered, then grinned. "We're not all that picky."

I snorted in unison with Bones, the sound so exact in echoing our skepticism that the other three stared at us before they began laughing. Goblin barked, tail wagging. He was in the cutest little shoes for the frozen ground and a little body jacket.

Making a mental note to pick him up some clothes the next time I went shopping, I let the guys laugh. It wasn't long before we split up. Voodoo and Legend left in one vehicle, while Bones, AB, Goblin, and I took the other. As usual, Goblin and I had the back seat and he was sprawled with his head in my lap while I gave him good firm scritches under his chin.

The action helped with my jangling nerves. Head back against the seat, I stared out the window though I wasn't really looking at the white painted landscape as they headed east—well, pretty sure it was east.

"Did you guys figure out why Bones' tracker didn't work?" It was a random thought, floating up to the top as I tried to focus on anything else.

"Electrical overload," AB said, shooting a glance at me over his shoulder. "They also had jamming equipment in that place. Not ideal, but we'll work out something that isn't so easily fried."

"It wasn't easily fried," Bones commented. "They used a lot of electricity."

I grimaced, hating the idea of his torture. Another mile drifted past and the quaky feeling in my gut grew more intense. "What made you guys decide to turn mercenary?" Where that question came from, I couldn't really say. "I mean, I know you were military. But now you're not. You take jobs like getting stolen people home, sourcing intelligence and..."

What else did they do? Assassinations? Takedowns? What exactly did you call a mercenary's various tasks? Their "services"?

For some reason that conjured the image of a website where you could scroll through the various job offerings and optional add-ons.

When neither one answered me immediately, I sighed. "Sorry, you don't have to answer that. My thoughts are kind of all over the place."

"I don't mind answering, Gracie," AB said, glancing over his shoulder again. "But I don't think it's the same reason for each of us and it's kind of a team thing..."

"So, let's put a pin in it for now and we'll sit down to a full team debrief after this is done." Bones cut a look at me in the rearview mirror. "There's a lot we should all sit and discuss."

Like what happened later? Or what was happening now? Or...

Instead of settling my disquiet, the idea of a full team meeting regarding their past, our relationship, and what the potential future held just made it so much worse. A chill seemed to settle deep into my bones and I shivered, despite the warmth of Goblin on my lap and my own jacket.

"Have I ever mentioned how much I struggle with patience?" It came out a grumble, a complaint, and *almost* but not quite a whine.

"I would never have noticed," AB said with absolute sincerity. "You are the absolute personification of stoicism."

Another snort escaped, and a smile broke out of the nervous cage closing in on me. "No one has ever called me *stoic* before."

"He's not calling you stoic now," Bones said in dry observation. "He's saying you are the picture of stoicism. Not exactly the same thing."

"You have a point," I conceded. "You are far more stoic than I am."

He grunted, but the faint curve of his lips gave him away. For some reason, the banter helped. Goblin helped where he sprawled against me so I could pet him. AB's playful looks and easy winks helped. Bones' terse demeanor and gruff comments helped.

At the same time, I swore I had an entire hive of bees buzzing under my skin. Every mile we traveled away from the airport, the more intense the feeling. My breathing grew shallower, and my pulse seemed to race.

By the time we turned onto a quiet residential street, the houses spaced just far enough apart to give the illusion of privacy, the buzzing in my chest had become a roar. Not bees anymore—this was a swarm. A living, crawling, stinging thing that filled every inch of me.

I couldn't breathe.

I didn't realize it at first, not fully. I thought maybe it was just nerves, the anticipation of getting closer, of being back *here*, so near Amorette's life, her work, her world. But when Bones slowed the SUV and AB reached for the garage remote clipped to the visor, the tightness in my throat became unbearable.

My hands started to tingle. Then they went numb.

Goblin shifted in my lap with a little concerned whine, and I barely noticed. The pressure in my chest was getting worse, like a boulder had been dropped on me and I was being crushed slowly beneath it. I couldn't pull in enough air. My vision blurred at the edges, white blooming in the corners like someone had turned on a too-bright light.

I was dying.

Oh God—was I having a heart attack?

I curled forward instinctively, wrapping my arms around Goblin and pressing my face into his fur. My breath came in shallow, gasping pulls that weren't helping. The cold air in the car felt too sharp. Like I was breathing in ice.

"I—I can't—I can't—" The words barely came out. I felt like I was underwater.

"Grace?" Bones' voice cut through the roaring in my ears. It wasn't calm. Not like usual. There was an edge to it.

We hadn't even made it to the house yet. The SUV slowed to a jerking halt and the next thing I knew, Bones had the back door open. Cold air rushed in, but I couldn't care.

He was crouched beside me a second later. Goblin shifted out of the way but didn't move far, staying pressed to my side, tail thumping once against the seat before going still.

"Dollface, look at me," Bones said, voice low and firm. "You're okay. You're not dying. You're having a panic attack."

"I—I c-can't—" I couldn't stop trembling. Couldn't get a breath in deep enough. Couldn't *think*.

"AB, grab the med bag. There's an inhaler in there and the grounding kit. *Now*." Bones' hands cupped my face, and I tried to meet his eyes, but everything was so *bright* and *loud* and *wrong*.

"I can't do this," I whispered. "I can't—I can't—"

"You're not going anywhere right now," Bones interrupted. "You're safe. You're not alone. You hear me? We're right here. You're not alone."

"Here." AB shoved something into Bones' hand, and a moment later a small, cool plastic piece was pressed against my lips.

"Just breathe. You don't have to think. Just do this with me, okay? In." He pressed the inhaler and the medicine flooded my lungs with a bitter, metallic taste. "Hold. Good. Now out."

I tried. God, I tried. Tears streamed down my face, and I wasn't even aware of them until Goblin started licking them gently.

"We're going to do the 5-4-3-2-1, Grace," AB said from somewhere nearby. I couldn't look at him. I couldn't do *anything* but shiver and shake. "Bones has you. Goblin has you. You're not in danger. You're not in the dark. You're not alone."

Bones shifted beside me, one arm wrapped around my shoulders now, his chest pressed against my side. He was solid and warm and *real*.

"Five things you can see," AB prompted. "Just say them. Anything. You don't have to think hard."

My gaze darted around, desperate and blurred. "Uh... steering wheel. Dashboard. Bones' jacket. G-Goblin's face. My—my boots."

"Good. Four things you can touch."

"My jeans... Bones' arm. Goblin's fur. The leather seat."

"Three things you can hear."

"Your voice," I choked out. "Goblin... whining. My—my breathing."

"Two things you can smell."

"Dog," I said. A weak, rasping laugh escaped me. "And mint."

"That's the inhaler," Bones murmured. "Last one, Doll-face. One thing you can taste."

I didn't even hesitate. "Fear."

They didn't laugh. Thank God, they didn't laugh.

"Okay," AB said, voice gentle. "Now you're back. That's all we needed. You're here. You made it."

I was shaking like a leaf, but the world had slowly started to come back into focus. The roaring in my ears dulled. My chest didn't feel like it was going to implode. And Goblin... God, that sweet baby didn't leave my side for a second. He licked at my fingers, then curled tighter against me, as if he could shield me.

"I'm sorry," I whispered, forehead pressed to the top of his head.

"Don't you *dare* apologize," Bones growled, but it was pain not anger. "You think we don't know what that feels like? You're allowed to panic. You're allowed to feel. Don't ever be sorry for it."

"We've all been there," AB added. "Hell, Bones punched a hole through a wall once during one."

"*You* punched a hole through a wall," Bones muttered.

"You *made* me punch the wall," AB shot back.

Somewhere in the middle of that absurd little exchange, I started breathing again. Really breathing.

"I didn't expect it to hit like that," I admitted, voice raw.

"You've been holding it together with duct tape and spite," AB said. "Don't be shocked when the tape gives out."

Bones shifted back slightly so he could look at me, brushing a thumb under my eye to wipe away the tears. "Next time, tell us it's building up. We'll help you bleed it out before it breaks loose."

I nodded. "Okay." Then, after a pause, "Thank you. Both of you."

"And Goblin," AB added. "He's the MVP."

Goblin woofed softly as if in agreement.

I gave his ears another scratch and finally straightened, the ache in my chest dulling. It wasn't gone. But it wasn't going to drown me now.

The guys gave me a few more minutes. Then Bones helped me out of the SUV, and Goblin hopped down to follow us. We were here. We were doing this.

And no matter how badly I wanted to fall apart again—I wasn't alone.

Not anymore.

TWENTY-SIX

ALPHABET

The safehouse was decent. Not our best, but far from our worst. Suburban, quiet, middle-of-the-road in that Virginia cookie-cutter way, with just enough space to spread out and not feel boxed in while also close enough to the neighbors that screaming would draw attention.

Which was great—unless you needed to do something messy. That made this a base of operations only. If we had to take prisoners or wage a war, we'd need to move. Still, we could do worse—at least they got food delivery here.

Speaking of which...

Me: *Get pizza. Do we know Gracie's favorite? Maybe grab some cinnamon roll stuffs or the pretzel bread sticks.*

Lunchbox: *She okay?*

Me: *She will be. Mild panic attack. Hit her with inhaler, and hydration. She's showering. She needs food and comfort.*

Voodoo: *Check her pulse 30 minutes post shower, and keep it easy. This isn't her first one...*

No, it wasn't. But it was her worst, at least in my opinion.

Me: *We have her. Goblin has her.*

Of all of the backup we had on this mission, Goblin was the best.

Lunchbox: *We'll be there in under an hour. Two more stops. Make it 90 to get the pizza.*

It was growing dark outside, so that would work. Between the time change and the flight, we'd spent most of the day in the air. For once, I was glad that flying east cost us time. It meant it was too late to dive in to that meeting immediately and gave her time to recover.

I set up in the dining room, which we were absolutely *not* using to eat. The big, cheap table gave me space to fan out my gear. Three laptops, each running off separate VPNs, one hardline connected through a buried signal repeater out back. Took me thirty minutes to get everything linked up and encrypted, and another five to push the deadbolt firewall layers I liked to have humming in the background while I poked around places I had no business being.

Bones hovered just long enough to install a few hidden cameras inside and out, check the windows, the basement egress, and stash a gun behind the pantry shelving. We had motion alerts set, two separate wireless feeds, and a panic protocol if anything went sideways. Goblin wandered through once, gave me a sniff like he needed to confirm I was still doing my job, then plopped himself under the table near my feet. He was loyal. Probably smarter than half the analysts I used to work with, too.

The shower turned on upstairs. Grace. She hadn't said much since the panic attack, but the shell-shocked look in her eyes had eased. Some. She was quiet, but not numb. Alert, but not twitchy.

Still—every sound from up there? Pretty sure all three

of us clocked it. Not because we didn't trust her. Because we *did*.

"She's not gonna break," Bones said behind me as he came in, tracking snow onto the floor. "But she's carrying more weight than she knows."

"Yeah," I murmured, not looking up from my screen. "She'll keep walking with the knife in her gut until someone tells her to sit down."

He grunted in agreement, then stepped around the table and crouched beside me. I angled the second laptop toward him. "Wanna help?"

"Depends on what I'm helping with," he said, but his fingers were already flying over the keys, pulling up one of the dummy profiles we'd created.

"We got into Sinclair's firm's client portal using an old vendor login. Real estate partner in Colorado forgot to update his security after he quit. System still thinks he's on the payroll."

Bones snorted. "Rookie mistake."

"Yeah, well, thank God for that. I'm in. Now I need to drill down into Sinclair's schedule—meetings, hearings, conference calls, anything the firm tracks."

I leaned forward and typed in a secondary search on the third laptop. "While you do that, I'm scanning the firm's internal calendar and building access logs. If we can confirm what days Sinclair actually *shows up* to the office versus the bullshit he inputs in his calendar? We can start planning around where to intercept him."

"Cornering a lawyer," Bones said. "I like this job more and more." The lack of humor in his voice decried that statement, but I got it.

"Not just any lawyer. *The* lawyer." The tone of my voice

flattened, the weight of it pressing down behind my ribs. I kept my hands moving. Click. Scroll. Query. Execute.

I needed the rhythm. The focus. Because if I thought too long about the fact that Grace's sister worked for this guy, and the more we looked, the more it seemed like he was involved, the more I thought about just scratching him off. The trash didn't always take itself out, sometimes you had to burn it.

"Don't forget to breathe," Bones said without looking up.

"Don't forget I can erase your entire financial footprint if you piss me off," I shot back.

He smirked. "That's adorable."

Goblin huffed like he agreed with him. Little traitor.

"Okay," I muttered, refocusing. "Sinclair logs into the firm's internal system most mornings between eight fifteen and eight thirty. Same IP. Home office—Georgetown area. He doesn't use the building keycard until around ten. That lines up with the data I'm seeing on the security logs. So either he works from home part of the morning, or he's lying about it entirely."

"He got court any of those days?"

"Only Wednesday," I said, tapping a key to bring the docket onto the second screen. "Circuit court, family law case. Weird."

"Why weird?"

"He doesn't usually handle these types, he's more corporate schmooze than family defender."

Then again, maybe his client was one of his corporate schmoozes.

"He's the rep on record, though," I continued "That means *he* has to show up."

"Where?" Bones asked.

"Alexandria Courthouse. Eleven a.m." I rubbed the bridge of my nose. "That's our window. Midweek, tight security at the courthouse, but he'll have to park nearby. If we wanted to spook him into a mistake—"

"We don't spook," Bones interrupted, his voice low. "We don't warn. We watch. We wait. Public confrontation is going to be far safer than one in his office. Once we've got him, then we send her in to see him."

I leaned back and blew out a slow breath. "Then we watch. And wait. Wednesday's our best shot. Unless we get lucky and he walks into a bar alone."

"He's not the bar type."

"Yeah," I said. "He's the suit who pours himself a double of whiskey in his home office after gaslighting his client into thinking she's safe."

Bones didn't argue. Just went quiet. The kind of quiet that meant his brain was already cycling through scenarios and backups and the best way to apply just enough pressure to make a man crack.

The shower stopped upstairs. We both went still for a half-second. Goblin's ears perked up, but he didn't move from under the table. Then we heard the creak of the bathroom door and her footsteps padding softly down the hallway toward the guest room.

We didn't say anything, but I felt Bones' tension ease by degrees.

"Let me know if she comes down," I said. "I want her to see this. Not all of it, but enough to know we're not shooting blind anymore."

"I'll bring her a cup of tea," Bones said, standing and cracking his neck. "She likes the honey vanilla one."

I nodded, not remotely tackling the comment of Bones making her tea. It was absolutely cute, but right now, she needed and *deserved* the care. "I'll make the maps. You run through the intel on his schedule and once we brief her, we'll let Gracie decide how she wants to do her approach."

Bones looked at me for a beat. "You sure?"

"No." I tapped the keyboard again and brought up Sinclair's personal calendar—the one he hadn't shared with the firm, but which was syncing in the background through his assistant's device. "But she needs to be part of it." She needed to be the one to break him even if it broke her.

She'd already broken once today.

And still? She got up.

Which meant when it was time—when we had this bastard in our sights—Grace would be the one to confront him. The shock of the meeting might do exactly what we wanted it to do and jar a confession out of him.

Liars often needed time to perfect the lie, rock them enough and the truth could be shaken free.

If he was involved...

Then we'd bury him.

By the time Lunchbox and Voodoo made it to the house with supplies—food, clothing, and electronics along with weapons—Gracie had come back down, showered and in better spirits. She was still paler than I'd like. The surprise on her face when Bones brought her the cup of tea almost made me laugh.

Her soft thank you, though, that was the kind of thing that wrapped a noose around me and yanked tight. The three of us worked, Gracie reading the reports we'd put together, Bones pulling more on Sinclair and his partners, as well as his senior associates.

It wasn't *quite* a boutique firm, but it was definitely one where the partners made the decisions and the people at the bottom were the ones left doing all the heavy lifting. I was right about his corporate leanings. He handled a lot of foreign trade negotiations, acquisitions, and mergers.

In no way was he a *family* attorney, that made me dig into the person he was representing in the Alexandria Family Court. His client was a man named Emanuel Mendoza—no photos were handy, no social media footprint, and no associated corporation.

Who the fuck was Emanuel Mendoza? The more I dug, the less I found and that just about set off every alarm I had. I was still chewing over that when we took a break from the computers to eat the pizza and get the debrief from Lunchbox and Voodoo.

They were pretty succinct in their summation of the firm, its security, and access. "It's not the easiest place to penetrate," Lunchbox said as he added another slice of pizza to Gracie's plate before he took a bite of his own.

She'd gone for the straight pineapple pizza, no meat, no veggies. Just cheese and fruit.

I kind of liked it.

They brought two large versions of it—one with a hand-tossed crust and the other thin. She preferred the thin, I took the hand-tossed.

"So," Lunchbox said when they finished going over everything they'd picked up. "What is the plan?"

As a group, we all looked at Bones. He grunted then downed an entire bottle of water before he rose to get a beer. He brought back five bottles and opened one after the other for us. When he handed one to Grace, she gave it the most inelegant little sniff before knocking back a long drink.

Amusement curled through me. She loved to yank his chain and she was so damn good at it. Good for him. Good for all of us really. Bones actually slept more these days. Lunchbox had gotten more creative in not only his cooking but his explosives. Voodoo had relaxed for the first time in —forever really.

As for me?

Gracie made me smile. She also made me want to put down a lot of assholes so she never had to deal with them again. Unfortunately, the world tended to frown on the eliminate the problem at the root theory. Still...

We had been cleaning up a lot over the past several months. That we let O'Rourke go... Well, I was still mulling on that one too. "Before I forget, I got an update on O'Rourke." It had come in thirty minutes earlier, but I was a little too focused on Mendoza to worry about that asshole.

"If he's not wearing a toe tag somewhere," Voodoo said. "We can skip that briefing."

A flicker of a smile over Lunchbox's face, but there was no mistaking the tension that tightened his eyes. Bones merely glanced at me. "Do we care?"

"Probably not, but in the interests of keeping us all aware, he's surfaced at a golf resort outside of San Diego. The broken leg is definitely slowing him down." The walk out of the desert on that broken leg probably hadn't been fun either.

Not that any of us cared when we dropped his ass off in the middle of nowhere, about three miles from no one gives a fuck and ten miles from anywhere Google maps had pictures. Not killing him was the only favor he'd earned by helping us get Bones back.

"Anyone of note at that resort?" Bones asked.

"No one we care about. But I have a program running to flag the people checking in and out, running it against a list of known problems. We'll see what we see."

One nod. "Then leave it for now. If he sticks his head out again, we'll blow it off. If he keeps his distance, he can keep his skull."

Gracie grimaced, but she didn't look green.

"Now," Bones continued. "Here is what we know and what we need to decide so we can go forward..."

TWENTY-SEVEN

GRACE

Even with food and their attempts at being light-hearted, the evening had settled into a heavy, almost oppressive quiet. The panic from earlier clung to me like static under my skin — a low, relentless hum that wouldn't quit. It wrapped me in scratchy wool, tightened at my throat, and made every small sound feel like a threat, so that smiling felt like wearing a costume I couldn't breathe in.

I curled up on the sofa in the unlit living room. The place's sparse furnishings and spartan aesthetic kind of appealed to me. Light crept in via the slats in the blinds and around the edges of the curtains. Not a lot of light, just the dim glow of the street lamps.

After dinner and the briefing, we'd split up and I'd gone up to sleep. It was the first time in a while that I'd just gone to bed by myself. I hadn't asked any of the guys to join me and they all seemed pretty busy. Staying in bed though, proved even more challenging. My thoughts kept racing, piling on each other until they threatened to break out of my skull while the knot in my stomach refused to go away.

Each time I closed my eyes, I kept seeing Amorette but only from the corner of my eye. Each time I tried to look at her directly, she just... disappeared like so much smoke. We were finally in Virginia, finally going after her boss, and maybe, just maybe, going to get some answers.

So why was I actively dreading meeting Mark Sinclair? Why did I just want to leave? I never wanted to abandon Am. So what was my problem?

Bones found me there, curled up on the sofa, my knees drawn to my chest. The soft click of a door opening upstairs and another closing barely registered. I didn't even look up until he spoke.

"Grace?" His voice, a low, concerned rumble cut through the silence like a knife.

The last thing I wanted to do was talk and I really didn't want to break down again. Even as I met his gaze, I couldn't figure out how to verbalize that. How to—

"Grace?" The way he said my name when he repeated it, soft and questioning just added to my heart ache. I didn't want anyone to see me like this, all vulnerable and broken. It was too late, however, he crossed the room, his steps not making a sound because he moved like a ghost.

His presence draped me like one of those weighted blankets. Glancing upward, I met his gaze and the concern reflected in his eyes damn near undid me.

"What's wrong, Dollface?" he asked, his voice gentler than I'd ever heard it. Kneeling in front of me, he placed his hands lightly on my knees. Warmth radiated out from him alerting me to the chill that iced over me.

"Couldn't sleep," I managed to say. My voice barely climbed above a whisper, rough like sandpaper. "Tried for a while. Gave up. Came down here to think." The words tasted like ash in my mouth, bitter and hollow. Bones nodded, his expression unreadable, and for a moment, we just sat in silence.

"About what?" he finally asked, his gruff tone a gentle prod.

I hesitated, the words catching in my throat, but something in his eyes urged me to continue. "About everything," I said. That seemed so—lame somehow. Everything could mean the pizza we had for dinner as well as the tracker they had to dig out of me a few months earlier. "About us. About what's happened. What comes next. What might happen."

I pressed my lips together to stop the damn tremble when it started.

"I'm scared," I said, trying to encompass the "everything" in one emotion and I wasn't all that positive that word was even right. "Scared to go back. Scared to go forward. Scared about what I'll find."

Chickenshit never got anyone anywhere and yet the quaking inside of me seemed to increase with each word. Curling my fingers into my palm, I tried to still the trembling vibrating its way through me.

"Tell me?" The entreaty was a request, not an order. That alone made me want to tell him.

Blowing out a breath, I let one my hands settle over his. "I'm probably just overthinking it..."

"Maybe," he said, with a shrug. "But until you talk about it, I can't really give you an informed opinion."

There was just something about the rough timbre of his voice as he said *informed opinion*, that made me smile. "You and I usually yell it out."

"So?" He threw the challenge down. "Do you need an argument to let it out?"

"No..." I sighed, closing my eyes as I gripped his hand. He turned his hand over until he could cradle my palm with his. One breath. Two. Then, I opened my eyes once more. "Ever since you found me...or the Vandals found me and got me out, I've been so focused on finding Am. Then on what was in the way to finding her. Getting home. Getting away from you guys."

I gave him a small smile of apology, but he just nodded his head and squeezed my hand.

"It was always about the next thing we had to survive so I could get back to the hunt. Or get to the hunt at all. Even the past few months while I found a way to *wait*, I kept telling myself one more thing, then we would do this and find her."

Tears I didn't want to shed clogged my throat and I tilted my head back, trying to keep them in.

"And now, we're close, you're worried that the answers you find won't be the ones you want to find."

Each word landed a staccato blow against my heart. "I'm scared that we're not going to find any answers. That she really is gone..."

My voice dropped to a ragged whisper at the end. I didn't want to manifest that. I didn't want to even put that out into the universe, yet, here we were.

"I'm scared that we will find answers but the answer is she is gone... forever." As hard as I fought to keep the tears contained, a hiccup of a sob escaped. Bones shifted, his hands sliding under me as he lifted me up and sat back on the sofa with me in his lap. "I don't know what's worse. Not ever finding out or finding out that she is gone."

Because either way, I would have lost her.

The tears slipped past the boundary, sliding down my face one after another. Nothing kept them inside and when he pulled me closer, I pressed my face into the crook of his neck. With care that once upon a time, I couldn't have imagined he possessed, he rubbed my back in slow circles.

The dam broke and real sobs tore out of me. I didn't want to cry but that seemed to matter even less right now. The emotion ripped through me like a hurricane, flattening me in its wake. Losing Am would kill me. For months, that was exactly what I fought against even considering.

She had to be alive.

She had to be out there.

She had to be—because if she wasn't, then I'd never see her again.

I had no idea how long we were there, but I cried until my eyes were swollen, my nose snotty, and my face a blotchy mess. I'd soaked the collar of his shirt. The greenish yellow remnants of his bruises were still visible over that collar. A lot had healed.

But not all of them. He was still hurting, but he was here with the others. They were all here, working on this for me just like they promised.

"Dollface." He cupped my chin again, then slid his hand up to my cheek before gliding it into my hair and fisting it. The pressure soothed some of the jagged feeling prickling over and under my skin. "You with me?"

I blinked.

A tear escaped, sliding down my cheek and carrying the salty dampness to the corner of my mouth.

"I'm here," I said after a long moment, probably too long. The wound inside me split wide open, bleeding without mercy, and I had no idea how to stop it. No clue how to stitch it shut and keep my focus where it needed to be — on Mark Sinclair, that law firm, and playing Am like my life depended on it.

No, not my life—Am's.

A stroke of his thumb glided over the upper curve of my cheek. "You are *not* alone."

Four simple words and they sliced right through the noise in my head, arresting my attention.

"You will never be alone on this quest. We will be with you every step of the way." It was a promise. An oath. "You are the priority, you have been for far longer than I wanted to admit. That makes your sister, *ours* to find as well."

The emphasis on "ours" was not lost on me.

He searched my eyes as he continued to trace his thumb against my cheek in a petting motion.

"We *will* find her. Alive or dead."

I flinched.

"I know you don't want to think of her that way, so don't. That's not your job. Your job is to focus on finding your sister and pouring all of that dynamite energy into finding her. I'll take care of the rest."

Swallowing around the lump in my throat, I raised my eyebrows. "You will?"

"Hell yes, I will. You have my word, Grace. No matter what we find, no matter how long it takes, we *will* find your sister." His voice was low, steady, assured. He meant every single word. Alive or.. No. We would find her.

He said to focus on the positive. I could do that.

"Bones?" At his raised brows of inquiry, I asked, "What's your real name?"

Amusement bled into his fierce expression, but he didn't retreat from where he kept one hand in my hair, the other on my face. He kept me right there with him, but I didn't want to run away. "Caylon," he said. "Caylon Gwyar."

I blinked. "That was the name on the passport at the hotel and on the card..."

He just hummed an affirmative.

Disbelief feathered through me. "You were using your real identity?"

"I wasn't hiding from anyone, Dollface. That was you."

I opened my mouth to argue, but snapped it closed when it hit me that he was absolutely correct. I had been the one who'd been trying to stay out of sight.

"Caylon," I said slowly, testing the sound of it. Voodoo didn't look like a Bryant to me, but Legend was definitely Legend and I wasn't using Lunchbox again if I didn't have to. But Caylon?

"You don't like it?" More humor flickered in his eyes.

"I don't hate it," I promised him. "Just not sure I can think of you as Caylon. Do you prefer Bones to Caylon?"

He gave a shrug. "I've been Bones for over sixteen years. I don't know that I'd remember to answer to 'Caylon.' Hell, Captain Gwyar sounds downright fucking odd to me."

Leaning into his hand, I half-closed my eyes. "I'll call you whatever you want," I said. "I just... it felt weird not knowing."

"Do you feel better now that you know?"

Lashes lifted, I met his gaze again. "I don't know. It definitely doesn't feel worse. Now I just have to figure out AB's."

His half-smile became a full one. "Would you like the intelligence, Dollface?"

I blinked again. "Doesn't that break like some bro code or something to tell me?"

"No. It's hardly classified. He just doesn't like how much shit he used to get for his name. Hence Alphabet."

Chewing on my lower lip, I turned that idea over in my head.

"If you want to know, Dollface, especially if it will help you feel better—he won't mind."

God, he sounded so absolutely certain. I wanted to be that certain. "I should wait for him to tell me. It seems only fair."

"If you change your mind..." He left the offer to hang there, but the intensity in his eyes didn't waiver. "Now, will you let me help you feel better?"

The husky offer stroked over my senses as deftly as his fingers caressed my cheek. I ran my tongue over my lower lip. "What did you have in mind?"

"You," he answered in that same, low, heated voice. "Me." Then he gave the room a sweep of a look before glancing back at me, The hunger suddenly blazing in his eyes sent shivers down my spine. There was nothing detached or distant about him.

"That's—very basic." It was actually a bit of a struggle to get those words out because the temperature in the room had gone from chilly to scorching in the space of a few seconds.

"I'm a basic kind of guy," he said without a hint of irony. He reached for the blanket I had over my lap and peeled it away. Then he was tugging me forward by the hips—wait, no, by my pajama bottoms.

I'd put the penguin-decorated fleece pair on more for comfort than anything else. He swept his gaze over them even as he hooked his fingers into the elastic waistband.

"Penguins." The dry intonation made me giggle.

"Not sexy," I said, feeling some of the anxiety drain away. "I know."

"The packaging never has to be sexy, Dollface." Then he peeled the fleece leggings straight down along with my panties. I slid half down until I was laying more on the seat than sitting on it and he caught my ass before I fell off. "It's what's inside that counts."

He took a deep breath and every muscle inside of me just *clenched*. All the witty comments and retorts dried up as all that ferocious power housed in his wild gaze sent liquid fire spilling through my system.

"You know..." I finally managed as he glided a hand along my leg to lift it up and over his shoulder. The rest of the sentence escaped me as he mouthed a kiss against the inside of my thigh. The scrape of his teeth had my pussy tightening even as the rasp of his stubble sent ripples up to turn my nipples taut.

The sweet, earthy heat of his breath teased right across my slit and I dug my fingers into the cushion. Not even the cooler air of skating over my skin could dampen the wildfire that little maneuver provoked.

"I know?" he prompted as he dragged one finger along my labia until he could circle my clit. The contact was right there, but he didn't quite connect. I'd gone from drowning in sorry to swept away by desire.

Huffing, I forced my gaze back to him. "What?"

One corner of his mouth quirked upward. "You said, 'you know...'"

I had?

"What do I know?"

I went utterly blank at the question. "No idea." And no, I wasn't going to try to fake it. "Don't care either."

"You sure?" Another stroke of that finger, the callused pad on his fingertip adding a hint of roughness to the soft tease. My hips bucked as I strained to follow his motion, but he pinned me in place.

"Bones..." I exhaled.

"Yes, Grace?" His voice—low, velvet-wrapped sin—brushed over my skin like a touch I craved far too much.

It wasn't fair, the way he looked at me. Like I was already his. Like he *knew* I would come undone just from the way he said my name. And God help me, I was. Melting from the inside out, undone by nothing more than that voice.

"Nothing," I murmured, throat tight. "Just... needed to say your name."

A downright devilish twinkle lit up his usually stern eyes, like mischief had slipped past the guard. It wasn't a wink, but it hit harder, hotter—more erotic than any deliberate flirtation.

"Feel free to say it as often as you need." The playful offer knocked the breath from my thoughts, leaving me dazed and a little undone. Before I could really process it, his finger found my clit.

The teasing path of his strokes grew tighter and added pressure to that bundle of nerves. It sent jolts of pleasure straight to my core. He didn't look away as he drove me right to the edge of orgasm. No matter how much I squirmed, though, he didn't let up on the storm of sensation that built within me to unbearable heights.

This time when his name fell from my lips, it was a plea. A demand.

A need.

When he pulled his hand away, I whimpered. "No... come back..."

"Shh," he hushed me, that same dark, decisive tone curling around the order like velvet and smoke. It was a command, a caress, and a promise—seductive and soothing all at once.

I didn't have time to process any of that because he slid

both of his hands beneath my ass and lifted me up to his mouth. Then his tongue, teeth, and lips alternated between licking caresses and deep, biting sucks that detonated my orgasm until I screamed.

Not seemingly satisfied with that once, he didn't let up. Unwavering in his devotion, he squeezed my ass as he thrust his tongue inside then stroked it back up to my clit. The demand in his touch was so fierce, it promised me a return to that edge and he barely let me come down from one orgasm before he smashed me headfirst into another.

The intensity wrapped around me, squeezing out every drop of pleasure only to infuse me with another layer of want and need. Then he moaned and I splintered. The sound vibrated against my core and I fisted his hair even as I ground upwards against his mouth.

I wanted everything he was offering. Wanted it. Needed it. Demanded it. Bones delivered on every single part, wrenching another flood of release from me that had my back bowing and my mind whiting out.

When I surfaced once more, it was with a sensual haze draping everything. Bones watched me, his eyes dark with desire and his cock throbbing against my thigh. He'd moved, stripped his clothes, and... he was *right* there. All masculine heat and contained energy, a tempest in a bottle.

"You with me again?" he murmured, his voice a low purr.

"Always." It was a promise, and a confession. From the first moment Bones touched me, I swore he'd understood my body even better than I did. I adored everything he did to me. Even more now that he let me touch him too.

"I'm a greedy man," he confessed, and there was an unexpected softness beneath the hunger. "Greedy for your pleasure. Your laughter. You."

"So…" I tried to cobble together the patchwork of thoughts that kept breaking apart. Particularly because he'd gotten naked at some point. I was still in my sleep tank, but I really didn't care about me.

Not waiting for me to sort out the syllables, he stroked a finger down my cheek to my lips then to my throat. When he wrapped his hand around my neck, I shuddered.

"Yes?" A query. A demand. An order.

"Yes," I said, more than happy to comply. Not that it rushed him along, the man's control was just… superhuman. He fisted himself with his free hand and began to stroke his tip along my slit. Tiny eddies of pleasure burst with each teasing touch.

He groaned, a deep, guttural sound that vibrated through his chest and into me.

"Legs around me," he issued the order with all the confidence of a man who would be obeyed. Since I absolutely arched to hook my thighs to his hips, he wasn't wrong. "Good girl."

He nudged at my entrance, a single, testing nudge. I was so damn wet and ready for him. He must have agreed because he didn't make me wait.

With a low growl, he thrust forward and impaled me in one smooth stroke. The stretch was right on the point of pain, utterly perfect as it shoved all the air out of my lungs. Another cry burst out of me as he sank balls deep.

Not waiting for me to adjust to his girth, he rocked his hips, thrusting, and his cock slid in and out of me in a rhythm that was both brutal and beautiful. His breath seemed to be coming in the same ragged explosions as mine.

Every thrust ended with him bottoming out. I locked my legs to his hips and wrapped my hands around his forearm as he tightened his grip on my throat. He wasn't squeezing, not quite, but he kept me in place as he pounded into me with far more control than I possessed.

A genuine smile creased his face and it made my heart stop. Every push of his dick ignited sparks of pleasure in my system. The coils of pleasure and pressure, tightened to almost unbearable and, yet, he continued to drive me back onto the sofa.

I was so damn close. Too close. Bones stared down at me, his eyes almost perfectly dark as he held my gaze captive while he sheathed himself inside of me over and over. When he tightened his hand on my throat, the pressure expanded and blinded me as the pleasure exploded.

My body convulsed as my inner muscles spasmed around him. The orgasm ripped every thought from my head until I was just a creature of sensation, riding him as he slammed into me over and over again. It didn't take him long to follow me, his cock pulsing as he came in a rush of heat.

We stayed there, locked together. Bones eased his hand from my throat, letting it rest against the sofa. Our bodies entwined, his forehead pressed firmly against mine. The rapid panting of our breathing mingled the air between us, a dance of desire.

When I surged forward, he met me with a kiss that sparked like a live wire — a sudden blaze that lit up every nerve, igniting something wild and electric inside me.

The raging fire between us had already mellowed, and the kiss deepened as he teased my tongue with his. The softness called to my own, asking, teasing, offering and shifting from erotic demand to something far more profound.

His lips, once urgent, grew gentle, tracing mine with a

reverence that sent shivers cascading down my spine. The tension melted from his body, replaced by a slow-building warmth that wrapped around us like a shared breath.

The world around us fell away, fading into silence, leaving only the pulse between us — real, raw, and alive. In that moment, there was no past, no future. Just now. Just us. A sanctuary forged in the quiet press of lips and the space between us.

CHAPTER

TWENTY-EIGHT

LUNCHBOX

The courthouse steps loomed ahead like a bad omen in good lighting. The architecture was clean, symmetrical, and self-assured. It was also cold, distant, and far too open for my tastes. The same could be said for Grace, I guess. Except right now, she wasn't Grace.

Today, she'd taken the role of an attorney: Amorette Black, her twin sister. She walked with a kind of purpose that said power, class, and assurance. It was almost spooky how well she vanished into this role. We'd never met her twin, but Grace possessed a kind of innate sensuality and playful charm that filled her every interaction whether she was throwing a brick at our heads or teasing us in bed.

This role as her sister? It wasn't her. They might be identical, but I'd never mistake one for the other. They were so different, beautiful—but different. Gracie?

She was *ours*.

"She's going in," I said, low into the mic.

"Copy that," Alphabet replied from the van a block

279

down. "Got eyes on north and east. Goblin's chewing something, I think it used to be a protein bar."

Goblin made a rude noise in the background. Alphabet laughed. Considering we got protein bars for the Staffy, he'd probably scored himself a treat. I shifted against the stone planter where I'd taken a seat to "eat" lunch and have a coffee.

It was cold out here, the air bitter and dry. It had snowed recently, but they'd had more than enough time to clear the streets and sidewalks. There was still snow frozen on the green spaces, but everything else was dry and clear.

For now.

The sun had been out the day before, but today had started out steely gray and seemed determined to take an icy turn. I checked my watch as Grace made it to the top of the steps.

"She looks like she's going to war," Voodoo mused in my ear. "Anyone else turned on by those heels?"

I snorted, but before I could reply, Bones said, "Too sedate. She needs more height and definitely more color."

"She could take an army," I said easily enough. "It's not the shoes."

"Nope," Alphabet said, though the smile in his voice echoed down the comms. "It's definitely that sway she just added to her hips."

Grace paused at the top step and glanced back. While she didn't look at any of us specifically, she did adjust her sunglasses with her middle finger. I damn near laugh out loud.

"How is her tracker reading?" Bones asked.

"Five by five," Alphabet said. "Give us a little kiss, Gracie, when you get inside. Want to make sure it stays that way."

"Hmm." The little hum carried. Since she was "working," she could hear us and we could hear her, but she wasn't supposed to talk to us.

"Almost wish we weren't working," Voodoo mused. "We could play a game of who can get her to swear loudest."

"Focus," Bones ordered. "She's inside."

"I got her." Voodoo was already in the building and had a backup comms for her in case hers triggered the metal detectors. It shouldn't, but never say never.

It was hard not to stare at the doors to the courthouse like I could see through them. Maintaining a relaxed posture wasn't that challenging. Sounds filtered in via the comms.

Security.

Why was she there?

Meeting another attorney from her firm.

Which one?

Mark Sinclair.

Ah. Second floor.

Step on through, but the briefcase has to go through the x-ray scanner. And she's in,

"Excellent." Alphabet was pleased. The ID passed muster. Of course it did, but still.

"Miss Black..." A voice called and I cocked my head to the side.

"Fuck," Voodoo muttered. "Incoming image." I didn't have to imagine him snapping a photo and sending it to us. My phone dinged a few moments later. Five foot four, blonde, with impossibly long hair, dressed in a pantsuit, but looking pale and worried.

"Miss Black," the woman said again. I could almost *feel* the deep breath that Grace took.

"Joan Reilly, homemaker, recently divorced, re-entering the workforce—she's actually also enrolled at Northern Virginia Community College working on an administrative degree. Two kids. Piece of shit ex—oh, and he's in jail. Your sister represented her briefly last year on a housing matter—they were trying to evict her. Your sister got it halted and then turned around. Reilly is her maiden name. She never took her husband's." The swift thumbnail from Alphabet carried a genuine note of admiration.

I didn't disagree. Hard life for the woman, but she was surviving.

"Ms. Reilly," Grace said. Oh, that was unsettling. Even her voice changed. Still warm, but with... a different note. I couldn't quite put my finger on it. "It's good to see you."

"You too!" There was a rustle of fabric but a video had also popped up on my phone. Voodoo had a good view of the interaction. The woman had embraced Grace, a brief, polite type of hug that suggested a far friendlier relationship than an attorney and former client. "I heard you'd moved on to a different firm."

"I'm sorry, were you trying to reach me?" Grace's tone was calm, controlled and very much in charge, though it held distinct notes of care.

"I was, but it was kind of very last minute. Ronnie is being a dick."

"Ronald Grant," Alphabet was already reporting. "He's in jail, on month five of a thirty-eight month stretch."

Grace touched a hand to Reilly's arm and moved them aside from the foot traffic. "I thought he was still in jail."

The woman let out a long sigh. "He is, but his parents are suing me."

A frown tightened Grace's expression. "Visitation?"

"Checking," Alphabet said, but Reilly was already nodding.

"I don't... his father is abusive. I don't mind his mother seeing them. She's a good grandmother, and I wish I could convince her to leave her husband. He's worse than Ronnie."

"Guy's got a record and she's not wrong," Alphabet said with a whistle. "Wouldn't hurt anyone if he got hit by a bus tomorrow."

"Are you trying to work out an agreement with her?"

"Yes." Another long, almost wet sigh as the woman folded her arms. The weight of it all seemed to be crushing her. "I told Phyllis—his mom—she's more than welcome to come spend time with the kids at my place. I've even invited her to a couple of the birthday parties and to the park. But her husband...he wants Nathan to spend weekends with them, and more..."

"Nathan, age seven, and Matilda, age five." Alphabet was definitely feeding her what she needed.

"We need to move her along," Bones said, though it wasn't unfeeling or harsh. I doubted he liked hearing the defeat in this woman's voice anymore than we did.

"Nathan?" Grace said slowly. "Not Matilda?"

The angle hid half of her face, but her mouth had firmed. Yeah, she'd caught that too. Reilly nodded. "He doesn't care about Matilda, just Nathan. Wants to man him up and a bunch of other misogynistic bullshit. I just want him to be safe and that man is always drinking, yelling, and hitting his wife. I will *not* let Nathan be exposed to that."

"Tell me you found someone good to represent you." Even as her sister, the steel came out in her voice. Or maybe they both possessed that. Would make sense.

"I do! Melinda Cho. You recommended her last year

when we were talking about the house and about future family issues. Ronnie can't see the kids because I have a restraining order and he's in jail. I don't even have to take them to see him. But his parents..."

Now Grace reached out to take Reilly's hand and clearly, she was squeezing it. "Good, Melinda's tough as nails. Listen to her and make sure you do everything by the book, but also document everything. You are still doing that right?"

"Oh yeah, I never forgot that lecture. I've logged all their calls, everything he's said, all the things I've witnessed both before and after. I also have some photos—they're old family photos of Ronnie's but you can see the abuse in the pictures. Bruises that pop up in odd places. The lost look in Phyllis' eyes."

"I'm glad you're still doing it. Every piece of data helps and if you have a clear log that shows you have documented each movement, that is evidence a judge can take into account." Then Grace held up her hand. "I'm so sorry, Ms. Reilly..."

"I told you, you can call me Joan. You said I could call you Am, but it seemed kind of weird to yell that in here." She huffed out another breath then caught Grace's hand again for another squeeze. "You have to go."

"I do. Listen to Melinda. Keep documenting. Maybe see if your mother-in-law will go to a counseling session—or a shelter."

Was it me or did Grace really want to help this woman? Some of it was the part, sure, but she was really focused on her.

"I don't know, but I'll try. Please, go, I don't want to make you late."

A flash of a quick, almost apologetic smile on Grace's

face before she turned to continue. I caught the moment she spotted Voodoo. There was a brief moment of recognition but her expression didn't ripple.

Good girl.

"Guys," she almost said it on an exhale.

"I'll see what we can do," Alphabet answered. "But not right now. Let's focus on Sinclair while we're here."

A single nod of acknowledgement.

She took a controlled breath then headed toward the bank of elevators before she paused and glanced at the stairwell. The elevator was a tight location, one entry, one exit. But Voodoo was already up and heading for the stairs. The image cut in and out as he climbed.

"Sinclair is..." Alphabet told her which courtroom and which judge. The whole plan hinged on what Sinclair did when he saw her. "Voodoo, you'll have to lose the phone video if you go into the courtroom. Switch to lapel camera."

"Got it." The sound of a door closing carried.

He made the switch to lapel cam before he was out of the stairwell. The video feed cut, and the new one took a moment. It came back in, low resolution and a little snowy, but definitely visible.

Grace was leaving the elevator along with a few others. She scanned the different signs, then headed for the one for Judge Wharnack's courtroom.

Wharnack. That name sounded like he should be a cartoon character. I took another swallow of coffee.

"Deep breaths, Dollface," Bones said, his voice steady and calm. "You're panting. Pause. Take a breath. This is *your* op. You have the control."

A few steps from Wharnack's courtroom, she stopped and put a hand against her abdomen. She took a controlled breath. Another. Then another. The rigid line of her shoulders eased and her expression shifted to neutral.

She'd buried all of her usual fire under layers of plausible deniability and an airtight demeanor. "Ready," she murmured the word, it was barely audible. Then she was moving. As she opened the door, a bailiff was right there at the door and he glanced from her to Voodoo then motioned for them to take a seat.

Grace moved toward the third row back from the front. Voodoo took the last row and he had a good angle for her.

A better angle for Sinclair.

There was a hum of white noise, and two attorneys were at the front of the court talking to the judge. No clients visible, maybe the clients didn't have to be here?

We still didn't have a bead on Mendoza, so we'd work on that.

The white noise vanished, then the judge motioned the attorneys to step back. Sinclair was easily recognizable, even without his standard firm portrait.

Hyper-slick. Corporate veneer. A guy who used his clients like leverage, his assistants like furniture, and everyone else? Collateral.

I wish we had some zoom capability. Sinclair looked pleased with himself, for all of three seconds. He blanched when he caught sight of Grace. No way to mistake how all the color drained from his face and how *stared* at her like he'd seen a ghost.

I cracked my knuckles.

Mark Sinclair was guilty as fuck.

CHAPTER

TWENTY-NINE

GRACE

I felt it before I saw him.

That shift in the air—an almost imperceptible pressure drop, like the room had collectively inhaled and then forgot how to breathe. My heels struck the court-room floor with crisp, calculated taps, the rhythm of someone in control. I counted them. Three steps in. One heartbeat. Two.

And then there he was.

Mark Sinclair.

He looked exactly like his picture, almost insultingly so. Smooth lines, slicked-back hair, smug jawline, and a designer suit so expensive it practically had an ego of its own. But that smugness cracked the instant our eyes met.

I didn't smile.

I didn't blink.

I didn't breathe.

And neither did he.

For a second—maybe less—he just stared. No greeting, no recognition twitch, no fake professionalism. Just raw, naked *fear*. The kind you try to hide behind a poker face, but it leaks out through your eyes anyway.

I'd worn my sister's favorite lipstick. Not mine. She liked tones that bled confidence. I'd also worn her scent—a sharp blend of citrus and heat. It burned in the back of my throat every time I breathed in, but I needed the armor.

Because I wasn't Grace right now.

I was Amorette—attorney, cool-headed legal warrior, and exactly the woman Mark Sinclair never wanted to see again. If I had any questions before, I had *none* now.

His Adam's apple bobbed. His fingers twitched on the folder in his hand. I watched him try to recover, try to paste on that polite little smirk he probably used on every junior associate he was two seconds away from backstabbing.

It didn't work.

And I *savored* it.

A polite nod was all I gave him. Just enough to be formal, not enough to be familiar. Because in this courtroom, I didn't need to shout. I didn't need to slam doors or throw accusations. All I had to do was sit down, cross one leg over the other, and let him stew in the silence.

He wasn't the only one watching.

I could feel the weight of Voodoo's gaze from the back row. I knew Bones, AB, Legend—all of them—were hearing every shift in my breathing, every pause in my steps. I didn't let myself think about that.

Not right now.

Right now, this was about *Sinclair*.

I almost hoped he tried to escape. Almost.

But I wanted to be the one who confronted him, who got the truth, and if that required beating it out of him—a shiver went through me though I maintained and didn't react—I wanted to be the one who punched him.

Even if the guys could do it harder.

"Mr. Sinclair..." The judge's voice cut through the roaring silence that had ballooned out from where my gaze held Sinclair's. His jerk to pivot and face the judge, broke the eye contact.

My pulse rabbited for a moment, the rapid and intensely *hard* thud of it, beating in my ears.

"Breathe." Bones.

One word in his voice and the vise around my chest eased allowing me to take a long, deep inhale. It helped. The judge was talking to Sinclair and the other attorney. I barely registered what the content was, I just kept my gaze fixed on Sinclair.

And he *knew* it.

He *had* to know, I was still watching him.

That I hadn't looked away.

That I wasn't going to.

Whatever thread of composure he'd managed to reel in for the judge's benefit seemed to fray by the second, and he couldn't figure out what to do with his hands. He set the folder down, then picked it up again. Smoothed a nonexistent wrinkle from the sleeve of his jacket. Shifted his weight from one foot to the other.

And still—my gaze stayed locked.

I didn't need to speak to make him sweat.

I *wanted* him to wonder how much I knew.

I wanted him asking himself how Am was here. If she was just an attorney who quit—well, we both knew that had been a lie. If I hadn't been dead certain of it before

The judge kept talking, oblivious to the slow bleed of panic radiating off Sinclair. He responded to a question with a clipped, "Yes, Your Honor," but his voice wasn't steady. Not really. Not if you were listening close enough.

I was.

He glanced at me again, quick and sharp, like a man checking for a sniper on the roof.

I tilted my head.

Just a little.

Nothing dramatic. Just enough to let him know: *I see you.*

I remember.

I'm not going anywhere.

He dropped his gaze first.

Good.

Let him wonder what came next.

The other attorney was speaking now, something about rescheduling a hearing due to a missing affidavit. The judge looked annoyed but not surprised. My stomach turned a little. That was the thing with guys like Sinclair—they always played just close enough to the edge of legal to be dangerous, but far enough from it to avoid jail time.

This time, he'd miscalculated.

The bailiff moved to the front, murmured something to the judge. Sinclair turned toward the bench, and I saw his profile tighten. Jaw clenched. One hand flexed at his side.

He felt trapped.

He should.

I leaned back in the pew—just a breath. Crossed my legs in the other direction. Shifted my briefcase slightly, letting the faint glint of my bar ID badge—the guys thought of everything—peek out. Not enough to draw attention from the court.

Just enough for *him.*

His eyes cut toward it like a whip crack.

There it was again—*fear.*

Sharp and wild behind those calculated eyes.

He hadn't planned for me.

He never planned for me.

Now he was off-script. I'd seen that kind of sweat bead on a man's upper lip before. Trapped.

I didn't smile.

But inside, I was *grinning*. It was probably more of a grimace, a baring of teeth. Didn't matter. He *knew*.

He fucking *knew*.

I wanted what he knew. I wanted to know what he'd *done*.

The judge dismissed them both with a few closing remarks. Sinclair stepped away from the table, gathering his folder, fumbling with the clasp. His polished veneer was slipping, fast. The other attorney moved past him without a second glance—probably used to his particular brand of rattled arrogance.

Sinclair turned toward the aisle.

And I stood.

Smooth, fluid, unapologetic. He stopped short. Just a half-step.

Like he wasn't sure whether to go around me... or through me.

He wouldn't do either.

"Play it cool, Firecracker," Voodoo murmured in my ear. "Don't spook him. Much."

But I wasn't spooking him.

I *was the spook.*

I met his eyes again. Let the silence stretch like a blade between us.

Then—finally—he found the nerve to move.

One foot in front of the other. Past me. But not before he

whispered, low and fast: "I don't know what you think you're doing."

I turned my head, just enough that he saw the flash of my smile.

"I think you do."

He didn't respond. Didn't look back.

But his shoulders? They were hunched like he'd just walked into a storm.

Because he had.

And this time, he wasn't going to walk out clean.

I didn't move until he was out the door. Even then, I gave it a beat. Just long enough to let him think he'd left me behind.

Then I turned and followed.

The hallway outside the courtroom was quiet, sterile. The fluorescent lighting buzzed above, faint and mechanical. I walked with purpose, heels striking tile, each step deliberate, steady. This wasn't a chase. It was a shadow. I wasn't hurrying.

I was closing in.

Sinclair had a decent lead, but not enough to matter. I rounded the corner and spotted the door swing of the men's restroom just as it eased shut.

Of course he ducked in there. Coward.

I kept walking until I reached the wall across from the bathroom, where I set down my briefcase and crossed my arms. No fanfare. No theatrics. Just a quiet sentinel.

And I waited channeling my inner Bones. The absolute relentless patience of the man who said he would never stop and never give up.

He had maybe thirty seconds before the walls started closing in.

Sixty before the mirror stopped reflecting his confidence.

Ninety before his pulse betrayed him in his ears.

"Talk to me, Dollface," Bones said in my ear, his tone low and smooth. "You tailing him?"

"Bathroom," I murmured. "Waiting outside."

A pause.

"Copy that. How's he look?"

"Panicked." I glanced at the door. "Trying not to be."

"Poor bastard," Voodoo chimed in, humor dry as kindling. "Nothing like a power piss to make you reevaluate your life choices."

I didn't reply. My focus was on the door.

Ten more seconds passed.

Fifteen.

Then it opened.

He stepped out.

I caught the moment he saw me, froze like he'd touched a live wire. Color gone. Forehead glistening. His hair, so perfectly slicked back earlier, now looked slightly damp at the roots.

He hadn't just peed. He'd tried to regroup.

Didn't work.

I tilted my head, slow and deliberate, watching him. Reading him.

He wiped his palms on the sides of his pants. The folder in his left hand was crumpled at the edge now. Not enough to be obvious to a judge or client.

But I saw it.

"You following me now?" he asked, voice low, brittle around the edges. He didn't step back, but he didn't come closer either.

"I'm observing," I said, letting Amorette's cadence slide

out—smooth, educated, just cool enough to cut. "It's a free hallway, isn't it?"

He glanced around, like someone might pop out of the shadows to save him. No one did.

Because no one *could*.

"I don't know what kind of game you think you're playing," he said, trying to recover that clipped tone lawyers used when pretending they weren't panicking. "But if you're looking for some kind of settlement or blackmail opportunity—"

"Mark."

His name stopped him cold. Not *Mr. Sinclair*.

Just *Mark*. Familiar. Personal. Dangerous.

"You should be very careful about assuming what I'm after." I stepped away from the wall, slowly, not closing the distance, not threatening, just *present*. What had Legend called me? A grenade with the pin out?

He backed up half a step. Not much. Just enough.

His throat worked. "I don't know who the hell you think you are—"

"You do," I said, and this time I let it slip, just a *fraction* of heat behind the words. "That's why you're sweating."

He looked like he wanted to argue. But he didn't. Couldn't.

So I nodded, gave him one more look, and stepped past him. My shoulder brushed his sleeve, and he flinched like I'd burned him.

I kept walking.

Didn't look back.

Not even when he turned to watch me go.

I didn't go far.

Turned the corner, past the elevators, into a shallow

alcove near the stairwell—just far enough to be out of sight, just close enough to keep eyes on the hallway.

Sinclair hadn't moved. He was still standing in front of the bathroom like he wasn't sure whether to run or pass out.

Then—finally—he shifted. Straightened his shoulders. Took a sharp breath like he was about to head into a deposition. He tucked the folder under his arm and started walking.

Right past the courtroom. Straight for the elevators.

Smart boy.

When the panic hits, get to the car. Get to the phone. Get to whatever backup plan you thought was going to save you.

"Voodoo," I said under my breath, already moving.

"Got him," came the smooth reply. "He's heading toward the west doors."

I took the stairs down. No need to pretend anymore. My heels clattered against the concrete, fast and sharp.

I exited through the east side and looped around the building's perimeter. There was a courtyard along the front step, mostly empty. A couple of lawyers talking near the benches. A security officer scrolling through his phone. Nothing that would hide him.

"He's almost out," Voodoo said. "Lunchbox get ready to tag in."

Sinclair burst out the west doors with that stiff-shouldered walk people use when they *think* they're composed. But his pace was too quick, his gaze too shifty. He hit the sidewalk and cut hard left, heading down the block with a hand already fishing for his phone.

He didn't even notice me half a building away, following his every move.

"Got him." Legend's voice crackled quietly in my ear. "He's calling someone. Not on his work phone."

"Burner?" Bones asked.

"Yup."

"Working on seeing if I can grab it." AB's tone was distracted, but if it could be done, he'd do it.

Sinclair turned the corner at the end of the block. I followed, keeping my distance, my pace steady, even. I could still hear him through Legend's comms mic.

"No, she's here. I told you—I saw her. She looked right at me."

There was a distinct pause, then...

"No, I don't think it's Amorette. It's not—something's off. I don't know. I don't *know*. I'm telling you this isn't good."

Legend murmured, "He's scared. Voice cracking. He's headed for the garage."

My stomach tightened. Underground garage meant fewer witnesses, fewer exits. If he bolted—if he *panicked*—we risked losing him before we had what we needed.

"Lunchbox stays with him," Bones cut in, his voice the calm in the center of the storm. "Dollface, roll it back."

I stopped moving mid-step.

"Time for step two," Bones said, firm. "You did what you needed to do."

I hesitated. Just for a second.

I could still see him—Sinclair pacing by a black car, waving his hands as he hissed something else into the burner. His hair was sticking to his forehead. His back was hunched. He looked like a man already digging his own grave.

God, I wanted to watch him fall in.

But this wasn't about *me*.

"Copy that," I whispered and it hurt to back off.
I turned. Let the city swallow him.
Let Legend follow.
Let Bones plan.
Let Sinclair *sweat*.
Step one was complete.
Now it was time to take him apart.

CHAPTER

THIRTY

GRACE

Peeled off my coat in the back of the van and let the team's low chatter fill the small space like static. The windows were fogged from the heat, the traffic a little stop and go on our way to Sinclair's place in McLean. My hands moved without thinking, redoing my hair to pull it into a tight knot. I shimmied out of the skirt, swapping it for slacks that Am would have loved, tailored with clean lines and excellent pockets.

Goblin stared at me, tongue lolling out as I switched out the button-down blouse for a slightly looser, but no less professional one. It was more casual professional, than smart and sober professional. I paused to scratch Goblin between the ears and his tail thumped.

Petting him settled me as much as it made him happy. I swapped the lipstick for gloss. In the mirror of my compact I checked the line at the corner of my mouth and the hard set of my jaw. The face staring back didn't feel like mine. It was sharper. It was *Am*. It made me miss her so much.

Bones glanced back from the passenger seat, his expres-

299

sion measuring. "You remember everything for step two or do we need to go over it again?"

We weren't improvising anymore. We were executing. I stuffed the sensible heels into the bag with my other discarded clothes. For a moment, a waft of the Am's favorite perfume all citrus and heat came up as I zipped the bag closed. I breathed it in and let it comfort me even as I readied myself for what was next.

"I remember," I said, proud of how steady I sounded. It was one thing to suspect her boss and her firm, it was completely something else to have it confirmed.

Legend's quiet voice threaded through the comms then: "Sinclair didn't head to the firm. He went to a hotel in the city—The Whitcomb. Went straight up to a room he already had a key for. He's on the phone. Looks like he's meeting someone. Still talking fast." There was a crackle of static and then, softer, "He's pacing near the window. Probably trying to buy time."

McLean was still the objective. His estate housed safe boxes and three different servers—AB had mapped them all —and whatever he kept close to his chest would be there. If Sinclair was meeting someone in DC, it only made the estate quieter. Easier to work undisturbed. Easier to let Legend watch the hotel and catch whatever crossed the city between Sinclair and his ghosts.

"Keep him on feed," Bones said. "Legend, you stay with him. If he takes a piss, you should be close enough to give him a hand."

When I made a face, Voodoo grinned then winked at me. Some of the armor plating around me softened. I was safe here. Safe with them.

"Alphabet," Bones continued, "you're on external cams at the estate. Voodoo, you've got the locks and we need to be ready for any forgery checks. We get what we need, then we take care of him."

Forgery checks. "Do you really think he'll have high end art and other valuables?"

"Yes," Voodoo answered before Bones could. "Using art, gold, and diamonds—it's a way to keep money clean and to pay for transactions you don't want the government looking at."

"What about his wife? Is she still out of town?" That was another sticking point.

Sinclair had a Mrs. Sinclair. No children of his own. That was good. But I couldn't remember Am ever mentioning the wife. To be fair, I didn't really remember my sister talking about most of the lawyers she worked with in particular. She took confidentiality very seriously. Didn't stop her from telling me stories, but they'd always had the names redacted.

"I think she's dead," AB said, surprising me and I wasn't the only one who snapped a look toward him. "I don't have any proof and I haven't been able to track any reports of her demise or what could have been done with her body, but she's been 'missing' for months. First it was a trip, then a cruise, then visiting 'friends.'"

All of which could be reasonable.

"But there are no calls home, no emails, no photographs from these various destinations. The people she allegedly traveled with do not exist or if they do, they come across more as paid actors than anything else." AB ticked each item off in a cool, rational voice that said he'd dug down.

The van hummed through the outskirts and the map on Legend's feed pulsed: Sinclair at The Whitcomb, phone to his ear, a shadow of a hand sweeping across a hotel room window.

Voodoo tapped my foot with his and I reached for the flats to put them on. I needed to look like I worked in the office, it was part of the plan to get in. But I also needed to be able to move.

We took the exit toward McLean. The trees loomed taller here, estates folding into one another like secrets. Bones' voice was clipped. "We're approaching the house," Bones said for Legend's benefit. "Once we're there, Grace takes point to get inside. Lunchbox, you stick with Sinclair, if he moves, alert us."

"If he heads for the house?" Legend's question wasn't an unreasonable one.

A beat of silence as Bones twisted to look back at me. All I did was raise my eyebrows. I wanted the man to show up. I was ready to ask him all the questions.

"Let him. We'll take care of him once he's here." Bones glanced ahead once more.

I blew out a long breath, both relieved and exhilarated. Yet, the tension inside of me coiled inexorably tighter. We were close. But how close? As close as it felt, it also felt like a million miles still separated us.

The steel gray skies had darkened in the near hour long drive it had taken us in traffic to get from Alexandria to McLean. When Voodoo held out a hand, I slid mine into his and let him tug me from my seat to the one next to him. We were almost there.

"You're cold," he said, trying to warm my hand with his.

"Not really feeling it at the moment," I admitted.

"Two minutes," AB warned. The traffic sounds had grown considerably quieter after leaving the highway. From what I could see out the front, we were entering the very affluent area Sinclair called home.

We were almost there.

The van eased to a smooth, quiet stop on the edge of the circular drive—close enough to be expected, far enough to seem like we weren't desperate to make a scene. The house loomed in front of me, three stories of stone and old money arrogance, with a steep gabled roof, black iron fixtures, and enough carefully trimmed hedges to make Versailles jealous.

Just another Thursday in McLean.

I stepped out of the driver's seat, tugging the strap of my bag higher on my shoulder. From the outside, we looked like a very tidy scene: a clean, newer-model van that could belong to a realtor, a consultant, or—if you were a little sleep-deprived and had the wrong glasses prescription—a well-dressed soccer mom. Very subtle. Very boring.

Perfect.

I didn't glance at the trees. Didn't check my watch. Voodoo and Bones had gotten out a quarter mile back, disappearing into the thicket that surrounded the estate like it had something to hide. I knew they were on foot, getting into position to sweep the grounds once I opened the door.

"Comms check," Bones murmured.

"Loud and clear," I whispered, and clicked the clasp on my bag.

The walk to the door was measured and confident— Amorette Black, no nonsense, no nerves. By the time I reached the oversized double doors, I'd gone still inside, like someone had flipped a switch and all the noise in my head had gone dark.

I knocked once, firm but polite. The sound echoed.

Thirty seconds passed.

Then the door opened.

The woman who answered was in her mid-fifties,

maybe older, wearing a muted floral blouse with dark slacks. She looked startled to see me—properly startled, like I'd just materialized on her front step instead of walked up to it. Her mouth opened, and she said something in rapid-fire Spanish.

"¿Pero qué haces aquí tú solita? No me dijo que venía nadie—"

Then her expression shifted, and she corrected herself quickly, her words slipping into English like a practiced code-switch. "Oh, I'm sorry. I forgot you don't speak Spanish."

I tilted my head, just a fraction, offering the exact kind of self-effacing smile Amorette might've used when someone spilled wine on her heels.

"No worries," I said lightly. "I'm so sorry to bother you this afternoon. I was just with Mark in court down in Alexandria, and of course he forgot some files. Then he had to go straight to the Whitcomb and asked me to stop by here and grab a few things."

The woman's shoulders relaxed with that specific weariness I recognized in service workers who'd done this dance a thousand times.

"Of course he did," she muttered, then caught herself again. "No, I mean—yes, come in, of course. I remember you from before, you've been here, yes?"

I nodded like it was the most natural thing in the world. "A couple of times, yes. I'm just here for the files. He said they'd probably be in the study, or maybe the upstairs office?"

She made a soft sound of sympathy and stepped aside. The door clicked shut behind me as I crossed the threshold and took in the house.

Inside, it was warm—too warm. The kind of curated

comfort that tried a little too hard to be welcoming. The walls were all creamy whites and soft lighting, with tasteful art, thick rugs, and furniture that had never been sat on by anything less than a well-dressed donor or a discreet mistress.

"We had a cleaning team through yesterday," the housekeeper said as she led me forward. "Everything should be in place, but if anything is out of order, I apologize. Mr. Sinclair can be... unpredictable."

"Oh, trust me," I murmured, smiling. "I know."

"Status?" Bones asked in my ear.

"I'm in," I murmured, following the woman deeper into the house. "Main hall. No signs of other staff yet."

"Find out how many are in the house," he said. "We're almost there."

I nodded slightly, then glanced toward the kitchen. "Did his wife make it back in town?" I asked, soft and casual, like it wasn't the question I'd been dying to ask all night.

The woman froze. Just for a second. Her hands clutched at the end of a dish towel she'd carried with her.

"No," she said after a beat. "Not yet. Still traveling."

Still.

Traveling.

"Of course," I said.

Liar.

I glanced toward the wide staircase at the end of the hall. I knew where I needed to go. I just needed her to let me.

"Is anyone else here?" I asked, just as casually. "He didn't say if anyone else would be working."

She shook her head. "No, no one else. Just me. The gardener came earlier this morning, but he left around a couple of hours ago. And the alarm is off—he likes it off when someone's home."

Perfect.

"Thanks," I said, pausing by the stairs. "I'll be quick. Then I'll lock up behind me."

"I'll be in the laundry," she said, with another tired smile, already turning back down the hallway. "Yell if you need anything."

She was still choking the dish towel as she walked. Why did she have a dish towel if she was working in the laundry? Maybe folding them?

The moment her footsteps faded, I exhaled and ascended the stairs two at a time.

"House seems clear," I said into the mic. "Only the housekeeper is here and I don't think she's a threat. But..."

"But?" That was AB prompting.

"I don't know," I said. "Just—felt weird."

"Trust your instincts," Voodoo said. "We're almost there. Get into his office and lock yourself in until we're there."

Adrenaline spiked and a wave of hot-cold slid over me.

"I'm going." I reached the landing, hand already brushing the small flash drive hidden in my jacket pocket.

Step two had officially begun.

The upstairs hallway was quiet—too quiet for a house this big, with this many doors. Each one loomed as I passed, closed and silent like a mouth holding secrets behind its teeth. But I didn't hesitate. I had to check behind a couple of doors before I found the right one.

Thankfully, they were all unlocked. Once I located the office, I pushed it open gently, slipped inside, and shut it behind me. The lock was a smooth brass turn. I rotated it with a soft *click*, then leaned my back against the wood and finally let myself breathe.

The office was colder than the rest of the house.

The curtains were drawn against the gray of the outside, and the room's palette was darker—navy, deep mahogany, and steel. Books lined the walls with obsessive precision. A matching set. Expensive, but barely touched. Everything in the space was curated, performative. But the real value here wouldn't be in the display.

It would be in what he tried to keep hidden.

My eyes swept the room. There was supposed to be a safe in here, probably a wall one from what the guys said. That would come later. To the right, a slim, fingerprint-locked drawer—which meant it held something personal, something he wanted fast access to.

But first?

The computer.

A sleek black monitor sat in the center of the desk like a mirror to the man who used it: pristine, clinical, and probably hiding a hundred filthy truths.

I moved to the desk, pulled the chair out just far enough, and pressed the space bar.

It blinked to life. No password. Either cocky, or recently used. Either worked for me.

From my pants pocket, I drew the slim flash drive AB had handed me earlier. Matte black, no branding. I slotted it into the port on the side, heart steady, fingers sure.

"It's in," I murmured.

"Copy that," AB said. "I'm on it. Shouldn't take long. You've got maybe five minutes before it starts mirroring data."

I nodded, eyes already moving again, scanning the

shelves, the walls, the floors for hidden compartments or floor safes. Something.

I knelt briefly to check under the desk, noting a scuff on the baseboard that didn't match the others. But before I could dig deeper, something rustled behind me.

I froze.

Not the creak of floorboards, not the soft sound of wood settling.

This was the unmistakable scrape of movement.

I turned slowly.

And the world narrowed to a pinpoint.

There was a man standing near the bookshelf. A man who hadn't been there when I locked the door.

I knew him.

God help me—I knew him.

One eye stared at me, flat and cold, the color of stormwater. The other, milky white and sightless, sat in a socket made crueler by the angry scar that bisected his eyebrow, cut across the ruined eye, and slashed down to the corner of his mouth. The skin was tight and shiny from where it had once burned. Or been cut.

The scar looked worse than I remembered.

And I remembered *everything*.

He smiled, if you could call it that. One corner of his mouth tugged upward. There was no warmth in it—just familiarity and something far more terrifying.

"Well," he said, voice a hollow scrape I'd heard in too many nightmares, "I'd almost given up on seeing you again."

Shock shattered into terror, and my breath caught sharp in my throat.

He took a step forward, not rushed. Not angry. Just certain.

I couldn't breathe.

"It's good to see you again, Pet," he murmured, that name curling around my ribs like barbed wire.

In my ear, someone was talking.

"Grace? Status?"

"Gracie, say something—"

But I couldn't hear them.

All I could hear was the sound of my own heartbeat slamming like a drum against my chest as the man who'd wanted to own me stepped closer, and the walls of Mark Sinclair's office closed in.

His smile curled like smoke. "I've missed you."

And just like that—every escape route vanished.

Grace and the team will return in DARE, the epic conclusion of the Blood Brothers saga.

AFTERWORD

And here it is... the end of the penultimate book in the Blood Brothers saga. Yes, I know, cliffhanger. But still, buckle up because we're not done yet! We have much more to do with Grace, Bones, AB, Legend, and Voodoo.

xoxo
Heather

Website:
heatherlong.net
Reader group:
facebook.com/groups/heatherspack

DARE

This is DARE. This is the endgame. Bring the fury. Bring the desire. Bring everything you think will break us—because we're already survived the flames.

Grab Yours Now

ABOUT HEATHER LONG

I *love* books. Not just a little bit, but a lot. Books were my best friends when I was growing up. Books didn't care if I was new to a town or to a class. They were always there, my trustiest of companions. Until they turned on me and said I had to write them.

I can tell you that my own personal happily ever after included writing books. I've always said that an HEA is a work in progress. It's true in my marriage, my friendships, and in my career. I am constantly nurturing my muse as we dive into new tales, new tropes, new characters and more.

After seventeen years in Texas, we relocated to the Pacific Northwest in search of seasons, new experiences, and new geography. I can't wait to discover what life (and my muse) have in store for me.

Maybe writing was always my destiny and romance my fate. After all, my grandmother wasn't a fan of picture books and used to read me her Harlequin Romance novels.

ALSO BY HEATHER LONG

82nd Street Vandals

Savage Vandal

Vicious Rebel

Ruthless Traitor

Dirty Devil

Shamelessly Loyal (Novella)

Brutal Fighter

Dangerous Renegade

Merciless Spy

Reckless Thief

Fierce Dancer

Dirty Dancer

Bay Ridge Royals

Shamelessly Loyal (Novella)

Battle Lines

Deceptive Truce

Wicked Surrender

Violent Chaos

Desperate Victory

BLOOD Brothers

Burn

Lure

Own

Oath

Dare

Blue Ivy Prep

Problem Child

Mad Boys

Party Crashers

Money Shot

Bravo Team Wolf

When Danger Bites

Bitten Under Fire

Cardinal Sins

Kill Song

First Chorus

High Note

Last Word

Chance Monroe

Earth Witches Aren't Easy

Plan Witch from Out of Town

Bad Witch Rising

Fevered Hearts

Marshal of Hel Dorado

Brave are the Lonely

Micah & Mrs. Miller

A Fistful of Dreams

Raising Kane

Wanted: Fevered or Alive

Wild and Fevered

The Quick & The Fevered

A Man Called Wyatt

Going Royal

Some Like it Royal

Some Like it Scandalous

Some Like it Deadly

Some Like it Secret

Some Like it Easy

Heart of the Nebula

Queenmaker

Deal Breaker

Throne Taker

Lone Star Leathernecks

Semper Fi Cowboy

As You Were, Cowboy

Shackled Souls

Succubus Chained

Succubus Unchained

Succubus Blessed

Shackled Souls (Omnibus)

STANDALONES

Kiss of Fate (w/Blake Blessing)

Taste of Karma (w/Blake Blessing)

I'll Be Home... (w/Tate James)

Overexposed (w/Tate James)

Switchboard Duet

Talk to Me

Don't Let Go

Untouchable

Rules and Roses

Changes and Chocolates

Keys and Kisses

Whispers and Wishes

Hangovers and Holidays

Brazen and Breathless

Trials and Tiaras

Graduation and Gifts

Defiance and Dedication

Songs and Sweethearts

Legacy and Lovers

Farewells and Forever

Hellos and Happily Ever Afters

Wolves of Willow Bend

Wolf at Law

Wolf Bite

Caged Wolf

Wolf Claim

Wolf Next Door

Rogue Wolf

Bayou Wolf

Untamed Wolf

Wolf with Benefits

River Wolf

Single Wicked Wolf

Desert Wolf

Snow Wolf

Wolf on Board

Holly Jolly Wolf

Shadow Wolf

His Moonstruck Wolf

Thunder Wolf

Ghost Wolf

Outlaw Wolves

Wolf Unleashed

www.ingramcontent.com/pod-product-compliance
Lightning Source LLC
Chambersburg PA
CBHW031551310726
48971CB00008B/2717